Your Tempting Love
(The Bennett Family, Book 5)

LAYLA HAGEN

Dear Reader,

If you want to receive news about my upcoming books and sales, you can sign up for my newsletter HERE: http://laylahagen.com/mailing-list-sign-up/

Chapter One

Christopher

Thump. Thump. Thump.

I almost step on a tennis ball while crossing the lobby of my office building. Picking up the neon green orb, I look around until I locate the owner: a small girl, maybe four or five years old. She's sitting on the couch in the waiting area with a serious problem on her hands: her toys have spilled out of her backpack, and she's desperately trying to shove them back in.

Bennett Enterprises is large enough that we added an on-site daycare a while back, but this is the first time I've stepped on a toy. Instead of heading up to my office, I stride in her direction, returning the ball.

"You lost this."

The girl snaps her head up, her blue eyes wide and thankful as if I just saved the day.

"Thank you." She grabs it from me with both hands, squeezing it to her chest like it's her most prized possession before shoving it in the backpack. She's in a frenzy, hopping down from the couch to collect the toys from the floor, pushing her dark brown hair away from her face.

"What's your name?" I ask her.

"Chloe."

"I'm Christopher."

"Wow! Both our names begin with C."

Sitting on my haunches until I'm almost level with her, I lean in, whispering conspiratorially, "That's because we're cool."

An ear-to-ear grin lights up her small face, and she seems to momentarily forget about her troubles. Then she directs her focus on the reception desk. Ah, she must be here with a visitor. That explains why she's in the waiting area. Visitors must check in at the reception desk first, so they're directed to the correct floor. Currently, there's some commotion going on at the desk, so it looks like little Chloe still has some waiting to do.

"This is yours?" I ask, picking up a small Rubik's Cube that slipped just under the couch. Chloe nods, holding the backpack open so I can drop it inside. Color me impressed. I'm the Chief Operations Officer of Bennett Enterprises and a shareholder. Throw any issue my way, and I can fix it. A Rubik's Cube? I'm stumped.

"Chloe," a female voice says behind me, "we can—"

Several mishaps occur at the same time. At the sound of the woman's voice, I abruptly rise to my feet, turn around, and *boom.* Straight-on collision. Stepping back, I realize the woman is carrying a cup… and spilled all its contents on my shirt. On the plus side, the beverage was lukewarm, not hot. But my shirt looks as if I crawled across a muddy street.

"I'm so sorry. It was hot chocolate. It'll wash out," she says, demanding my attention.

Damn.

She's tall, with brown waves falling over her shoulder, green eyes piercing me. Her full lips could tempt even a saint into sinning, and I'm no saint. Meeting a beautiful woman is hands-down the best way to start a day, even if it comes with hot chocolate on my shirt.

"I'll pay for your dry cleaning." Her shoulders turn rigid as she assesses the damage to my shirt.

"Don't worry about it," I reply, because by the looks of it, she has enough to worry about already. When Chloe tugs at her hand, I put two and two together. Chloe is here with her, which means she must be her daughter. Instantly I check her hand for a ring because I'm not *that* kind of sinner. There's no ring.

"His name starts with C," Chloe tells her. "Like mine."

"Oh! You're Christopher Bennett, aren't you?" If possible, her shoulders tense even more. That's not the usual reaction I cause in women.

"Yes."

"I'm Victoria Hensley. We have a meeting in ten minutes."

This day just got a hell of a lot better. She's the interior decorator my sisters Pippa and Alice recommended to decorate my new apartment. They insisted she's very talented, and after I witnessed the great job she did at Alice's restaurant and Pippa's house, I was sold.

"Pippa told me there's an on-site daycare, and I can leave my sister there during our meeting," Victoria continues.

Ah, now I remember. Pippa told me Victoria is looking after her younger siblings after they lost their parents in a boating accident last year. I can tell Victoria wants to shake my hand, but Chloe stubbornly holds on to her right hand.

"Sure," I counter. "Go settle Chloe in. I'll be

waiting upstairs in my office."

"Do you think the other kids will like my toys?" Chloe asks Victoria.

Victoria smiles down at her sister, and I'll be damned if it's not the sweetest smile I've ever seen. "Of course they will."

Apparently, Victoria's smile only affects me, because Chloe puffs her cheeks, not convinced.

"You've got so many toys," I say, patting her backpack, "I'm sure they'll find something they like. It's really nice of you to want to share toys. When I was your age, anyone touching my stuff was an enemy. You're cool."

Her puffy cheeks give way to a grin again. Mission accomplished.

Victoria frees her hand from Chloe's grip, and as I shake it, she inspects the damage to my shirt. I bet she's calculating the odds of gaining me as her client after this mishap.

I'll have to turn on the charm to full power in my office, just to put her mind at ease, of course.

***

Victoria

Way to make a first impression, Victoria! After dropping off Chloe, I chastise myself all the way to Christopher's office, looking forward to proving myself to him. His sisters might have recommended me, but that doesn't mean he'll go with me if I don't convince him.

The moment I step inside his office, some of the tension bleeds from my shoulders, as Christopher offers me a friendly smile. I inspect his eyes to check whether the smile is perfunctory, but the warmth in them tells me he is genuine. Christopher Bennett is a damn fine sight to behold. Handsome face with a perfectly groomed three-day beard, broad shoulders, solid six feet of muscles—he's the type of man who can dominate a room with his presence without even trying.

When I stop in front of his desk, I can't help ogling his shirt. What a mess I made of it. He catches me inspecting the stains, and his smile deepens. He points to the chair in front of his desk. "Take a seat."

I do just that, crossing my legs and brainstorming for the best way to start with a clean slate.

"Everything worked out with Chloe?" Christopher asks.

"Yeah."

"How many siblings do you have? Pippa must have told me, but I forgot."

Usually, I don't go into details about my personal life with clients, but Christopher's interest seems genuine.

"Three. Chloe, Lucas, who is nine, and Sienna. She's seventeen."

Christopher nods thoughtfully. "That sounds like a full house."

"It is." I can't help smiling. "It gets crazy sometimes."

"I know what you mean."

"True. Your sister Pippa said you are nine siblings. That must've been something while growing up."

"Yeah. To be honest, I think my parents might know what you mean more than I do. I was causing all that craziness. At least part of it."

His easygoing nature surprises me. I've worked with men in powerful positions before, and most were cold, even stuck-up. But Christopher doesn't take himself too seriously, even if he has a corner office with a brilliant view of San Francisco.

We're interrupted by a knock on the door, and his assistant steps inside. "Christopher, your next appointment is here early."

Shoot.

"Half an hour early?" he asks skeptically. His mouth sets in a thin line, his eyes losing some of their spark. Ah, I bet he's a shark in business meetings.

His assistant shrugs. "I can tell them to wait."

"No one likes to wait. We'll wrap up here quickly," he tells her, spurring me into a panic. Nodding, his assistant leaves the room again.

"Sorry for cutting this short, but those are partners with whom we're renegotiating some contracts. Nothing's worse in a negotiation than a partner pissed off he had to wait, even if it's their fault they arrived early."

"I understand."

"I'll be honest, Victoria. I saw the pictures with your portfolio, and Alice and Pippa spoke highly of you. I've seen what you did for them, and I think you can make any place look like home. I'm great at my job and have a number of other talents." A smile tugs at his lips. "But decorating is pig latin to me."

And there he goes with that self-deprecating humor again, mixed in with an unexpected dose of cockiness. But something in the way he delivered the line about "a number of other talents" makes me want to know more instead of having me roll my eyes.

"What are you looking for?" I ask.

"Thing is, I have no idea." He leans back in his chair, lacing his fingers on top of his head.

"I can work with that," I assure him.

"You can? You're magic, then."

"Close to it. I've been in this business for eight

years. I've worked with people who had a wide array of tastes. Why don't you show me the plan for your apartment, and I can run some ideas by you right away?"

"No time right now. Besides, I don't want to hurry this. I receive the keys to my apartment in six weeks, so we have time."

"Then e-mail me the plan and any pictures you might have, and I'll pitch you a few ideas in a reply. You have my contact information."

"I do."

We rise from our chairs in unison, and as he walks me to the door, I say, "Let me pay for the dry cleaning of your shirt. I'm really uncomfortable."

"Would you be more comfortable if I got rid of my shirt?" His voice is laced with boyish playfulness and the hint of a dare. I open my mouth, fully intending to blatantly ignore his question, but other words slip out instead.

"Do you often offer to strip for women you just met?"

Hell no! I can give good banter when it's required, but he's a potential client. Banter has no business here. His dark brown eyes widen. Clearly, he wasn't expecting this.

"Do you often spill hot chocolate on men you just met?"

"Touché."

"For your own peace of mind, I keep spare shirts in my office. I just didn't have time to change into it because you arrived early. And so is the next meeting, but I'll change the second you leave. Unless you want to watch?" He winks, and my mind spins.

"Send me that floor plan," I say, proud of keeping it professional.

"Will do." Wiggling his eyebrows, he adds, "While changing my shirt. Multi-tasking is one of my talents."

"I never asked what those talents were."

"One of my many faults is that I volunteer too much information. But you never know when it might come in handy."

Shaking my head, I can't hold back a grin. "Pippa said you used to be a big troublemaker as a kid."

"That's still true. The only difference from then is now I'm trouble with a capital T."

Chapter Two

Victoria

"Good night, Victoria," Chloe says, hugging her teddy bear, her wavy brown hair splayed on her pillow, her eyes heavy with sleep.

I kiss her forehead lightly before whispering, "Good night."

"Will you stay with me until I fall asleep?"

"Sure thing, sweetie."

Placing the book I was reading to her on the nightstand, I turn off the light and slide in beside her. Chloe nestles her small body against mine. Keeping my gaze trained on the moon visible through the window, I listen as her breathing pattern becomes increasingly calmer. Mom used to read to her sometimes before bed, and now I do. It's our way of keeping Mom's memory alive.

Once I'm one hundred percent sure Chloe is asleep, I silently leave. Lucas's and Sienna's rooms are on the other side of the hall, and they are blissfully quiet. I tiptoe down the corridor on my way to the staircase, but the boards creak beneath my feet anyway. *Damn.* The floors at our old house used to creak too, but those were of the cute "parent-approaching-alert" variety, whereas these are of the "earthquake-alert" variety.

The death of my parents brought many changes. One of them was that two months after burying them, we had to let go of the only place where we could still feel their presence: the old house. Our new home is smaller and farther away from the children's school than I wanted, but we live in San Francisco, and housing is exorbitant. This was the best we could afford. We're still learning to call this our home. All our furniture and most of the decorations are from the old house, but it takes more than that to make a place home. We'll get there eventually though.

With a sigh, I shake my head, trying to push the thoughts away. Thinking about my parents always brings on a wave of sadness, and I don't want to let in the pain tonight. I have so much to be thankful for—most of all, that the kids weren't on the boat with my parents the night of the accident. Losing them all… I shudder at the thought.

Social services almost took the kids away. They stepped in after my parents died to make sure I'm a fit guardian. In the beginning, I thought it was because Lucas and Chloe were adopted, but then I found out social services often assist when parents of minors pass away. The problem is they were not convinced that I'm a fit guardian. I fought tooth and nail so we'd all stay together, but social services is keeping a close eye on our case, checking in with us monthly.

Stepping inside the living room, I smile widely at the sight of the gigantic hat sitting on the coffee table, still waiting to be "glittered up." Chloe's preschool is organizing a costumed picnic in October. Though it's only September, I started working on her costume to make sure it'll be ready in time. Chloe is going as the Mad

Hatter, the glittery version. Kneeling beside the coffee table in front of the couch, I eye my phone, my palm itching to check my e-mails again, but I decide to ignore the urge and finish the hat.

Tonight I'm all tied up, waiting for Christopher Bennett to reply. I received a message from him with the plan for his apartment after leaving his office, and I sent him the pitch two hours later. I haven't heard from him since, which is normal. It can take days for a potential client to get back to me, but my stomach is in knots. I really need to sign him on as a client to replace the one who unexpectedly ditched me last week. And if I'm honest, Christopher Bennett intrigues me. From the sweet way he talked to Chloe to the borderline shameless way in which he joked with me, everything about him is refreshing and fun. I have a feeling it'd be a blast to work for him.

Because I'm not a hypocrite, I also can't deny that the man is a sight to behold: broad shoulders, strong build, eyes I could lose myself in—which is out of the question, of course. Taking a break from glittering up the hat, I can't resist the temptation of scrolling through my e-mails for the hundredth time. To my surprise, there's one from Christopher in my inbox.

I like your ideas and definitely want to work together. When are you available for a call to talk about the next steps?

I type the response back so fast I nearly break a nail.

I'm available now if you want to talk. Seeing his number below his signature in the message, I add, **I can call you, or you can call me.**

I type my number, even though he has my business card. As I press Send, I do a small happy dance around my living room, shaking my hips to the memory of a catchy tune I heard while driving this morning. My phone beeps with an incoming call seconds later. I recognize his number and immediately answer.

"Thank you for getting back to me so quickly, Mr. Bennett."

"I think we can drop the formalities, Victoria."

The way he says my name, in a low baritone… damn. I can practically hear the smile in his voice, and my mind immediately conjures up the way his almost-sinful lips curl up to form a smile, revealing dimples at both corners of his mouth. Jeez, I can't believe I memorized that. In my defense, it's a great smile, and those dimples would turn even the strongest woman to mush.

"Thank you for calling me back so quickly, Christopher."

"That's more like it. So, what are the next steps?"

"First of all, I fell in love with your apartment already. I'd love to be able to turn it into a home for you." His apartment, a huge condo at the top of a high-rise, would be a dream to decorate. Since Christopher bought it while still in construction, he had some structural changes made, turning it from a five- to a two-bedroom apartment. This has resulted in delightful and spacious rooms.

"Thanks. Before going into more detail, I have one question. Why did you leave the company you worked at?"

Oh, damn. I was hoping this wouldn't come up. I have an answer ready, of course, but I prefer to avoid the topic. I worked at that company for eight years, putting in long hours and a lot of dedication. When my parents died, things changed. My siblings became my priority. My boss, a woman I had respected almost to the point of worship, decided I wasn't a "good fit" for the company anymore, and fired me. Losing my job was one of the reasons social services didn't think I was a fit guardian. At twenty-nine, I started my own business, which has been exciting and nerve-racking.

"I needed more flexibility for my siblings," I tell Christopher honestly.

"Got it. So, what are the next steps?"

"Which of my pitches didn't you like?" I've found that the easiest way through this is to eliminate the choices that don't fit the client's taste.

He doesn't miss a beat. "The third and fourth one."

Interesting. Those proposals were modern and minimalistic, the way his office is. I assumed they'd be his favorites. Then again, it's possible he didn't choose the furniture in his office. The multi-story office building exuded power in a way that wasn't ostentatious, but rather spoke of quiet, bone-deep strength. It was elegant too, with its sleek surfaces and minimalist designs.

"And which one did you like most?"

"I liked elements from all the other proposals, but I can't single out one I liked best."

In short, he still doesn't know what he wants, but that's normal at this stage. Sitting again in front of the coffee table, I make some mental notes, my mind already bursting with ideas for his apartment.

"The next step would be for you and me to look through furniture and design catalogs together," I inform him. "This will give both of us a better idea what you want. I can mark some items I think you'd like in advance, but it's really best if we take an hour or two to comb through those catalogs. I can bring them to your office. When do you have time this week?"

"I have back-to-back meetings every day, but I can do Thursday after seven o'clock."

Damn. One of my unique selling propositions is that I'm flexible, trying to accommodate the clients as much as possible, but as a rule, I don't do any meetings after six. The kids and I make a point of eating dinner together, like a family, and I don't want to change that.

"Is four or five o'clock possible on any day? I can also come up early in the morning."

"Afraid not. As I said, my schedule is packed."

I carefully consider my next words. Twice I've had the unpleasant surprise of clients dropping me when they found out about my siblings. They thought I wouldn't be able to commit one hundred percent to their project. But I have a hunch Christopher isn't like that. His sisters weren't either. I adored working for Alice, as well as for Pippa and her husband, Eric. They were a true team, and the love between them was so apparent, I often felt like a third wheel.

At any rate, Christopher saw me arrive with Chloe today. If he'd thought the kids are in my way of committing to his project, we wouldn't be having this conversation. I decide to go out on a limb and be honest.

"The kids and I eat at six thirty every evening, and I—"

"Say no more," Christopher cuts in. "That's nice. When I was a kid, we used to have a designated dinnertime too. It really helped keeping things in check. I'll tell you what. I'll drop by your house one evening after dinner, if that's okay with you?"

Wow. No client has offered this before. Warmth fills me, relaxing my limbs.

"Perfect. Thank you. I do have a designated area for my home office. But in the interest of honesty, I rarely receive clients here. The kids haven't fully grasped the concept of quiet."

"They're kids. If they're quiet, something's wrong. Don't worry!" Christopher laughs a lovely, melodic sound.

"When do you want to stop by?"

"Thursday okay?"

"Sure. Shoot." In my enthusiasm, I flapped my free hand a little too energetically, hitting the glitter bottle. I catch it right before it lands on the carpet. "Glitter disaster averted."

"What?"

"Chloe's going as the Mad Hatter to a preschool thing, and I'm making her a glittery hat, and… now I'm rambling. Sorry." Biting my lower lip, I barely suppress a groan. "I seem to have the tendency of making a fool of myself when you're involved. First the hot chocolate, now this. But I do promise I'm a consummate professional."

Christopher is silent for so long, I fear he's about to serve me a line like "I think I'll find myself another decorator" when he bursts out laughing. "You're something, Victoria. For the record, the Mad Hatter is a great costume idea. I never had better ideas than a zombie, vampire, and pirate."

"Really? I had the craziest costume ideas. Things took a turn for the unoriginal toward the end of high school though. I dressed up as sexy bunny one year for Halloween just to spite my parents." I realize one second too late what I just said and how this doesn't belong in a professional conversation at all. Me and my big mouth, damn it. "Right… I seem to go from bad to worse tonight. How about ending this call, so I can keep up any pretense of seriousness?"

"Bad idea. I'd like to continue this conversation.

It's the most fun I've had in a while."

"Me too," I reply honestly, feeling an instant kinship with him.

"So you were something of a wild child?"

"Exactly. My parents were great people, and I was still a terrible kid. To be honest, my wild side persisted up until college. Then I had to tuck it away, step up, and be all serious. I gave my mom and dad white hair. I mean… I didn't do dangerous stuff, just crazy enough to cause trouble."

"Ah, you're a girl after my own heart." His low tone awakens a deep and powerful longing inside me, and I do my best to ignore it. "What was the craziest thing you did?"

"Once we were vacationing in Texas, and my best friend was with us. We snuck out at night and went swimming. Mom almost had a heart attack. And she didn't even know the worst part. We went skinny-dipping." And cue my return to inappropriate lane. This man has a dangerous effect on me.

"Do you still go skinny-dipping? If yes, I'm in dire need of swimming lessons. Actually, I'd settle for you wearing your sexy bunny costume while teaching me."

I let out an audible breath, heat spearing me at this unexpected turn of the conversation. Yeah, in his office, I suspected his humor is the kind that's sprinkled with inappropriate comments, but I have an inkling that was just a preview.

"Sorry, I was out of line," he says.

"Yes, but I did bring up those topics, so… we were both misbehaving. Can I ask you a favor?"

"Sure."

"Please think up some wildly inappropriate childhood stories and share them with me on Thursday. I feel like I'm at a distinct disadvantage here."

Yet again, his laughter fills the air, and before I know it, I'm grinning ear to ear too. "You've got it. So how inappropriate are we talking? Just funny, white-hair-inducing for my parents, or…?"

He doesn't finish the sentence, but his meaning is clear. I fear I've unleashed the inappropriate side of him with my incessant rambling.

"Funny will do," I say, and my voice doesn't sound quite right.

"Great. See you on Thursday. Also, and I'm just putting this out there, I wouldn't mind seeing that sexy bunny outfit someday if you still have it."

"You're a bad man, Christopher."

"I suppose it would be unwise for me to add that I wouldn't mind seeing you wear it?" He says this with the slightest hint of laughter in his voice, but I can picture his luscious mouth curled up at one side, his dark eyes full of mischief and lust. *Damn, damn, damn.*

"Very unwise, Mr. Bennett."

"We're back to Mr. Bennett? Let's end this call before I become so inappropriate that you call me something ridiculous like Sir or Your Highness."

Oh God. This man is hilarious, and I could talk to him for hours. Which is precisely why this is the best time to end the call.

"See you on Thursday, Christopher. Have a good night."

"You too."

After the line goes dead, I focus on the hat again. It's been a long time since I had so much fun talking to someone. A thought nags at the back of my mind that I should keep things professional. Christopher Bennett isn't a friend, he's a client, and I've learned the hard way that crossing professional boundaries can have dire consequences.

Besides, I'm the girl with the plan, always have been. Before my parents passed away, the plan was to rise to the top of the career chain in a design and decoration company, and when I'd achieved that, I'd focus on my private life. Now the plan is to give Lucas and Chloe a happy childhood, like the one Sienna and I had, and focus on raising them. My personal life will have to wait.

I focus on the hat again, determined to make my sister a kick-ass costume. Still, I can't help grinning as I rewind the conversation in my mind. That man definitely has a great sense of humor and a way of twisting words that leaves my skin simmering.

In his office, he said he's a troublemaker with a capital T these days. I have a feeling trouble doesn't even begin to cover it.

Chapter Three

Christopher

"Hey, brother," Pippa greets me, swinging open the front door to her house. "Come in."

I follow her inside, shrugging off my jacket and putting it on the hanger. My sister's house has the feeling of a home to it, which is what I hope Victoria will achieve with my apartment. The rental I'm currently living in feels like a hotel, and I can't wait to move out. The house is oddly quiet given that twin three-month-old babies, Pippa's husband, and his thirteen-year-old daughter, Julie, all live here. From my previous visits, I know the odds of everyone being quiet at the same time are slim.

"Are Julie and Eric home?"

"Nah, Eric's picking up Julie from a friend's house. They'll be home in about an hour. Are you hungry?" she asks.

"Always."

"You're lucky. I haven't cooked dinner, but Alice brought some goodies from her restaurant."

"Alice is here?"

"Yep, she's with Mia and Elena in my bedroom. She should join us any second though. The twins were almost asleep when I came to open the door."

Damn. I was hoping to catch the twins awake because I haven't seen the little firecrackers in weeks. I'm counting the months—okay, years—until they're old enough to start pranking people. My identical twin Max and I were the family's pranksters as kids. I have to pass on the gift to others. My two oldest brothers, Sebastian and Logan, are married, and Max is engaged, but only Pippa has kids.

As we enter the kitchen, I eye the take-out boxes from Alice's restaurant on the wooden table in the center and attack one right away. Roast duck leg is my favorite dish on Alice's menu. Every time I eat it, I thank my lucky stars Alice decided to go into the restaurant business instead of joining Bennett Enterprises.

My oldest brothers and Pippa founded the company more than a decade ago, and it's become one of the leading players in the high-end jewelry market. Max and I joined the company too, but the rest—Alice; the other set of twins, Blake and Daniel; and the family's baby, Summer—went on different paths. Summer is a painter, Blake opened a bar and Daniel a business that centers around offering customers adventures and extreme sports.

"You didn't tell me why you were stopping by," Pippa says, grabbing a take-out box herself and sitting at the table.

"Are you implying I can't visit just to see you and the girls?"

A few weeks ago, Pippa surprised my brothers and me by suggesting we extend our collections by developing a line of engagement and wedding rings. She's the designer at Bennett Enterprises. Each collection always carried a few models, but we've never focused extensively on those. From a purely business perspective, there were other profitable niches to tackle first. Despite wedding rates going down and divorce rates going up, Pippa insisted love would never go out of style, and Bennett Enterprises could position itself as a leader in the segment. Pippa's exuberance when presenting her vision for the line convinced us all to look into this.

"You were using your business tone when you said you'll stop by," she remarks. My sister's ability to read into everything will never cease to astonish me.

"You're right. It's about your proposal to develop a line of engagement and wedding rings."

Pippa stops chewing, and her eyes widen as if asking, *And?*

"We researched the market in more detail, and the numbers look promising. We'll go forward with this."

Pippa squeals, jumping from her seat and hugging me. When she pulls back, she's grinning.

"But I have one question, and I want you to be honest. Are you sure you're up to it?" My sister has been working from home since the twins were born three months ago, delegating everything that she could, including some key design aspects. But, I suspect she's still taking on more than she can handle.

"Yes. I'm passionate about this! I know I can do it."

"If you change your mind at any time, let us know. We can always do this later on."

She shakes her head with vehemence. "I'm up to it."

"Okay."

"Christopher!" Alice exclaims, joining us in the kitchen and sitting on the counter. My sisters look nothing alike. While Pippa is tall and blonde, Alice has inherited Mom's small frame and dark brown hair.

"How's your apartment coming along?"

"I'll get the keys in six weeks. I had the first meeting with the decorator you two recommended."

"And?" Pippa and Alice ask in unison.

"She seems to know her stuff, sent me a few proposals. I liked them."

"She's a dream to work with," Alice says. "Super efficient and very friendly."

"Very hardworking," Pippa adds. "I love her style too. I wish I could wear as many colors as she does and not look ridiculous, but that takes talent."

Right. I had no clue what they were talking about because I was too busy fantasizing about what's under her clothes. Men don't notice those things anyway. I'm about to point that out when I catch my sisters exchanging glances. Suspicious glances.

When Pippa says, "I have no clue how that woman is still single," I finally catch up with the program and groan.

"Please tell me you didn't recommend me to work with her just to set me up."

"Not just to set you up," Pippa clarifies. "She's really good at what she does."

"I thought you'd give up your matchmaking ways after getting married," I tell Pippa honestly. My sister was married once before, and that ended with a nasty divorce. After that, she had a hand in my oldest brothers getting married, but we all thought matchmaking was a therapy of sorts for her, that she'd give up after she found her own happy ending. Apparently not.

"What gave you that idea?" Pippa says, genuinely shocked. "I had to take a break what with the pregnancy and the birth, but now I'm back in my full capacity as a matchmaker. Alice is my helper."

"Since when did you go over to the dark side?" I ask my other sister.

Alice shrugs. "It's fun."

I wolf down some more roast duck, mystified about not seeing through this before. My mother's ability to read other people has unfortunately only been inherited by my sisters.

"Girls, please stay out of this."

Alice tilts her head in Pippa's direction. "I liked him more when he was clueless. He was a much easier prey."

"But you've been single for so long," Pippa remarks.

"It's not a disease, you know," I deadpan.

"You're not still hung up on Felicity, are you?" Alice asks bluntly. "You two were together for a long time, and then you broke up out of the blue."

Yeah, that's not exactly the whole story. Felicity and I started dating in our senior year of college. A few years later, I thought it was time I proposed. Sure, we were still young, but I could see us building our future together. On our anniversary, I planned a long, romantic evening, which ended with us on the Golden Gate Bridge, me on one knee, popping the big question, and Felicity saying no.

I was dumbstruck. She said something about marriage being like shackles and that she felt it would hold her back from pursuing her dreams. When I asked what those dreams were, she said she didn't know yet, but wanted to discover herself.

Every word felt like a slap. She'd never, not once, shared those thoughts with me. She was a teacher and seemed more than happy with her job. I thought we were building something together. Obviously, I was delusional.

She *thanked* me for the proposal because it made it clearer that she needed to be alone for a while. Among our irreconcilable differences, she mentioned that I had it all figured out, but she needed to figure herself out, alone. She emphasized the word "alone" a few times more, as if she thought my skull was too thick and she needed to drill the rejection into my brain.

Afterward, I tried to make sense of everything, to gauge if she gave me signs and I had missed them. I came up blank, concluding that women's minds are up there with the world's greatest mysteries.

I never told my family or anyone else that I proposed, because really, my ego can't take any pitying looks.

The opportunity to move to Hong Kong and expand Bennett Enterprises there came up a few months later, and I jumped on it. A change of scenery was just what I needed. Working hours in Hong Kong were long and brutal because we were just starting out there, but I welcomed the workload. It didn't leave me time for much personal life, only casual dating, which was a much-needed change. I intend to keep that change now that I'm back in San Francisco. Casual means superficial, and superficial can't lead to any ego bruising or heartbreak.

"No, I'm not hung up on Felicity," I tell my sisters. "I haven't spoken to her in years."

"Excellent." Alice claps her hands. "You can start fresh, then."

"What are my chances of convincing you to give this a rest?"

"Zero." Pippa smiles sweetly at me. I have come to fear that smile. It usually means she has *plans.* "But we've done our part, so aside from the occasional nagging, this is up to you."

Yeah, *that* sounds very reassuring. I do like Victoria; she's fun and gives good banter even when she's trying not to. Not to mention those perfect curves of hers are burned on my retinas. I've had more fun on the phone with her than I've had talking to a woman in years. But I have no time or desire for anything more than casual right now, and even though I've only met Victoria once and spoken to her twice, I suspect she's not the type who does that. I wouldn't try to do casual with a woman who's raising two kids and a teenager. I'm not an asshole.

Placing my empty take-out box on the table, I say before either of my sisters gets any more dangerous ideas, "I'll be going, then."

"Can you drive me to my place?" Alice asks, jumping down from the counter. "My car is in for routine maintenance and—"

"You like being driven around by your brothers?" I ask.

Alice grins. "What good is it having a gazillion brothers if they don't even drive you around?"

"Sure, I'll drop you off."

After saying good-bye to Pippa, Alice and I leave. The moment I drive away, Alice asks, "Do you have time to sit down with me for a few hours sometime? I wanted to pick your brain on some operations stuff."

"Sure, what about?"

"When I opened the second restaurant I didn't anticipate how much more complex it would be. I know that certain things can be streamlined. The way I currently run everything is eating away at my profitability."

"Do you have money issues?"

"No, but I don't like throwing money away. Just want to pick your brain, but you're living up to the Bennett name in terms of hours sitting on your butt in your office. Do you have time?"

I wear my workaholic badge proudly. I was a wild child until college, much like Victoria. The summer before my senior year, I interned at Bennett Enterprises. After the first week on the job, I had a troubling realization: if I wanted anyone to take me seriously, I had to act the part. People regarded me like Sebastian and Logan's little prankster brother, and me cracking jokes the entire time didn't help.

So I put on a suit, joked less while at the office, and worked hard. Slowly, I climbed inside the company until I took over as head of operations. I'd like to think it was all my hard work, but the truth is, my last name being Bennett contributed. Which is why I work my ass off. When you're handed chances, you do your best to prove you're worthy of them.

"You share my last name," I tease Alice. "That means I'm obligated to make time for you and drive you around."

"Well, don't I feel special."

"How about this for feeling special? I'm also obligated to kick anyone's butt who crosses you."

Alice holds up one finger as I stop at a red light.

"Those are big brother duties. Last I checked you're younger, so you're off the hook. You can just annoy me."

"Of course I'll make time for you, Alice," I assure her. The last thing I want is for my sister to worry about her business. "We can sit down and talk about this sometime next week. This one is crazy."

"All joking aside, it's a good thing Victoria's helping you decorate. It's a big time suck otherwise."

"Agreed. I'm going to her house Thursday evening to go over some brochures."

"Ooh, you'll meet her siblings. They're adorable."

"I already met Chloe. By the way, how can a twenty-nine-year-old have a four-year-old sister?"

"Chloe and Lucas were adopted. Victoria told me once that her parents wanted more children, but after her, they didn't have any luck until twelve years later when they had Sienna. Afterward, they felt they were too old to have more kids, but Mrs. Hensley was a maternity nurse. One of her patients wanted to give up her son after he was born, and the Hensleys adopted Lucas. A few years later, the same woman gave birth to a little girl and put her up for adoption too. The Hensleys took her in as well."

"Victoria's parents sound like great people. Any tips about going to their house? Victoria seemed nervous about it. I think she's afraid the kids being loud will bother me. I told her I don't mind at all, but…."

As I come to a stop in front of Alice's building, I turn around to face her just in time to catch her smile.

"Bring them some ice cream. They'll love it. Ben & Jerry's, chocolate cherry and coconut flavor. And thank you for driving me home."

She climbs out of my car and through the car window, she flashes me a smile that resembles Pippa's "I have plans for you" smile a tad too much.

Chapter Four

Victoria

My goal on Thursday evening is to make the most out of Christopher's time and keep the encounter 100 percent professional. No allowing his smoldering gaze to affect me. No bonding over inappropriate stories. Fifteen minutes before his arrival, I'm coaxing the kids into watching a movie while I spend time with Christopher in my office. Sienna and Chloe are sitting on the couch already, focusing on the TV, but Lucas isn't convinced.

"I want to meet him too," Lucas says, pouting. Ever since Chloe told him about her encounter with Christopher, he's been pestering me about an introduction too. Sienna gives me a sympathetic look.

"He's a client," I say to Lucas gently. "No meeting the clients, remember?"

"But Chloe already *met* him," Lucas insists.

"By accident," I repeat for the hundredth time. Separating my personal life from the professional one isn't an easy task when my office is at home, but I do my best trying to set boundaries. "He's an ogre, anyway. You don't want to meet him."

I kiss Lucas on the cheek, and he makes a gagging sound, rubbing his cheek vigorously. "You can't do that anymore. I'm too old."

"If you don't listen to me, I'm going to kiss you

some more." As an afterthought, I add, "In public. At school."

He straightens up, adopting a stoic expression, then joins Chloe on the couch seconds before the doorbell rings. I practically sprint to open the door.

"Hi," Christopher greets me, his eyes raking over my body, resting on my hips a tad too long, making me blush. Behind him, the sky is a mix of heavy clouds and streaks of clear blue and orange, as if the heavens aren't quite prepared to let go of the summer, or allow autumn to take over.

"Come inside."

The second I close the door, the sound of feet shuffling informs me that the kids are on their way here. So much for them staying in the living room.

"Christopher," Chloe calls. Lucas is right beside her, inspecting Christopher. Lucas's hair is exactly the same shade of dark chocolate as Chloe's, while Sienna's and mine are a few shades lighter. Lucas is a tad too tall for his age, while Chloe is smaller than other four-year-olds, something Lucas endlessly teases her about. Sienna mouths "I'm sorry," and I smile, letting her know it's not the end of the world. After all, Christopher was lovely toward Chloe on our first encounter.

"Hi, Chloe." He ruffles her hair good-naturedly. "I brought the three of you something."

"Ice cream," Sienna exclaims. "Ben & Jerry's with chocolate cherry and coconut."

"That's my favorite," I remark, wondering how he guessed.

Sienna shakes Christopher's hand, introducing herself, then snatches the ice cream out of his hands.

"You have great taste," she informs him. "We love Ben & Jerry's."

"Glad to be of service. And you must be the man of the house, Lucas."

I'm pleasantly surprised Christopher remembers his name, and I melt as he smiles at my brother.

"See, Victoria," Lucas says, "he's not an ogre. He's nice."

Blood rushes to my face, embarrassment rooting me to the spot. *Mental note: Never say anything in front of the kids that would embarrass you if they repeated it in front of anyone else. Ever.*

Out of the corner of my eye, I peek at Christopher. His lips are pressed together, as if he's trying hard not to burst out laughing. Not that I'm blaming him.

"Who wants ice cream?" Sienna asks, holding up the box. Chloe and Lucas answer in unison. "Okay, let's go. Thank you, Christopher."

They disappear into the living room, yet I can't bring myself to meet Christopher's eyes, still ashamed from Lucas outing me. A buzzing noise startles me.

"Sorry, I've got to answer this," Christopher says, placing his phone to his ear. "How did it go?"

The person at the other end of the line speaks quickly, but I can't make out any words.

"I don't care," Christopher says harshly. "We're not caving in. That's our offer. He can take it or leave it. We've invested millions on this."

I study him in silence, trying to reconcile the powerful businessman before me with the man with a tomboyish charm who brought the kids ice cream.

After he finishes the conversation, he shoves his phone in the pocket of his pants, opening his arms wide. "I'm all yours now. Promise."

"First things first, sorry about the ogre thing. I told Lucas that because he was insisting on meeting you, and I thought it would put him off. I try not to mix my personal life with my professional one, but...."

"Don't worry," he says with a rueful smile.

"Follow me."

He walks in step with me as I lead him through the house all the way to the office. "Thank you for bringing them ice cream. It'll keep them occupied. You sure have a knack for kids."

"Grew up in a big family," he says simply. "Knowing how to keep the small ones occupied was a basic survival skill."

I find myself grinning and wishing to know more, but business is calling.

"Besides," he continues as we step into my office, "I'm invading your personal time. The least I could do was bring them goodies." Leaning slightly forward, he says in a low tone, "I and my inappropriate stories are all yours."

He pins me with his gaze, and being the object of his focus messes with my senses. My skin buzzes with awareness as I catch a whiff of his cologne: mint, wood, and something else I don't recognize. I barely restrain myself from leaning in closer and discovering what the mystery ingredient is. *What has gotten into me?* Last time I got entangled with a client, things went bad fast. It was a mistake, and I've learned my lesson. Business and pleasure don't mix. With my siblings in my care, I can't afford to make mistakes any longer.

Clearing my throat, I step away from him, gesturing toward the couch and pointing at the catalogs on the coffee table. My office is small, with a simple wooden desk and an ergonomic black chair behind it. In the far left corner are a small, light green couch and a miniature coffee table. Behind the couch is a room divider in the shape of a floor-to-ceiling bookcase, filled to the brim with books. It looks like a regular bookcase, and I masked the entrance to my room with a tall plant.

The two-story house seems big on paper, with three bedrooms upstairs and a bedroom on the ground floor. In truth, the house originally had two bedrooms upstairs, which have been remodeled into three tiny ones. My favorite part of the house is definitely the living room. It's spacious, the large window and glass door opening into the backyard allow in plenty of light. Most of our activities, eating included, take place in the living room. Because there was no spare room I could use as my office, I had to split my bedroom, with the result that both the bedroom and the office are a tad on the small side, but I love them.

"Let's look through these catalogs, tell me what you like most. We'll go from there."

Christopher and I comb through the material, and I slowly grasp what he likes. He leans toward warm, traditional designs, which I suspected after our phone conversation.

I write down the pieces of furniture he seems especially interested in, and already have a clear idea which shops I'm going to use in his case. Over the years, I've built a network of suppliers, and I regularly work with them. They are relatively quick, I can pull in favors, and most importantly, they don't overcharge. Even though all of my clients are well off, I don't want them to overpay.

"Okay, this was productive," I exclaim about an hour later, after we finish perusing the material.

"What's the next step?"

"I want us to go to a shop, so you can look firsthand at some of the pieces of furniture you liked."

Christopher grimaces. "But we just looked through magazines."

"I know, but seeing them live is different. You might decide you don't like some of them after all."

"Not really a fan of shopping."

"I can work based on what you've chosen from the catalogs, then."

Christopher scoffs, running his hand through his hair. "Nah, I'll do it. I actually want to like the place I'll live in. Now I'm in a rental that came fully furnished, and it looks like an office. Before this, I lived in Hong Kong for a few years, expanding our business. That apartment also came fully furnished, and I felt like I was living in a hotel the entire time. Hated it, but I didn't want to put in the effort to change it. Now I want home to actually feel like home. I'll look over my schedule tomorrow and let you know when I have time."

"Great."

Christopher focuses on my pen, which has a small figurine of a Disney princess on top of it. I really should stop borrowing pens from Chloe.

"How are you juggling looking after the kids and running your own business?"

"The business side runs rather smoothly. The other one is more challenging," I say honestly. "But mostly, it's a lot of fun. It's as if I'm reliving my childhood all over again. I don't know what it says about me that I remember about the struggle of choosing whether to wear my glitter boots or pink boots to school. That either I have a great memory, or I still have the fashion sense of a four-year-old. I wish I had paid more attention in my P.E. class so I could help Lucas with—"

I swallow the rest of the sentence, embarrassed. I don't dare glance at Christopher, who is suspiciously silent next to me. Staring at the coffee table as if it's the most interesting item in the world, I say, "I'm sorry. I'm not usually a chatterbox. I mean, I am, but not with clients. You just… well, you seem so easy to talk to and so trustworthy."

"So it's my fault. Interesting. What convinced you I'm trustworthy? My offer to strip for you in my office or asking you about swimming lessons?" He laughs, and I can't help joining in.

"Sorry, back to your question. So yeah, in a nutshell, I am handling things all right most of the time. I like to focus on the positive things. And I enjoy working for myself. I'll be honest that striking out on my own wasn't easy. I depend heavily on recommendations, and the chase for new clients can be exhausting, but I'm glad I get the chance to spend more time with the kids, and being my own boss has its perks."

He tilts his head to one side, watching me intently. "Such as?"

"Being able to divide my workload as I need, wearing comfortable clothes when I'm in my office, sometimes nothing more than panties and a sleep shirt."

Nononononono, I did not say that last part out loud. Judging by the way Christopher's eyes instantly darken, I did say it. To hell with my big, traitorous mouth.

Dropping my head in my hands, I draw in a deep breath.

"My fault again, right?" he asks playfully. "Something about my incredibly good looks and inescapable charm makes you talk about your underwear?"

I cross my legs, biting the inside of my cheeks. "I swear this is atypical behavior—"

"No worries. I do believe one doesn't come

across good-looking men like me very often. Also, I still owe you some inappropriate childhood stories."

"Better not," I murmur. "This has already gotten out of hand pretty fast."

"Okay. But I do have a question for you."

"Shoot."

"Were you wearing a sleep shirt when you talked to me on the phone, Victoria?"

"The.... Yeah, I...," I stammer, unable to form a coherent thought, much less sentence. Desperately I attempt to whip my thoughts into place, but Christopher makes that impossible by inching closer to me on the couch.

He dips his head slightly, and I inhale sharply, the whiff of his cologne alerting my senses. Oh! Musk. That was the mysterious ingredient I couldn't identify before. His proximity makes my hormones go haywire, and my heart skips a beat. Judging by the look he gives me, he knows this. A man who looks like him will be aware of the effect he has on women.

"Were you wearing a thong under that sleep shirt?"

His words have an atomic effect on me, sending a heated jolt right through my center. *Well, this conversation got out of control fast.* Christopher seems to be thinking along the same lines because he pulls back, rising from the couch and pacing around the room.

"You should know something about me," he offers. "I have no filter."

"You don't say," I say, my voice tight with shock, still a little off-balance from the exchange. What just happened? I can't believe he had the balls to talk about my thong, and I definitely can't believe the way my body reacted to his words.

Christopher opens his mouth, but before he utters one single word, the door bursts open. Lucas saunters inside with Chloe hot on his heels rubbing at her eyes. Her bedtime is in half an hour, and she's already sleepy.

"It's eight thirty," Lucas announces, and I can't help smiling.

"I promised them I'd be done by this time," I explain to Christopher.

"It's a good thing we're done, then." Checking his watch, he adds, "I even have time to catch the soccer game at nine."

"You're a soccer fan?" Lucas asks.

"Big fan."

Chloe climbs in my lap, resting her head against my upper arm and yawning.

"Did you play soccer in school?" Lucas continues with the interrogation.

"Yeah. I was really good at it. Still am. My family plays often, even now."

Lucas smiles, as if Christopher just told him there will be two Christmases this year. "Could you give me some pointers? Coach me? Tryouts for the team are in a few weeks, and I really want to earn a spot. Dad was supposed to train me, but…."

His voice fades, and I suck in a deep breath. Chloe sighs deeply. I kiss the top of her head and wish I could do the same with Lucas, except I don't think he'd be happy with being kissed in front of Christopher.

My heart squeezes for my brother. I'm no good at soccer, having played volleyball at school and hating every minute of it. My Aunt Christina and Uncle Bill live nearby, and my uncle offered to help him train, but Lucas wasn't keen on it, possibly because Uncle Bill isn’t very good at soccer. But asking Christopher isn't right. He's a stranger to him and my client. I can't let the professional and personal boundaries blur even more. Also, I am one hundred percent sure Christopher has a full schedule.

"Sweetie, Christopher is busy. We'll find someone to coach you, okay? I promise."

Lucas doesn't budge.

To my surprise, Christopher says, "Sure, I can give you some tips. I coached my younger brothers years ago when they wanted to make the team. Victoria and I will figure out when the best time is."

There is so much hope in Lucas's gaze. And light… more light than I've seen in months. I'll have to find a way to thank Christopher for this.

"Here you are," Sienna exclaims, entering the room. "I left you two alone for two minutes with clear instructions to stay in the living room."

Chloe smiles coyly, then hides her face in my arm.

"It was more than two minutes. You talked on the phone for a looooong time." Lucas grins like the little devil he is. Sienna rolls her eyes at him.

"It's okay, Sienna, we were done anyway. Lucas, Chloe, go with your sister into the living room. I'll walk Christopher out."

The kids grudgingly follow Sienna out. Christopher and I leave the office too.

As soon as we're on the front porch, I shudder. The crisp autumn air raises the hair at the nape of my neck, and I rub my arms in an attempt to warm myself. The porch is my second favorite part of the house, after the living room. Come Halloween, there will be pumpkins along the entrance, and come Christmas, we'll unpack the family's decoration boxes, and the house will look like we're Santa's elves.

"About Lucas." Christopher begins, snapping me to reality.

"I'm sorry he cornered you like that," I say honestly.

"No problem. I can drop by." He rubs his jaw, his brow furrowed in concentration. "My schedule is packed during the week, but I can do weekends."

"Weekends would be great. Thank you. It'll mean a lot to him." My throat suddenly clogs, and I switch gears to professional again. "Let me know after you check your schedule with your assistant. I'd like for us to go shopping as soon as possible since some furniture can take a long time to be delivered. It won't take more than two hours."

He groans. "Hate shopping."

"I promise I'll make it worth your while."

He grins at this. "Any chance I get to see you in your thong? I can clear up my schedule for an entire day if thongs are in the cards."

"Christopher! No more no-filter lines or unintentional flirting."

A slow smile spreads on his face. Leaning in, he shoves a strand of hair behind my ear, his fingers lingering at my earlobe. The slight touch sets all my nerve endings on fire. "Who said it was unintentional?"

Chapter Five

Victoria

"Crap!"

The curse escapes my lips as I push my body to the limit, doing the last of my sit-ups. Once I'm done, my body goes lax, and I lay my head on the exercise mat. Once upon a time, I used to go to a gym, but now I'm working out from home. I like the privacy, but I have to admit that being around other people who were going through the same hell was a great motivator. My breath is labored, and I close my eyes, attempting to cool off. My abs and booty are going to hurt like hell tomorrow, but it's all worth it to stay in shape. I do the routine three times a week, on the floor of my living room after the kids are asleep.

I push myself up on my elbows when my phone beeps with an incoming call. I put the phone on loudspeaker and lie back on the floor, trying to compose myself.

"Hi, Isabelle."

"I'm interrupting your workout again," she exclaims.

"Don't worry, I was done. Now I'm trying to remember how to breathe normally."

Isabelle is my business partner and my best friend. We worked together at the old company, and after I started my own business, she asked if I needed a partner. I was happy to say yes because it was reassuring to know I wasn't completely on my own, and I loved the idea of working with my best friend.

"I want to run a few things by you, boss," she says, making me cringe. Even though we're partners, I realized early on that Isabelle relies on me for the heavy decision-making, and she wants my approval for everything. The problem is I've never been much of a leader, and being practically thrust in this position hasn't been easy. I listen to her patiently, offering my opinion.

"Great. See you Friday at lunch, then," she finishes. We have a weekly meeting where we bring each other up to date and draw plans for the next week, assessing whether we're on to meet our monthly goals.

"Sure."

After hanging up, I notice I have a text message waiting for me.

Christopher: Finally found time for the shopping trip.

Swallowing hard, I hover with my fingers over my phone, a familiar longing taking hold of me. Since his cryptic "Who said it was unintentional?" good-bye one week ago, we've only texted once. He told me his schedule was packed for the entire week, so he couldn't fit in the shopping trip. His weekend was also full already, but he assured me he could train Lucas the next weekend. We still haven't scheduled the shopping trip, hence his message.

Grinning, I begin to type back. Damn it, what's the spell this man has on me? Whenever I hear from him—or think about him—my face splits into a smile of its own accord. Midway through typing, I decide to call him instead. Sitting on the floor with my legs bent in a yoga pose, I dial his number and hold the phone to my ear.

"I was beginning to think you wanted to bail on the shopping trip," I say instead of hello once he picks up.

"I already admitted I hate shopping, but I'm a man of my word. Found time on Thursday or Friday after lunch. Can you make it on either day?"

"Friday works. And on Saturday we're on with Lucas's training?"

"If you're still up for it."

"I am."

"You're great for doing this." The more I think about it, the more I appreciate his gesture. In fact, I'm pretty sure it's one of the reasons why I smile like a lunatic every time I think about him. "I wanted to help him, but I'm no good at soccer. I could teach him shenanigans galore, but he's a bit too young for that."

"What kind of shenanigans?"

"Oh, sneaking out through the window when he's grounded, things like that."

"You do know you're the one who's supposed to be the one grounding him, right?"

"Shucks, you're right. Conflict of interest."

That's another role I've been thrust into that I'm not really fit for—being a parent. I love being the kids' sister, but joking aside, I often lie awake late at night, wondering if I'm parenting them the right way. I wish parenting came with a set of instructions.

"You sound like me. When my younger brothers turned fourteen, the first thing that occurred to me was that I had to teach them how to flirt. Weirdly enough, when my sister was born, the only thing I could think about was to protect her from any guy in existence. Feel free to call me out for being sexist or having double standards."

Adorable is what I want to call him, but I smartly remain silent. I rise to my feet, pacing the living room, suddenly filled with too much energy to stay put. Who *is* this man, and why do I feel like I could talk to him forever?

"I knew I couldn't be the only weirdo who wanted to pass on hard-earned knowledge," I reply.

"We weirdos have to stick together."

My stomach flutters at the word "together."

"In fact, you know what? I can teach him some shenanigans on Saturday," he offers. "I assure you I'm on top of my game."

"I have no doubt." Without realizing, I add, "Why are you so nice to us?"

Silence hangs in the air for a few seconds. When he finally speaks, his voice is gentle. "My sisters told me you lost your parents. I can't even begin to imagine how hard that is. Spending a few hours with Lucas and giving him feedback isn't an effort for me, but it looks like it's a big thing for him."

"It is. For me too. Thank you. See you on Friday."

"Don't forget you promised to make the time worthwhile," he teases, and my skin instantly heats up, even more so as I recall the thinly disguised flirting that followed my statement the last time I saw him.

"Victoria?" His voice is a notch huskier and music to my ears. I have a hunch he and I are thinking about the same thing.

"Yeah?"

"We could dance around this some more, but considering we can barely keep from flirting whenever we're in the same room—sometimes even on the phone—I think it'd be smart to admit we're attracted to each other."

Wow. I wonder if I'll ever know what will come out of this man's mouth next.

"Are you always so direct?" I ask him, trying to ignore the way my heart seems to have skipped a beat.

"I try to be."

"I have no idea how to continue this conversation," I tell him honestly, wishing I could carve a hole in the ground and disappear into it.

"Well, this would be an appropriate time to tell me that you have a lover, one who is very jealous and possessive."

"You gave this imaginary lover so much thought already."

"Imaginary?"

"Hate to disappoint you, but yeah." My mild mortification has turned to curiosity now, energy zinging through my veins, infusing my mood with something resembling euphoria.

"Damn. I was hoping you'd have some strong arguments, something to deter me from flirting the pants off you."

Oh, what I'd give to see his face right now. Not even Christopher can say this with a straight face. But as I formulate my answer, some of the euphoria fades, reality setting in.

"I do, they just don't include a boyfriend."

"I'm all ears."

"For one, I don't get involved with clients."

"That's excellent."

In my mind, I can picture him checking off a list with a red pen.

"And I'm really focusing on the kids. We're just

learning to navigate through life on our own. My siblings are my priority right now. I'm the only adult they can look up to as a role model, and… I feel like we've been drowning ever since the funeral. We went through so many changes, and now we're finally reaching a balance." My voice catches and I take a deep breath, steadying myself. Damn it, I didn't mean to dump all this on him.

"A very legitimate reason." His tone is softer now, and I detect something more than heat or amusement in his tone. Possibly worry.

"Enough to keep you from… what was the phrase?" I know exactly what the phrase was, but I want to hear him say it again.

"Flirting the pants off you."

"Yeah, that. You know, I just thought we might make it through an entire conversation without any inappropriateness."

"Are you implying I have no self-control? 'Cause you'd be absolutely right." He is weird but in the best kind of way.

"Christopher," I admonish, even though my voice doesn't hold much severity. In fact, I'm dangerously close to bursting into laughter. "Here's a challenge for Friday. Keep your words in professional territory. Do we have a deal?"

"Okay, promise," he answers quickly. A little too quickly. I'm tempted to question his statement, but the saying "don't look a gift horse in the mouth" crosses my mind.

"See you on Friday, then. Have a good evening."

"You too, Victoria."

After I click off, I head to my bedroom, planning to finish reading the book I started yesterday before calling this a night. Sliding under the covers, I pick up the book from the nightstand, noticing an unread message from Christopher on my phone.

Christopher: How about my eyes? Can they remain unprofessional? 'Cause keeping both in check is too much.

Victoria: And we already established you don't have much self-control.

Christopher: Around you, apparently not. I promise I'll be as obvious as possible so you can call me out on it.

This man! He is unbelievable. The problem is, when it comes to him, I'm not doing too well with this self-control thing myself. I'm tempted to text back some challenge, but like the good girl I am, I place the phone back on my nightstand instead, turning away from it and trying to concentrate on my book and my to-dos for tomorrow. I have to buy some school supplies for Sienna and Lucas, and Chloe wants a new toy. She didn't tell me what kind of toy, only that she wants something she can cuddle at night. She already found a name for the unknown toy: Mr. Cuddles.

Alone in my double bed, I hug my pillow tightly, wishing I had something, or someone, to cuddle. Better still, I'd love to have strong arms to envelop me at night, someone to whisper naughty things in my ear and reassure me that everything will be fine. A vision appears in my mind: dark eyes, strong shoulders, a sinful mouth. I smile against my pillow at the same time I chastise myself. *Off-limits. He's completely off-limits.*

Maybe I'll buy a Mr. Cuddles for myself too. I could nickname him Christopher.

Chapter Six

Victoria

"We should pop open a champagne bottle," Isabelle says on Friday during our lunch meeting. We're sitting at a cafe downtown, going through our financial plans for the month. Two more clients signed with us this week, which is always a reason to celebrate, but even more so because they came from recommendations. That means a lot to us. It shows our clients are happy enough with our services to recommend us to their friends. Dad always said recommendations are the bread and butter of a business.

"We'll put that on our endless to-do list, but for now, how about toasting with our hot drinks?"

We clink our glasses spiritedly, before returning to our lunch.

"By the way," she continues, "Helen and I were thinking of a weekend-long escape and drive out to L.A. What do you say? Maybe your aunt can watch the kids?"

A year ago, I would have said yes in a minute. Helen is our other best friend, and the three of us frequently went on impromptu weekend trips. Now, however, things are different. I'm lucky Isabelle and I work together so at least I see her on a regular basis. I haven't seen Helen in a long while.

“Nah, I have plans with the kids. Maybe another time.”

"Okay. How is Christopher Bennett's project coming along?"

"He's very cooperative," I say instantly. "I wasn’t expecting him to want to be so involved. I'm meeting him this afternoon after Ms. Parson's."

"How is he as a person?" Isabelle presses. "There's so much about the company in the press but rarely about the family itself."

"He's… not what I expected." I hesitate for a split second whether to tell her more, but the truth is, I need to talk to someone, and Isabelle is my best friend. "He came to the office to look through catalogs, and then Lucas cornered him about soccer, and now he's coming to my house on Saturday to give him some pointers."

Isabelle leans back, surveying me. "Do you like him?"

"He's a hard man not to like," I admit with a sigh. "He's nice to the kids, has a body to die for, is the funniest man I've met, and really knows how to lay on the charm."

"Whoa, girl. You haven't gushed over a man in… since forever, actually." Sitting up straight again, she drums her fingers on the table, and I know the warning is on her lips.

"I know he's a client," I say quickly. "And I've learned my lesson. Mixing business with pleasure brings a lot of headache."

"Amen to that." Over the years, we both were burned by this. To our defense, working sixty-hour weeks leaves little room for personal lives. Isabelle went out with a colleague back at the company we both worked at, FortyStarsDesigns. After they had broken up, the atmosphere in the office was unbearable. Also while at FortyStarsDesigns, I fell for a client. After I had slept with him, he tossed me away like I was a broken toy. One of the next clients came because of his recommendation, and during our initial meeting, he asked me if my sexual services were included in the price. I felt so dirty that not even a long shower in which I vigorously scrubbed myself helped.

So when Isabelle and I started our business, we made it a rule that we won't date any clients. In truth, I don't plan to date at all for now. Every action, including whom I choose to date, will impact the kids. I won't deny I'd love to be held and cuddled once in a while. I love cuddles. They make me feel loved and safe, and I haven't felt safe since I buried my parents. I can't explain it, but sometimes I feel like I'd been wrapped in a blanket all my life. Now suddenly the blanket's gone, and I'm permanently cold. But a girl can't have it all, I suppose.

"So you're sure you won't fall for his charms?" Isabelle presses.

"Yep. He's the most shameless flirt I've encountered, but I can go toe-to-toe with him. I can't afford to make any mistakes."

***

Later that afternoon, with half an hour to spare until my meeting with Christopher, I do a little window-shopping, right until I spot a familiar and gorgeous red sweater that Sienna was looking at online last week. Taking out my phone, I snap a picture and send it to my sister. She calls me within two seconds.

"Is that the sweater I was hoping to find on sale online?" she asks in one breath.

"You tell me, but I think it is. The price tag isn't

in the pic, but it's on sale. Do you want me to buy it?"

"Are you serious? Oh my God, yes." She lets out a squeal so loud, I'm afraid my ear will ring for the next few hours. My sister is an unusual seventeen-year-old. She is rarely moody, never rebellious, and generally seems like an old soul. Mother used to say Sienna missed the 101 course on how to be a teenager. But the one thing that absolutely fires her up is fashion.

"You'll have it tonight."

"Thanks, Victoria. You're the best."

After ending the conversation, I walk in and buy the sweater, then hurry to my meeting with Christopher.

Armed with a million ideas for his apartment, I wait for him in front of the furniture store. One of the reasons I like to do a shopping tour with my clients is because I learn a lot about their tastes as I watch their reactions while they're in the store. Going with them through catalogs helps, but sometimes they like an item in a picture and hate it upon seeing it in real life. Christopher arrives precisely at three o'clock, flashing me a smile that seems to say he's up to no good.

"Hello, Victoria." From the way those two words tumble from his lips, and his gaze rakes over my body, it's clear he intends to follow through with his promise to be as obvious as possible, but I don't intend to call him out on it. I have the nagging suspicion that it would lead us down a rabbit hole. Though I feel my cheeks heat up, I stubbornly keep my mouth shut. I'm wearing a bright yellow dress that shows no cleavage and ends up just a notch above my knees, and I paired it with red ankle boots. My coat is the same color as my boots. Yeah, I love colors. Sometimes I overdo it, but wearing brightly colored clothing just fills me with positive energy.

Overall, my appearance doesn't scream sexy in any way, but the intensity in Christopher's gaze makes me feel utterly naked.

"Nice tie," I remark, and it occurs to me that it's the first time he's wearing one in my presence. For some reason, he doesn't seem comfortable wearing it.

"I forgot I had the stupid thing on. I hate them."

"Why wear it if you hate it? You're your own boss, after all."

"Believe it or not, it helps in some meetings, especially with banks." In an instant, he removes the tie, shoving it in his pocket. "Much better." Even without the tie, he exudes power and authority—thanks to the dark gray suit he's wearing. Still, his mischievous expression betrays him, giving him a youthful charm.

"Ah! It was one of those meetings. Yeah, I have a special suit I wear when I have a meeting with my bank adviser. It says I have a stick up my ass and never stray from the beaten path. Now, give me all the money in the world." I'm surprised that even someone of his caliber still has to work to impress the bank. Then again, the loans Bennett Enterprises asks for probably have quite a few more digits than mine do. "I'm glad you made time for this."

"Hey, just because I don't know jack shit about decorating doesn't mean I don't want to have a say in the things I'll buy."

"I've had clients who gave me carte blanche. I gave them a general concept, and they pretty much left me to my own devices."

He pinches his brows together, rubbing his jaw. "How did that work out for them?"

"Good for some, not so well for others. Which is why I prefer to window-shop with the client. Shall we go in?" I ask. Christopher surveys the four-story shop as if it's his own personal hell. "I promise it'll be quick and productive."

"And fun. That's the most important part." He leans into me slightly, unleashing the full power of his gaze on me. "You promise to make it fun?"

"Only if you promise to keep your eyes from wandering."

"Touché. After you."

The store is unusually quiet when we enter it, with only about a dozen customers shuffling around.

"Hi, Donna," I greet the first-floor supervisor, who is currently with a young couple, showing them a selection of curtains. She gives me a quick nod, but she winks at Christopher. My insides tighten, as I lead Christopher further inside the building, then up to the next level. I suppose he's used to this kind of attention from women. Curiosity grips me all of a sudden. Did he return Donna's blatant ogling? *Doesn't matter. He can do whatever he wants.*

"I called the store to check which of the items you liked from the catalog are on display, and they have quite a few. We can start by looking at the couch you chose. It's in a different color, but you can test to see if it's comfortable enough for you."

When we arrive in front of said item, Christopher plops himself on the U-shaped sofa.

"It's comfortable," he says as he runs his palm over the armrest. "Perfect." Christopher stands up, stretching his legs. While we check out the chestnut table and the chairs next, two warehouse workers move out one of the huge couches available on display. Their orders must be not to disassemble it, and the poor men have a hard time moving the giant around.

"I worked in a warehouse one summer," Christopher says unexpectedly.

"You did what?" I asked, stunned.

"Yes."

"How come? I thought your family…."

"By the time I was in high school, we had plenty of money. I think my parents feared us kids would grow up to be self-entitled brats."

"Which would have been a real possibility."

"Yeah. So for my sixteenth birthday, I asked for an exorbitant computer so I could play my video games. My parents and oldest brother made a deal with me. I had to find a summer job, and if at the end I still wanted that computer, I had to use my earnings, and they'd pay the difference. I was a sixteen-year-old with zero skills except pranking and playing video games—two things that don't belong on a résumé, unfortunately. My options were limited, so I ended up working in a warehouse."

"What happened?" I ask, entranced.

"When I received my paltry checks, I realized they'd barely make a dent in footing the bill for my computer. And working side by side with people who had to live on a slightly higher paycheck kind of made me feel like a self-centered schmuck. As my dad put it, it taught me the value of hard work and money. I ended up saving that money and continued using the computer I already owned, which was a good one anyway."

"Wow, your parents are so smart. That's a brilliant tactic. I'll keep it in mind in case I ever need to apply it to the kids. Any other wisdom?"

"Parenting tips, you mean?"

"Yeah."

"Nothing comes to mind right now."

"I've read some books on the topic," I confide in

him, "but I don't feel like much of a parent. It's a work in progress."

"Everything is," he says encouragingly. "Don't be too hard on yourself. I'm sure my parents made mistakes too, but there were so many of us that by the time they got to me, they'd already perfected their techniques."

"That's really encouraging," I tease, but already feel better. We return to inspecting the table and the chairs, and in the end, Christopher declares he likes them, insisting the chairs be fitted with leather seats and backrests as well.

"Next on the list?" he inquires. "This really is efficient."

"Told you it would be."

He trails behind me as I lead him to the next section. "Let's go to the bedroom," I murmur, head bent to check my list.

"Ah, my favorite words to hear from a woman," he whispers into my ear. I swirl around, which turns out to be a big mistake because I've miscalculated the distance between us, and my face ends up inches away from his. On top of that, the motion made me dizzy, and I lose my balance for a split second. Christopher places his hand on my waist, and the gesture electrifies me, lighting up every nerve ending. My pulse quickens, and I lick my lips nervously. Another big mistake. Christopher's gaze zeroes in on my mouth with an intensity that makes my knees weak. "You okay?"

"Yeah."

He lets go of me as I step back, trying to gather my wits. "Sorry about that."

"It's understandable. I sometimes cause that reaction."

"What reaction?" I ask, genuinely confused.

"Blushing cheeks, weak knees," he says with a straight face.

I become acutely aware of the heat in my cheeks. "Can you be serious for a moment?"

"Why? Serious is overrated. That's what I do at the office all day. It's nice to get a break when I leave it."

"You're so far past unprofessional right now."

"I know. I'm downright shameless, and proud of it." He lets out a long whistle, shaking his head. "And you haven't seen anything yet."

Crossing my arms, I take a step back. The more distance I put between us, the better. "You promised to behave."

"Come on, Victoria. I kept it professional until now." Christopher's eyes light up, like those of a kid when he receives a new toy. "Don't I deserve any points for that?"

"Your cocky self-assessment just wiped out every single point."

"That's not really a fair point system now, is it?"

"Christopher, can we go back to our to-do list?"

He tilts his head to one side, as if considering his words, then smiles devilishly. "You're right. We were about to go in the *bedroom*."

"Look, I might have given you the wrong impression with all that no-filter talk, but those were just slips. I'm—"

"You're not going to deny we have chemistry, right?"

My shoulders slump. "There's no point denying it, is it? We don't have to act on it though."

"I know." His gaze—determined and smoldering—keeps me captive. My breath catches. Damn, those are some strong alpha vibes. "It would be so much fun though."

I chuckle, despite myself. "You were searching for a reason not to act on it when we spoke on the phone."

"I still am. It's just proving to be difficult."

"Come to think of it, you never said why you *need* a reason."

Christopher shoves his hands in his pockets, his brow furrowing as if he's weighing his thoughts carefully. He's silent for so long that I can't help a sense of foreboding creeping up my spine.

"Oh no," I groan. "You're one of those 'wham, bam, thank you, ma'am' types, aren't you?"

"No, but let's just say that even though my older siblings are getting married so fast, you'd think they're in a competition, I'm not about to follow in their footsteps."

He seems to be talking to himself more than to me right now.

"Are you rehearsing this speech for someone?" I ask.

"Some members of my family are into matchmaking. I'm next on their list, and I need some solid reasons for them to back off."

"Is your family as hilarious as you are? Pippa and Alice seemed fun but not quite on your level."

"I like to think I take the cake, but they're all a hilarious bunch, especially my younger brothers, Blake and Daniel."

I barely repress my laughter and the urge to ask more questions. His family sounds like my kind of people.

"So where does that leave us?"

He tilts his head to one side, scrutinizing me. "I can't give you my word I'll behave, but I'll try to."

"So we're good?" I ask suspiciously.

"One hundred percent." He purses his lips, clearly wanting to add something more, then just extends his hand, as if saying "After you." Relieved, I take the lead, showing him the way to the bedroom area.

"This is what you chose." I point to a king-sized bed with a lighted headboard. "Don't bother sitting or lying on it though. It has the wrong mattress. For someone of your height and build, you need a firmer one." I walk over to the nearest bed, checking the tag on the mattress. "You can try this one."

After inspecting it for himself, he gives me his stamp of approval.

"I'm making an inhumane effort not to say anything inappropriate. I hope you appreciate it."

"What were you going to say?" I challenge.

"I was going to invite you to try the mattress with me. Or the shower. That's next on the list, isn't it?"

"Yeah," I acknowledge.

"I have simple criteria: two people must fit inside it comfortably."

In the second it takes me to register his words, my cheeks heat up, and I'm sure they're the same intensity of red as my boots.

"That's why it'd be perfectly appropriate to ask you to test it with me."

"Christopher!"

"I know, I know!" He holds up his hands in mock defense. "I promised that I'd try. But it's a work in progress. Let's check out the showers."

Astonishingly, he does keep his promise, and we check off the shower in a matter of minutes.

"We're done," I inform him afterward. "You can go. I'll just check with the manager on the delivery dates on some of these items. We're not going to order anything yet, in case you change your mind, but we need the information. I'll e-mail you everything as soon as I'm out of here."

"I'll wait for you."

"Okay."

I return with all the information ten minutes later, only to find Donna chatting up Christopher. She twirls a strand of hair between her fingers, smiling constantly at him. Christopher nods and seems to give one-word answers. When she sees me approaching, Donna becomes flustered and gives Christopher her card.

"Call me if you need *anything*," she tells him with emphasis on the last word before taking off. I often come here with clients, but it's the first time Donna's hit on one. Not that I can blame her; Christopher is too sexy for his own good. Or mine.

Clearing my throat, I say, "Here's the list of the dates."

"Thanks."

"I leave you alone for two minutes, and you already collect a number?" I try to make it sound like a joke, but my voice is a tad too strained to pass off as casual. It bothers me, and it really shouldn't. Christopher shrugs, his expression unreadable.

"She's a nice person," I say as we walk out of the store side by side. "Recently divorced, likes Tiramisu."

Once outside, Christopher stops in front of me, cocking an eyebrow. "Are you trying to set me up with her?"

"No, I was just giving you some info for when you call her."

His jaw ticks, his eyes growing hard. "I'm not going to call her."

"No?"

"My incessant innuendos might have given you the wrong idea, but I don't flirt with everything that moves, Victoria. I only call a woman or respond to her advances when I'm interested. That's not the case with Donna."

Even though I know I shouldn't care, I can't help the sense of elation overcoming me.

"Okay."

Checking his phone, he says, "I'm going to grab a coffee before I head back to my office. Would you like one?"

"No time. . .and I can't believe you're a coffee person," I say, feigning disgust. "I knew there had to be something wrong with you."

"Don't tell me you're a tea person. You were drinking hot chocolate when I met you. I have it on good authority one should never trust a tea person."

"Yeah, I like hot chocolate but hate coffee. I'm a tea person through and through. There you have it. We could never work. "

He shakes his head, squaring his shoulders, but then his face lights up. "Should I bring breakfast tomorrow?"

"No way. You're coming to my house to help Lucas. Breakfast is on me. Do you have any preferences?"

"I'll eat anything."

"Okay. I really need to go now, or I'll be late for my next meeting."

Christopher closes the distance between us, and his proximity is all it takes for my senses to come alive. We'd been closer than this inside the store, when I practically spun around into him, but this is different. The chilly air forms a stark contrast to his cologne, and the smell all but engulfs me. Raising his hand, Christopher touches the hinge of my jaw with the back of his fingers. It's a light touch, really, but the effect is devastating.

"By the way, is it okay if I use your shower tomorrow?"

My throat dries up. "What?"

"I plan on showing Lucas some moves, and I like to shower after a workout or a soccer game."

"Sure. Of course. No problem."

"See you tomorrow, Victoria." Dropping his hand, he steps back, winking once at me before taking off. As I walk to my car a few seconds later, I try hard not to think about Christopher in my shower.

Chapter Seven

Victoria

I'm full of energy after the meeting with Christopher, and on the way home, I debate whether to take the kids out to dinner, and possibly a movie too. My mood takes a deep dive when I arrive home because a familiar car is parked in front of the house. It belongs to Hervis Jackson, the social worker assigned to our case. I had hoped he wouldn't visit this month. Over the last three months, he's been doing the monthly checkups over the phone, and I hoped he'd stick to that method. Social and family services are supposed to help in cases such as ours, but from the beginning, it's felt as if they're against me.

Steeling myself, I climb out of the car and head inside. I find Hervis in the living room, talking to the kids. He's in his late forties with short hair and premature lines around his mouth. He's also a master at pushing my buttons, getting on my every nerve.

"Ms. Hensley," he greets me.

"I would have preferred for you to call me beforehand. What if we weren't home?"

He ignores my question, instead surveying the kids. "I'm done here, anyway."

"You won't mind if Lucas, Chloe, and I go in the front yard, then," Sienna says. She has as much love for

Hervis as I do.

"Not at all," Hervis answers. Sienna and the little ones are out the door the next second. He turns to me. "The commute to the minors' schools is fairly long. That isn't much of a problem for the oldest one, but for the little ones, not the best."

"It's fifteen minutes longer than it was from the old house. I thought it would be best if they didn't change schools. One less new thing to adapt to. Their school is much better than the ones around here."

"That's true, but also more expensive."

And here we go again. *Breathe in, breathe out, Victoria.* I pace around the room, his stern gaze following me.

"Mr. Jackson, we've been through this. I can afford it. I've already proven I have an income—"

"Which varies heavily from month to month, depending on how many clients you have. Have you reconsidered finding an actual job? Steady employment and a steady paycheck?"

I fold my arms over my chest so he can't see I've curled my hands into fists. "We've been through this too. I'm more flexible working for myself, I can attend the kids' recitals and so on, and I can be home for dinner every night. I'm aware my income is variable, but even in the lowest months I've made enough to cover our living costs."

"Yes. Of course, having no mortgage helps," he deadpans. I taste bile at the back of my throat. The mortgage on my old parents' old house still had fifteen years of payments to run, and it immediately became clear my "then" salary wouldn't have been enough to cover the monthly payment. Not even by taking into consideration my parents' life insurance could we have kept the house.

So I did what I thought was logical, sold that house, paid the debt, and with the money left from the sale and the life insurance, I bought this house. I thought it would show my commitment to offer the kids a stable home. Hervis thought I was conning my siblings out of insurance money so I could live rent-free. Talk about perspective.

"I won't deny it helps. But I pay for their private school and make sure they have everything they need."

"How long are the minors alone at home every day?"

"Since school and preschool started, about two hours. However, Sienna is seventeen, and she's always with Chloe and Lucas when I'm not home. Mr. Jackson, I have to say, I understood your skepticism regarding my abilities to be the children's guardian in the beginning. I'd lost my job and clearly had no idea what I was doing. But I'm working hard to provide them with a stable home now."

"Ms. Hensley, I'm here to make sure you are indeed the best person to look after the young minors. You've made improvements, yes. I have noted that. Rest assured it's being taken into account. But we're talking about a span of a few months. That's hardly proof enough you're a fit guardian for another fourteen years until the youngest minor becomes an adult. I've been a social worker for twenty years. I've seen things that would make you sick to your stomach."

I do believe him. I cannot even begin to imagine the horrors he must have witnessed, even if indirectly. I also believe there are many wolves in sheep's clothing, but I'm not one of them.

"The best advice I can give you is not to stray from the straight and narrow path."

Chapter Eight

Christopher

When I walk up Victoria's porch on Saturday morning, I can hear a war waging inside the house.

"Chloe, you can't wear that shirt again. It's dirty. Take it off now." Victoria's voice sounds stern but tired.

"But I like it," Chloe retaliates.

"It's dirty and smelly," Lucas says. "Why do you want to be smelly?"

For a few minutes, I wait outside the door for the spirits to calm down, but things just seem to escalate. It's best if I announce my presence, even if I'm twenty minutes early.

The second I ring the bell, the voices die down but then start again, now as low whispers. After a few hurried orders of "behave" and "pick your socks up off the floor," the door swings open.

"Hi," I say.

"You're here early," Victoria exclaims. She wears a bright orange robe she desperately tightens around her. Clearly she meant to change before my arrival. Something is different about her this morning. There are shadows under her eyes, and she looks utterly disheveled. She looks down at the gym bag in my hand as if considering something.

"Should I wait outside, or in my car?" I joke

because she seems to need some lighting up.

"God, no." If possible, she gets even more flustered than before, shaking her head and opening the door wider. "Sorry, I'm a bit of a mess this morning."

"There's no need to explain yourself to me," I assure her as I walk inside. The little devils are nowhere to be seen. "Where did the kids disappear to? I heard them when I walked up onto the porch."

"Chloe agreed to change when she heard the doorbell. Sienna's helping her. Lucas went to change into soccer-appropriate clothes. Do you need to change?"

"Nah, this will do. I'll change into a new shirt afterward." I point to the gym bag, in which I packed a towel, shower gel, and a new shirt.

"Sorry for my outfit. I meant to change into something decent, but…."

And maybe it's because she seems to get more distressed by the second, but I resort to the one thing I know will take her mind off it.

"Hey, I'm a big proponent of indecency. You'd make my day if you told me you're wearing a camisole underneath that." Seeing her blush, I can't help leaning in and adding in a slight whisper, "And no panties."

My words have the desired effect of making her laugh. "I'm not even awake enough to come up with a witty reply to that. Let's go in the kitchen. I'll make you a sandwich."

As I follow her, I actually make an effort to avoid ogling her round, perky ass. Her robe is tightened around her middle, which highlights her other curves more than I wish it would.

"Do you ever leave the house wearing just your robe?"

"I know my choice of clothes is oddly colorful

sometimes, but I don't go out of the house in what's practically underwear."

"Not even to get the mail or something?"

She turns around as we enter the small kitchen. "What's with all the questions?"

"Just wondering if any of your neighbors saw what I'm seeing right now. I might have to kill a few if the answer's yes."

"Territorial much?"

Her question takes me by surprise, and damn, I haven't been territorial with a woman in a long time. Victoria keeps surprising me. Not only that, she makes *me* surprise myself, and that has never happened before. Maybe this is why, despite my best efforts, I can't tone down the flirting. Okay, scratch that. I'm not even making a decent effort. If anything, I'm looking for any opportunity to make her blush.

A slow smile spreads on her face. "Just think about all those men who saw me in a bikini."

I love this woman's spirit and talent for banter. Still, that doesn't make me less of an ass. All I want is to prop her up on this counter, bury myself inside her, and lure sounds of pleasure out of her delicious mouth.

"How do you drink your coffee?" she asks, snapping me out of my dirty, selfish thoughts.

"Black. I thought you were a tea person?"

"I am, but you aren't, so I bought a bag of coffee. It's the least I can do since you're willing to spend your day training Lucas."

The kitchen is small but practical. Placing my gym bag in a corner, I stand by the window, where I have a view of the backyard. There's a goalpost in place already.

A few short minutes later, she hands me a cup of steamy coffee and pours herself tea, then opens her fridge.

"What do you want on your sandwich? I have ham, cheese, vegetables…."

"Ham and cheese will do."

Shortly afterward she hands me a sandwich. I bite into it while I'm waiting for the coffee to cool down a few degrees since I don't have the patience to sip it slowly. Usually, I down it in a few gulps. I formed the habit over the years, drinking my coffee quickly before anyone interrupted me with a call or a meeting.

"Are you waiting for that coffee to cool down so you drink it in one guzzle?"

"Please tell me you don't have that weird people-reading ability all the women in my family possess. I'm a dead man otherwise."

"I'd love to say yes, but I'm a pretty bad judge of character. Something in your body language just tipped me off, I suppose."

"You're right. I usually wait until the coffee is almost cold, and then drink it in a few gulps. It's the quickest."

She squints her nose, looking more adorable than ever. "So you're not just a coffee drinker, but a lukewarm coffee drinker?"

"The worst kind," I confirm. "I don't drink it for the taste. In fact, I don't even like it, but I need the caffeine boost."

She holds up her cup, tipping it slightly in my direction. "Is tea sounding more attractive?"

"Never."

"I challenge you to take your time and enjoy your coffee in peace today. Admire the sky, the flowers."

"Maybe I'll just admire you."

She smiles coyly, sipping her tea. I sip my coffee.

"Hey, this is actually good. I wasn't expecting it since, you know...."

"I'm a tea drinker?" Her smile fades. Sadness settles over her as she sits at the small kitchen table by the window. "Mom and Dad were big on coffee. I learned to do it just the way they liked it when I was a teenager. They had this cute routine on weekends, which always started with them drinking coffee in the morning. They'd sit out on the porch, enjoying each other's company. Our old house also had a porch."

"The old house?"

"The kids and I grew up somewhere else. We had to sell the house after our parents passed away. The mortgage was more than I could handle. But we love this place too."

She offers me a smile, but her eyes are glassy, and damn if I don't want to call a real estate agent and buy that house for her and the kids.

"Tell me more about your parents," I encourage. "If you want to."

"They were the loveliest people. Mom was my best friend, and Dad was just... he was a character. Always up for a good laugh. They loved each other so much. Sometimes I caught them looking at each other, and there was so much love there. I sort of always assumed that love faded away with time, and the relationship was based on respect. But my parents were in love, even after all that time."

"My parents are like that," I tell her. "They still finish each other's sentences sometime. It's weird for all of us to watch. Also, it explains why there are nine of us. Though to be fair, there are two sets of twins."

She chuckles, which is what I was hoping for; seeing her sad makes me want to walk over and take her in my arms. That's a bad idea for many reasons, not least of which is I'd end up kissing her.

"Do you talk to your parents often?" she asks.

"Yeah. In fact, I'm heading to their house for dinner tonight. We're very close. Since I returned from Hong Kong, I swear Mom is hogging me even more than before."

"Good. Let her do it and enjoy it as much as you can. You never know when you won't have the chance anymore." Shaking her head, she adds, "Well, aren’t I a ray of sunshine today?"

"Are you okay?"

"Yeah. Just a rough morning. Sorry you had to walk in on a war."

"Technically I just eavesdropped."

She still looks uncomfortable, and I have a hunch I know why. Moving from the window to sit at the table, I say, "You don't have to put on the professional facade now. I'm not a client you need to impress, just a friend showing Lucas how to score. Ground rule for today: relax."

"You want to set the rules in my house? You've got balls."

"You have no idea. Do we have a deal?"

"Okay. Are my eyes red?" she asks, somewhat alarmed as thunderous steps indicate the kids will burst inside the kitchen any second now.

"I can't tell. They look beautiful, as usual."

Before she has a chance to reply, the three kids enter the kitchen. Sienna carries Chloe, who appears to be in a great mood. Lucas bounces in wearing his training gear, ball under his arm.

"Hi, Christopher," Lucas and Chloe say at the same time. Sienna just nods.

"Hey, everyone," I greet. "Lucas, ready to kick some ass?"

Sienna and Victoria shoot daggers with their eyes at me, but it's not until Chloe giggles, informing me, "We're not allowed to say bad words," that I realize where I'm wrong.

Lucas's grin is contagious. "Yeah, let's go in the backyard." We walk out of the kitchen, and as soon as we're out of the girls' earshot, he says, "And kick ass."

***

Lucas's enthusiasm magnifies once we're in the backyard, which is small but gives us enough space for practice. Putting the soccer ball down, he hunches his shoulders, dipping his head downward. That's a sign of lack of confidence.

"Let's do some warm-ups," I say.

Lucas stares at his toes, then back up. "Do you have time to warm up *and* give me pointers?"

"Yeah, kiddo. Don't worry."

He attempts to rush through the motions, obviously eager to get to the good part, but I make him do it again. Eventually, he gives in, doing everything by the book.

"Now, show me what you know, and we'll go from there."

I observe him for the next few minutes, in which he self-consciously performs the routine he learned at school. I make mental notes of the moves he does wrong and the techniques he can improve.

For the next few hours, I teach him everything I

think might be useful for tryouts. He absorbs everything with a voracity I recognize, and it reminds me of the long afternoons Alice spent practicing with me. Yeah, my sister was, and still is, hands-down the best soccer player in our family. When I was in high school, I finally shoved my pride aside and asked her to train with me. I desperately wanted to be the best on the team, to impress a girl.

Watching Lucas, I can tell there's something strong driving his motivation, but given his age, I suspect it's not a girl.

Four hours later, we're both tired. We only stopped for brief breaks to drink water. Now we're wolfing down sandwiches Sienna brought to us. I can tell Lucas would like to keep going, but he's exhausted.

"Do you think I have a shot at making the team?" he asks. "Dad would be so proud of me if I did."

Ah, and here's his reason. "Yeah, you do. When are tryouts?"

"In two weeks."

I try to remember if I have important meetings scheduled late in the evening from now until then. Screw it! If I do, my assistant will just have to move them around. "How about if I stop by a few times after dinner until your tryouts? I could give you more tips, watch you train."

Lucas freezes in the act of biting into his sandwich. "That would be so cool."

"I'll work out something with Victoria, then."

He nods, eating his sandwich at lightning speed.

"Hurrying somewhere?" I inquire. "You'll choke."

"Yeah, I have to shower and then water the flowers," he explains proudly. "I always do that on

Saturdays."

I stare at him, slightly thrown by his enthusiasm. "You're a good brother. When I was your age, I tried to weasel out of my duties as often as possible."

Lucas sits up straighter, squaring his shoulders. "I'm the man of the house. I can't wise out of my duties."

"Weasel," I say automatically.

"Yeah, that." After a brief pause, he says, "I want to help Victoria, so they let us stay with her."

"What?"

"That guy from social services was here yesterday. Victoria is always upset after that. I think they want to take me and Chloe away. We're adopted, you know."

Stunned, I mull over an answer in my mind, but nothing brilliant strikes me. "I know, but Victoria is your sister, and she loves you," I say simply. "She'd never let them take you away."

Judging by the apprehension on his face, he really fears that possibility. He glances toward the kitchen window before saying in a small voice, "Last night I heard her crying in her room. Victoria never cries. What if something bad happened?"

I stop chewing, the thought of Victoria crying not sitting well with me at all. The kid breaks my heart. I take one long look at him, trying to put myself in his shoes, but the truth is, I didn't have a care in the world growing up, while he's lost his parents. I suppose this creates some kind of insecurity running deeper than anything I know.

"Look, your sister loves you 100 percent. People sometimes cry without something bad happening. Maybe she just had a long day. Work can be stressful, or you just run into a jerk in traffic—"

"Bad word," Lucas informs me.

"Sorry! You run into a bad person in traffic."

"But how can I help?"

"Sometimes there's nothing you can do, but there is one thing that almost always helps. It's the big secret to dealing with women."

He shifts closer. "What's that?"

"Chocolate."

"Huh?"

"No matter if they cry or laugh, chocolate is always welcome."

"You sure?" he asks suspiciously.

"Buddy, having chocolate ready for every occasion is Survival 101. Trust me, I have three sisters."

This seems to convince him.

"So what do you do when someone makes your sisters cry?" he queries.

"First I give them chocolate. Then I have my sisters' backs. I protect them. That's what brothers do."

His face instantly lights up.

Chapter Nine

Christopher

The house smells like heaven when we step inside. I'm guessing Victoria's been baking some kind of pastry. I don't recognize the smell, but it transports me back to when I was a kid and Mom baked for us. This is what a home should smell like.

"What's she baking?" I ask Lucas as I follow him into the kitchen.

"Cookies. I hope she made some with cheese again."

"Cookies with cheese?"

"Yeah, we have cookies every weekend, and she likes to experiment."

We walk in on what appears to be happy hour in the kitchen. The girls are drinking lemonade and laughing their asses off. Sienna sits on the windowsill, munching on a cookie. Chloe sits on the table while Victoria braids her hair. Neither sees us come in, and I take this moment to study Victoria in silence. She changed into jeans and a tank top, and there is something incredibly sweet about the way she plants little kisses on top of Chloe's head while doing her hair. I like this tender, nurturing side of Victoria. But then again, I suspect there's little I wouldn't like about her.

"Boys," Sienna exclaims when she notices us. "I

didn't see you there. Which one of you will shower first?"

"Which means we stink badly," I say.

"How come I'm not allowed to be smelly, but they are?" Chloe inquires, looking honestly crestfallen.

"They played soccer, and they're sweaty," Victoria explains patiently. "But they'll shower."

I pop a few cookies in my mouth. Damn, they're good.

"Christopher said he can come by after dinner until my tryouts," Lucas announces, puffing his chest forward.

Victoria turns to me. "But don't you have work and meetings?"

"I'll shift things around," I assure her. The bright smile she offers me is the best damn payment in the world.

"I'll go shower first," Lucas says. After stuffing himself with cookies, he rushes up the stairs. Sienna and Chloe leave the kitchen too. After the girls leave, I take advantage of the fact that we're alone and ask, "Can I talk to you about Lucas?"

She frowns, nodding. "Sure."

Delicacy has never been my strong point, but I try to recount what Lucas told me in the gentlest way possible. Leaning with her back against the counter, Victoria becomes smaller with each word, and I feel like a jackass for making her feel bad, but she has to know.

"That poor thing. I had no idea he feared.... I'll talk to him. Thank you for telling me this."

"Why were you crying? If it's the social worker's fault, just give me his name. I can take care of him."

Unexpectedly, she smiles—and damn, I love how it lights up her entire expression. "You don't even need his address?"

"Nah, a name is all I need to find him. I'm resourceful like that."

"Quite a savior, aren't you?"

"If you want me to be."

"Thank you for the generous offer, but it's not necessary." Her smile falters. "The meeting with him wasn't even as unpleasant as it could've been, but child services aren't convinced I'm a fit guardian. They're keeping an eye on us, and it's exhausting to always be afraid that if I make one mistake, I could lose the little ones. But I never mentioned that to Lucas and Chloe, just to Sienna. They must have eavesdropped."

"How can child services doubt you?"

"I was fired from my job two weeks after my parents passed away, and I was running around like a crazy person in the beginning. I was a mess, and I suppose first impressions are hard to shake off. They're checking in periodically, making sure the kids are all right."

"I don't like to think about you crying yourself to sleep."

"I'm not a crybaby. It's not like I do this every night. It was just a way to let it all out, I suppose." She seems to shrink a few inches as she adds in a low voice, "I felt like a failure."

Almost without realizing, I cup her cheeks, tilting her head up so she can't avoid looking at me.

"You're not," I say automatically. "You changed your life to accommodate everything around these kids. I think you're amazing."

"You're a sweet talker."

"No, this is me being honest." I respected her from the beginning because I usually like people who are competent in their job, but in the meantime, she's shot up to the list of people I admire. Dropping my hands from her cheeks, I place them on the counter at her sides, trapping her. "When I sweet talk you, you'll know it."

"Really?" Looking first down on the left and then to the right, she takes notice that I've completely invaded her private space, but instead of pushing me away, she merely glances up at me, cocking an eyebrow. Right, she's still waiting for my answer.

"Yeah."

"Give me a clue."

"Your panties will drop all on their own."

Inhaling sharply, she tilts her head to one side, as if she suddenly found something interesting to stare at to my left. Her hair slides back with the motion, baring her neck to me. Her skin is almost translucent, and I detect a faint smell of peach, probably her shampoo or shower gel. I could get drunk on the smell of her skin, on her in general. I'm tempted to dip my head lower and trail my mouth up and down her neck, feeling its softness. I grip the counter hard, steadying myself. The smart thing would be to step back, but right now, I'm not smart. I'm taken with this woman.

"You're truly incorrigible, Christopher," she whispers.

"Does this mean you're accepting my general shamelessness and won't scold me for hitting on you?"

"I'm starting to get that it really doesn't make a difference if I scold you or not."

"And you like it."

"Now don't put words in my mouth." She juts her head back in my direction, and our mouths almost collide. She stops short of touching my lips, but she's so close I can feel her breath, can almost taste the sweetness of her mouth. She smells like cookies.

Walk back, Bennett. Walk back.

Instead, I lean forward until I feel her breasts against my front. A current of awareness zips through us, and my control nearly snaps when her soft nipples press against my chest. She's not wearing a bra. The temptation to cup her breasts overwhelms me, and feeling her nipples turn to hard buds sends a jolt straight to my groin.

"I'd say this is proof enough," I say in a low voice, desperately grasping for some humor to diffuse the sexual tension. I come up blank on laughs but find an unpleasant topic. "I shouldn't be so close to you when I haven't even showered yet."

"Christopher," she says in a low voice, fisting my T-shirt with both hands. "I like your smell. You smell like a man."

"Oh fuck. You can't say things like that and expect me not to kiss you senseless."

Turning to me, her eyes widen just a fraction, and she licks her lower lip quickly. I barely keep myself from leaning down and sucking that lip in my mouth.

"I've fantasized about lifting you up onto this counter and burying myself inside you since this morning." Just saying it out loud makes me hard.

"Oh." She sucks in her breath, squeezing her thighs together.

"You're the sweetest woman I've met, Victoria," I tell her honestly.

"And you're the most bizarre man I've met."

That one unexpected word breaks the spell. Through a haze, I step back. Victoria immediately crosses her arms over her chest, masking her nipples. They were showing nicely through the fabric of her shirt.

"Bizarre? Please elaborate."

"I didn’t mean it in a bad way."

"I can't think of a single time I heard the word bizarre to describe something in a positive way."

"You take your time to come here on a Saturday to help Lucas, you guessed my favorite ice cream flavors, and… I just meant you keep surprising me."

No idea why she chose those two particular things, but they probably mean something to her. An honest man would tell her my sister Alice specifically told me about the flavors, but… *not* being honest seems smart right now.

"I believe the word you're looking for is perfect, not bizarre."

"You forgot to add cocky to my description."

"It runs in my family. You can't hold inherited traits against me."

"Is that so?" She runs her fingers through her hair, shaking her head. A loud alarm makes us both jump, and she turns her attention to the oven. "Second batch of cookies done."

A delicious smell fills the kitchen as she takes them out, placing them on the counter.

"Lucas said you like to experiment."

"Yeah, this time I included a few with pumpkin." She leans over the counter, inspecting her work.

"Interesting. Can I taste?"

She glances at me over her shoulder, a satisfied smile spreading on her face. "Brave, aren't you?"

"I like to live dangerously. And I'm always a fan of spicing things up."

A red hue spreads up her neck as she hands me a cookie. It's still hot, but I'm impatient, so I bite into it almost immediately.

"Hey, this is good," I say, unable to hide my surprise. "So how come you do this every weekend?"

"Lucas also told you that?"

"Yeah."

She remains quiet for a few seconds, busying herself at the counter, her back to me.

"Mom used to bake every Saturday morning. I loved how it made the house smell. All warm... like a home."

She and I have that in common.

"I like to keep that tradition," she adds.

"See? More proof that you're amazing. And yes, now I *am* trying to charm you."

Victoria laughs heartily, turning to me. "My panties are still on, Bennett."

"Challenge accepted."

The tension between us is rising to dangerous levels again, but the sound of footsteps and voices cut right through it. Seconds later, Lucas bursts inside the kitchen.

"The new batch of cookies is ready. Awesome." Without further ado, he heads to the counter, attacking the cookies.

"I'd better go shower."

Sienna and Chloe enter the room, joining their brother by the counter.

Grabbing my gym bag, I say, "Sorry to interrupt the cookiefest, but would anyone care to point me to the shower?"

"It's down the hall, second on the left."

***

"I had a great time today," I tell Victoria later, as I'm preparing to leave. I usually plan the hell out of my weekends, be it friend visits or working out at the gym, only leaving a few hours unscheduled in case my family is up to something spontaneous—and they always are. It might sound weird to plan time for spontaneity, but I'd never get to keep up with what everyone in my family is doing otherwise. I want to make the most of every free moment, and I found that's best achieved by planning ahead.

Today was different. I cleared my schedule until dinner and came here without any expectation beyond teaching Lucas some moves and making Victoria blush. It's been a wildly different day compared with how I usually spend weekends, but I found it surprisingly nice, and I don't want it to end. I have a hunch anything that involves Victoria would have that effect on me. And the kids are definitely a bonus.

"Thank you for doing this, Christopher."

Damn it. My name in her mouth is a trigger. She opens the door for me, and I step outside but linger in the doorway, inches away from her lips.

"He's going to kiss her," Lucas whispers. Damn. He and the girls were supposed to be in the kitchen. I can't see him from my position in the doorway, but he's obviously watching us.

"No, he won't." That was Sienna.

"Kissing is gross," Chloe chimes in.

Jesus. Where are they? I peek behind Victoria, but I still don't see the little buggers.

"But maybe we'll have another sister," Chloe continues. That girl jumps to conclusions fast.

"She'd be our niece," Sienna says. "Besides, kissing is not how you make kids."

"How *do* you make kids?" Lucas asks.

"You have to—"

Right, time to break up that conversation. Victoria

seems to shake off her stupor, swirling around.

"Kids, eavesdropping is not polite," she says.

"But he wanted to kiss you," Lucas says. The kiss police emerge from behind the staircase leading upstairs. "We have to protect you."

I'd be perfectly on board with his plan if he were referring to anyone else except me.

Sighing, Victoria turns to me again. "In this house, there will always be someone listening," she whispers. A strand of her hair has caught at the corner of her mouth. I brush it away with my fingers, but instead of retracting my hand, I touch her lips, watching with satisfaction as they part in surprise.

"In that case, I can't wait to see you outside of it again."

Chapter Ten

Victoria

After shutting the door, I turn on my heels, inspecting my siblings. Sienna gives me an amused, if sheepish, smile, trying to shush Chloe, who tugs at her shirt, repeatedly asking, “How do you make kids?” Lucas stares at me, arms crossed.

"We need to talk," I tell them, doing my best mom impression. "In the living room, all of you."

Once inside, Sienna sits on the ottoman while the small ones take the couch. I pace around the room, looking for the right words.

Sienna breaks the silence. "We're sorry for interrupting the moment with Christopher."

"You didn't interrupt anything," I assure them. "That's not what I wanted to talk to you about."

"What, then?" Sienna continues.

Mulling the answer over in my mind, I realize I don't have a plan. I just want to reassure them that I'll never let anyone take them away. At the same time, I don't want Lucas to realize Christopher and I talked about him. He won't appreciate it. Biting the inside of my cheek, I take a deep breath.

"So, I have a confession to make," I begin, and the three of them perk up. "Yesterday evening, I cried."

Lucas grimaces. "Christopher told you what I told him, didn't he?"

Fantastic start. Sighing, I admit, "Yeah."

"Why were you crying?" Chloe asks. "Will they take us away from you?"

Sienna throws me a startled glance, a sign she didn't know the little ones were eavesdropping when I shared my concerns with her.

"No. No one will take you away, I promise."

"I thought grown-ups didn't cry," Chloe whispers, breaking my heart. That's because Mom never did, or at least we never got wind of it.

"Of course they do," Sienna says sensibly. "They just hide it better."

"Kids, I want you to know that whatever happens, I won't let anyone take you away."

Lucas and Chloe are both watching the floor.

"What if you get married?" Chloe asks.

"What—" I begin, but my brother interrupts.

"You're old enough to have your own kids," Lucas insists. "Will you still want us when you have your own kids?"

Wow, this is going extraordinarily well. Sienna runs a hand through her hair, alarm clearly visible on her face at the fears the little ones are harboring.

"Of course I'll still want you. I love all of you."

"But what if you fall in love?" Chloe asks.

"If I do, it doesn't mean I will love you any less, or that I will stop taking care of you." *Where are they going with this?*

"What if he won't like us?" Lucas asks, stunning me. "I've seen kids at my school with divorced parents. When they get a stepmom or stepdad, they hate each other."

"I promise you I won't date anyone I'm not one hundred percent sure likes you. And you also have to like him."

Lucas's and Chloe's faces break into the biggest smiles I've seen in months, and my heart suddenly feels lighter.

***

An hour later, I'm elbow deep as I attempt to build owls for a thing Chloe has at her preschool. The emphasis is on attempt because my owls so far look like deformed potatoes. The kids are in the backyard, and I can hear them bickering from here.

"Victoria!" Sienna pokes her head through the living room door. "Can I go to the movies?"

"With whom?" I ask automatically.

"The usual. The resident weed dealer and the head of an underground fight club."

"So, Ben and Emma?" I ask, referring to two good friends of hers.

"You got it."

"Smartass. What time will the movie end?"

"I guess around nine. I'll come straight home afterward." She bats her eyelashes at me, grinning.

"Sure, go. Have fun." She spends so much time helping with Lucas and Chloe that I'm afraid she isn't living enough.

Soon after Sienna leaves, I get the hang of making owls. They end up looking so cute that Chloe and I build a few for our home too. I can't help wondering how Mom did it. I don't remember ever seeing her cry. Sure, she lost her temper now and again, but she always seemed in charge, as if she could handle anything life threw at her.

After we're done with the owls, we settle in a companionable silence in front of the TV, watching a documentary about saving whales. Since it's Saturday, both Lucas and Chloe are allowed to go to bed later.

Today has been unexpected on so many levels. Christopher's presence here was everything I dreamed of, as well as everything I feared. I watched him and Lucas while they trained, and I could practically feel Lucas's self-confidence grow the more time he and Christopher spent together. The bad part is that we obviously can't control our attraction to one another. I almost climbed him in the kitchen… while the kids could have walked in on us at any moment!

My skin heats up at the memory of having him near me. Even talking about my parents wasn't as painful as *thinking* about them usually is, and I have a suspicion it's all because of Christopher. He was there with me, strong, resilient, and listening intently. With a sigh, I hug my knees to my chest on the couch, trying to put the day behind me.

We're all entranced in the documentary when my phone lights up with a message.

Christopher: My mother wants to ask you something about her kitchen furniture. Is that okay?

Victoria: Sure, I'll call her right away if you give me her number.

After Christopher sends me her number, I move away from the living room into my office, where my laptop is, and call her. She answers at once.

"Hello, Mrs. Bennett. Victoria Hensley here, Christopher's decorator."

"Hi, Victoria! Please, call me Jenna. Thank you for calling me so quickly."

"My pleasure. What are you looking for?"

"I want to add some cabinets to the kitchen, but the shop I've bought from doesn't stock the model anymore. I haven't been able to find anything similar enough."

"If you tell me the brand and model number, I'll look for it. I'm sure I'll find what you need." Jotting down what she dictates, my mind already races with potential shops that might still store it. Opening my laptop, I'm about to type the model in the search engine when Mrs. Bennett changes topics.

"Christopher told me you've got quite the soccer player on your hands."

"Yeah, my brother, Lucas, hopes to make his school's team. Christopher was very sweet to help him today. Dad was a great player, but unfortunately, neither my sister Sienna nor I were ever interested in it."

"I'm sorry for your loss, child."

"Thank you. It's been harder for the little ones." My throat clogs up. Damn, I'm overly sensitive today.

"Pain is pain, no matter the age. And having to raise three kids on your own on top of that is no small feat."

"You've raised nine. You're the authority on that." Tucking my feet underneath me, I can't help asking, "Were there days when you felt overwhelmed?"

"Every single day. Hard doesn't even describe it. It was beautiful, but raising them felt like an impossible task most days. Don't be hard on yourself. One day you'll look at them and won't believe they're adults."

Aunt Christina often tells me I'm too hard on myself when I share my concerns, but I've always feared she's just cutting me too much slack. Hearing this from Jenna Bennett helps tremendously.

"You raised wonderful adults," I tell her in all honesty. I've only met Christopher, Alice, and Pippa, but I think it's an educated guess to believe the rest of them are just as great.

"Sometimes I wonder if they all grew up in the same house. My children are all so different, and also the same."

"How do you mean?" I ask.

"The oldest trio always had a deep sense of responsibility, rarely stepping out of line. The younger ones were more relaxed, also because they had more opportunities. Christopher and Max pulled so many pranks, I swear they're responsible for all my white hair. Because the older ones shouldered most of the pressure, the younger ones had more freedom. Pursuing hobbies is one example. Max was in a band in college. Christopher and Alice were so good at soccer in college that they had professional scouts asking them to join teams."

"How about the youngest ones?" I inquire, eager to know more.

"Oh, Summer is an artist through and through, and Blake and Daniel are shameless. But they're all fiercely loyal."

I'm about to point out that Christopher is the most shameless man I've met—in a way that makes me laugh, and tingle in places I don't have any business tingling— but some things mothers don't need to know. Instead, I type in Mrs. Bennett's kitchen model in the search engine.

"Jenna, I found three shops where your particular kitchen model can still be ordered. I can call them up and find out which one can deliver the models you want quicker."

"Oh, no need, child. Just tell me the name of the shops."

After I rattle off the names and phone numbers, we say good-bye. And it's only after clicking off that I realize Ms. Bennett has asked me exactly one question about her kitchen, and it was something she probably could look up herself on the Internet. Of course, it could be that she's not using the Internet much, or Christopher might have asked her to make up a bogus reason so I'd call her and she could give me a pep talk, given my mini-meltdown today. The way she gently spoke about the days when everything felt impossible, the reassurance in her voice.... The more I think about it, the more I lean toward the second option. And here goes the tingling again, only now it's taking over a more dangerous part of my body—my heart.

Glancing down at my phone, I notice an unread message from Christopher. I must have received it while I was talking with his mother.

Christopher: I have a problem.

Oh crap. I wonder what he wants to change in the setup of his apartment. I inspect Christopher's folder on my laptop. I have a list of all the items he seemed interested in beside the ones he signaled as "the ones." In my experience, people sometimes change their mind up to one week after the shopping trip. When that happens, they often prefer an item they saw in passing to the one they decided on. In the early days, this led to a lot of back-and-forth hassle, which is why I try to jot down most of the items they seem interested in. It's also why I don't actually order the items after the first visit. I just check the estimated delivery date, and if one week later nothing changes, I place the order.

With Christopher's file in front of me, I text back.

Victoria: What is it?

A few minutes pass before he answers.

Christopher: I can't take my mind off a

certain brunette I met recently.

I have to reread the message three times before the meaning of his words sinks in. When it does, a lightness settles in my chest. I type and delete a few times, wondering what on earth would be an appropriate answer. Yet the longer I stare at my phone, the more tempted I am not to reply with something appropriate. In the end, curiosity gets the better of me.

Victoria: Why not?

I'm on pins and needles the entire time I wait for him to write back. An eternity seems to pass in the thirty seconds—not that I'm counting—it takes for his reply to appear on my screen.

Christopher: Because I like everything I know about her so far.

OhGod OhGod OhGod. He's not done yet; I can see that by the tiny dots appearing on the screen, indicating he's typing. I hold my breath, drumming my fingers on my desk, staring at the screen the entire time.

Christopher: She's smart and sassy, and beautiful. I've never met anyone who's so devoted to her siblings outside of my family. And she makes great cookies.

Until now, I never understood the concept of swooning. My entire body buzzes with awareness and emotion, and I'm at a loss for what to say. *This man.* He's a dream and danger all rolled into one, and I have absolutely no idea what to write back. My fingers are moving on the screen of their own accord.

Victoria: Cookies are really important to you, huh?

Christopher: Oh yeah, absolutely! So now I'm trying to find out if she's met anyone recently she likes.

My grin is so wide, my face is actually hurting. I have no clue how long I've been grinning, but I haven't felt like this since I was in high school, sending clandestine notes to a crush—sneaking it into his locker or backpack. Maybe it's because we're talking in the third person, but I type back with no restraint.

Victoria: As a matter of fact, she has. He has a dirty mind and zero filter, is a shameless flirt, and has a knack for raising her brother's self-confidence. He's a striking man. (Striking is an improvement over bizarre.)

I'm expecting him to reply with one of his legendary no-filter lines that has the effect of setting my entire body ablaze, but he surprises me.

Christopher: I want to know more about her. What does she do in her free time?

This gives me pause, as I make a mental inventory of my favorite activities. I don't have as much free time now, but I still try to cram some fun in between all the hard work.

Victoria: She loves books and movies and going out with her girlfriends. She also loves dancing but hasn't had time for it in ages. She's an avid foodie, especially if it involves unexpected or bizarre courses. (See? Bizarre is used in a positive way here.)

His response is almost instantaneous.

Christopher: What's her favorite drink/food/movie?

Slowly, I become aware of his game, and I can't help being pulled into it.

Victoria: She absolutely adores eggnog with extra caramel topping (outside of her working hours, of course) and thinks it's a pity it's not available year-round, and she never says no to pizza. Favorite

movie of all times: Gone with the Wind.

My fingers hover over the Send button, but I want to ask questions of my own too. So I add some.

Victoria: What's his favorite book/movie? Does he like dancing?

Then I press Send and become aware I've been chewing my nails. I'm trembling with excitement. *Trembling.* What spell does this man have on me?

Christopher: He likes to read and watch superhero stories, but he'll sit through a chick flick if there's a chance it leads to dancing. The horizontal kind. It's the only type of dancing he practices (and he's open to bizarre positions too).

Well, hell. Instantly, images start flowing in my mind of a naked Christopher. Though I have no proof, I'm sure this man knows his way around a woman's body. He'd know exactly how to touch me to send me over the edge, exactly how to kiss me to make me want more of him. God, I already want all of him, and he hasn't even kissed me.

With a sigh, I realize I'm not just excited anymore but also turned on. The ache between my legs is almost unbearable. Swallowing, I try to focus on the benign part of his message.

Victoria: Gone with the Wind is NOT a chick flick.

Christopher: It has chicks crying over guys. That makes it a chick flick in any guy's book. (Also, the blatant ignoring of the horizontal dancing topic has not gone unnoticed.)

Yep, I'll keep ignoring it. Not ready to open that can of worms.

Victoria: Superhero movies also have chicks crying/fighting over guys. Judgmental much?

Christopher: Nope. 100% in the right.

Well, now he's just awakening my mama bear side, who'd do anything to protect her favorite movie. Gripped by the intensity of our exchange, I can't help myself asking more. I can't even explain why this feels like a safe way to find out more about him, but I don't care.

Victoria: What's his favorite place in the city? What's his greatest secret?

Christopher. The Golden Gate Park. As for the secret, he can't tell you.

Frowning, I reach for the glass of water on my desk. I text him while downing a large gulp.

Victoria: Why not?

Christopher: Maintaining an air of mystery is a must, even if it means resorting to sneakiness.

I nearly spit out the water as I read that last word.

Victoria: Said sneakiness involves tricking me into talking to a certain Jenna Bennett?

Holding my breath, I wait for his answer.

Christopher: That was no trick. My mother is known to give some great advice, and I thought it would help. It was a completely selfless thing.

Victoria: It did help. Thank you. That was a very nice thing to do.

Christopher: If you were mine, I'd do many *nice* things for you. Feel free to replace nice with delicious, sexy, and romantic, depending on what you're in the mood for.

I would have pegged Christopher Bennett as many things, but not a romantic. He's such a pragmatic type, it never even occurred to me. I wonder if he'll ever cease to surprise me. I have no clue what to write back, and when he doesn't follow up, I return to the living room just as Sienna enters the house. I smile at nothing at all, my pulse at an all-time high, and my stomach full of butterflies.

Oh my. Be still my beating heart. I can handle fun and lust. But butterflies? They're traitorous little beasts.

Chapter Eleven

Christopher

"I need a refill." I hold up my empty glass as I rise from the chair, excusing myself from the table.

Three college friends flew into town this week, and we scheduled drinks tonight to catch up. I haven't seen two of them in five years, the third even longer. Naturally, I've brought them to my brother Blake's bar. Blake and Daniel are the younger set of twins in the family, but they are not identical. Up until last year, the running joke in the family was that Blake and Daniel were the “party brothers.” When Sebastian, Logan, and Pippa set up Bennett Enterprises, they made each member of our family a shareholder, whether they worked in the company or not, so Blake and Daniel lived off the dividends, attending one too many parties. This changed last year when Blake decided to open a bar, and Daniel, his extreme adventure- and outdoor-excursion business. After scoring a spot on various lists featuring San Francisco's top bars, Blake's place has become a popular stop for tourists and locals alike. I'm damn proud of him.

"Little brother, your barman skills are needed," I tell Blake, plunking my glass on the counter.

"Here you go!" He refills my glass with beer, motioning with his head to the blondie tending the other end of the bar. "My girl Amber here is interested in you."

I slice a glance at Amber, who smiles shyly.

"How come you're not interested in her?" I inquire. Back when he first opened the bar, he tended to be overly friendly with the female members of his staff.

My brother shrugs. "New rule—I don't hit on employees, which means I have to go to other bars to pick up women, and that gives me an opportunity to check out the competition. It's a win-win."

Amber is now openly staring at me, her smile changing from shy to suggestive. She's a beautiful woman. I know where this would lead, and it would be a fun night, but I have zero interest in her. A certain brunette has been hijacking my thoughts lately. A night with Victoria, now *that* I'd be interested in.

"Tell her I'm seeing someone else," I instruct him, "and try to let her down gently."

Blake shoots daggers with his eyes at me. "She explicitly asked me if you're seeing anyone, and I told her no."

"Tell her you weren't up to date."

"But—Wait, are you seeing someone? I didn't hear anything through the Bennett rumor mill. Now that I think about it, our sisters were coy when talking about you last time I saw them. That should have clued me in."

"Trust me, when it comes to Pippa and Alice, you'll see the clue only when it smacks you over the head."

Blake groans while I gulp down some beer.

"So, you're dating someone?" he presses. I swear to God, Blake is almost as nosy as my sisters.

"Not exactly, but the decorator for my apartment… I can't stop thinking about her. She's a great woman. Hardworking. Sweet. Sassy."

"And another one bites the dust," Blake mutters,

mixing a cocktail.

"What?"

"These symptoms… I've seen them before."

"What are you talking about?"

"Those puppy-dog eyes, thinking the sun shines out of her butt. In the past three years, I've seen three of our brothers fall to this virus, Bennettitis. It's an epidemic."

"You're annoying me."

"That's what siblings are for," Blake says. Leaning over the counter, he adds, "You do have Bennettitis. Mark my words. By the way, are you coming next Monday?"

“Sure.” My siblings and I try to meet every Monday evening here at Blake’s bar to catch up with each other, but lately everyone’s been busy, occasionally skipping it, to Blake’s annoyance.

Shaking my head, I raise my glass in his direction, then walk back to the group. They're currently immersed in a conversation about some shit we pulled during college, especially freshman year. Later, the conversation turns to the present. All three of them work at the same bank on Wall Street, and apparently, their after-work activities can be summed up in one word: strippers. What a cliché.

As the evening progresses, it becomes painfully obvious I have nothing in common with these guys anymore. Meeting up with them seemed like a great idea when they called to let me know they'd be in San Francisco, but now I'm about to poke my eyes out. I could have done a million other things instead, like go to the gym, or meet people I actually have things in common with.

I could’ve stopped by at Victoria's house. Over

the last two weeks, I've done that a few evenings, helping Lucas get ready for tryouts. Things between Victoria and me have moved beyond sassy banter to something else. No clue how to describe it, but I want more of it. I want *her*, and not just for one night. Victoria has gotten under my skin like no woman has in years, and that's dangerous. I got burned before, and I have no desire to go down that road again.

But Victoria's throaty laughter is addictive, and there's a sweetness to her that I can't get enough of. Spending time with her and her trio of misfits has become one of my favorite activities.

Far be it from me to admit Blake is right, but he *might* have a point. That Bennettitis virus must be airborne.

Chapter Twelve

Victoria

Four o'clock on Wednesday afternoon finds me in my car, waiting outside Lucas's school. He's having tryouts right now, and I was supposed to pick him up at five. I tried to busy myself, but excitement got the better of me, and I arrived one hour too early. Lucas forbade me from attending tryouts. I think he was afraid I'd embarrass him, either by kissing his cheek the first chance I got or shouting inappropriate encouragements from the sidelines. I've been known to do both in the past, so I don't blame him.

Drumming my fingers on the wheel, I turn the volume of the music louder, trying to fill the space and drown my anxiety from hoping he'll succeed. I have contingency plans in the works. If he made the team, we're going to pick up Sienna and Chloe and head to our favorite restaurant to eat cheesecake and celebrate. If he didn't make the team, I'm taking him for consolation cheesecake by myself. Lucas doesn't like company when he's upset, but the great thing about cake? It cheers you up no matter what.

Glancing at the clock, I groan, realizing I still have fifty-five minutes to wait. Right, this is going to be a long hour. I could whip out my laptop and work on a decoration plan for a new client, but something tells me I won't be able to concentrate. An angry whirl of leaves slams against my windshield, startling me. A gust of wind carries them away, clearing my view. Seconds later yet another gust blows, ripping more gold and copper leaves from the trees, their frail and brittle stems giving away. Rolling down the window, I inhale deeply, greedy for the autumn air. I love the smell of autumn—rich, earthy, and crisp—but not cold enough to pinch my nose.

After rolling it back up, I pull my e-reader from my bag. I sometimes carry it with me. A girl must always be prepared; you never know when you might have a few minutes to kill, and reading has the magic power of instantly relaxing me.

A few minutes later, I'm entranced in my book. So entranced that I jump in my seat when my phone chimes with an incoming message.

Christopher: How are tryouts going?

Frowning at the screen, I try to remember when I shared with him that tryouts had been rescheduled from Thursday to Wednesday, but I don't think I did.

Victoria: No idea. How do you know they're happening now?

My phone lights up with an incoming call this time, and I don't hesitate to pick up.

"Lucas told me," Christopher says instead of hello, and I swear the sound of his voice is the best thing I've heard all day. My muscles instantly liquefy, the tension gathered throughout the day melting. This is even better than reading.

"I didn't know he had your number. Maybe he snuck into my phone to steal it."

"Why do you sound so hopeful about that?"

"It would be a sign he's back to his prankster self. He's been very serious since… you know…." Placing the e-reader on the passenger seat, I add, "One of our *things* was that he'd try to guess the password on my phone. I changed it every time I visited my parents' house."

"I hate to disappoint you, but we exchanged numbers. We've talked a few times, and I gave him some more pointers. It was more of a pep talk, to be honest."

"Thank you," I say, truly touched. I'm also surprised he didn't mention this during our numerous calls and messages this past week. But I'm starting to understand that Christopher doesn't do things expecting payment, or even acknowledgment. He's genuinely a good person.

"How come you're not at tryouts?" he asks.

"Ha! I'm in my car, in front of the school. I've been denied access to the gym."

"You're one of those ubersupportive people who shout their head off the entire time, aren't you?"

"Yep. It makes it even more embarrassing that I have no idea what I'm shouting about."

"Bet you're precious."

"I think the word you're looking for is annoying."

"Nope. Sticking with precious. Still, I can't believe you were hoping he'd hacked into your phone."

"Well, it's not like I have anything to hide," I say, drumming the fingers of my free hand on the wheel, glancing at the clock.

"No traces of indecent behavior?"

"None," I confirm, even though he knows this very well, but as usual, I'm game to see where he's going with this.

"So, say he'd hack into your phone a week or two from now. Would you have anything inappropriate to hide?"

Ahh, of course. I should've guessed this was where he was going. I have absolutely no idea what to answer, but the situation requires some teasing.

"Who knows? I might meet a handsome man with blond hair and blue eyes, who could sweep me off my feet."

"I thought you already met someone," he deadpans, and by the frosty undertone in his voice, it's clear he's not appreciating my joke. Whenever Christopher teases me, he puts a smile on my face, and that's exactly the reaction I was hoping to get out of him.

Right, mental note: must work on my teasing skills.

"I have met someone," I say, surprised by the way my voice catches at the end.

"Now we're talking."

I can practically hear him smile, and my heart grows in size.

"You'd better lay it on thick," he continues. "Nothing less than 'he's the best thing to walk on this earth' is acceptable."

I suppress the urge to giggle, sliding down lower in the car seat.

"He makes me smile all the time," I confess.

"You deserve to."

"He also makes me blush a tad too much."

"Really?" His voice has turned thick and rich, like melted butter.

"Yeah," I confirm, suddenly feeling shy.

"Just one question. Does he also make you want to touch yourself?"

In the few seconds it takes for his words to register, my entire body heats up, desire bolting through me. I press my thighs together, attempting to quench the throb in my center.

"Christopher!"

"I take that as a yes."

"You're a bad influence."

"Best words I've heard all day." A loud crack alerts me that there's some commotion on his end. "My assistant just came into my office with a report I need to look at. Let me know about the tryouts."

With that dismissal, he clicks off, leaving me to wonder how he can switch from naughty to businesslike in the span of a second. Still, with some time left to kill, I pick up my e-reader again, attempting to lose myself in the book I was reading. Only my mind flies far too often to a certain bearer of bad influence, and I'm far too aware of all the places where my body aches for him.

***

"I made it," Lucas announces a while later after all but ripping the car door open.

"Congratulations." I refrain from leaving the car and congratulating him properly because the risk of hugging and kissing my brother for all his teammates to see is far too high. "Hop in."

After he climbs in and secures his seatbelt, I say, "How about picking the girls up and going for some cheesecake? At our favorite coffee shop?"

"Awesome. Can I ask Christopher if he wants to come too? I think I only made the team because of this trick he showed me. I was the only one who did it."

"Sure. Go ahead, ask him. But don't call him. Send a message. He might be in a meeting."

Nervously, I gun the engine while Lucas types on his phone. Seconds later, he exclaims, "He wants to join us. I'll tell him to meet us there."

A thin sheet of sweat breaks on my forehead because I wasn't expecting to see Christopher so quickly, especially after admitting the rather unorthodox effect he has on me.

***

"And then the coach told me I would be an assert to the team," Lucas exclaims through mouthfuls of cake. We're all at the coffee shop, listening to his play-by-play recount of the tryouts.

"You mean asset," Sienna corrects him.

"No. I'm sure he said assert," Lucas insists. Sienna looks away, snickering, while Chloe keeps muttering "asset" and "assert," as if she can judge the correctness of a word if she says it often enough.

I love this place. It's a quaint mom-and-pop coffee shop with a decor that seems stuck in the nineties, but cake recipes have definitely kept up with the times. What I especially like is that they have booths, which offer privacy.

Next to me, Christopher shakes his head, prodding Lucas with more questions. We haven't spent time alone since he joined us here, but the man is constantly touching me. He brushes my hand each time he reaches for his glass of soda, and his thigh rubs against mine occasionally, lingering a split second too long for it to be accidental.

"Okay, if everyone's ready, we should head home," I announce about an hour and a half later. There is a general sound of disagreement from the kids, but they don't fight me.

"I'll go ahead with Lucas and Chloe, get Chloe in her seat and everything, while you pay," Sienna offers after I ask for the bill.

"Great idea," I say, handing her the car key.

After slipping into their jackets, they take turns saying good-bye to Christopher and leave the coffee shop just as Ms. Winters, the owner, waitress, and all-around kick-ass woman who runs this business, hurries our way in obvious distress.

"There's a slight problem with the cash register," she says. "But it should work again in a few minutes. I'll bring you some Turkish delight to make up for it. It's a new recipe. I think you'll like it."

"Wow, thanks," I call after her, because she's already hurrying back to the front. I'd tell her I have no problems paying without receiving the receipt, but I know her golden rule. She never takes money without handing out a receipt for it.

Scooping out my phone, I text Sienna to start the car and turn on the heat because I'll be a few minutes late. As soon as I drop the phone in my purse, Ms. Winters returns with a small plate filled with Turkish delight.

I become acutely aware of Christopher's fingers trailing up and down my back.

"Thank you for including me in your celebration," he says.

"Lucas wanted you here."

Leaning into me, he whispers in my ear, "And you didn't?"

His proximity is intoxicating, and it prompts a confession out of me. "I wanted to see you so badly, I ached."

Christopher's fingers dig slightly into my back, and not really knowing what else to say, I pop a Turkish delight in my mouth. Oh my word, it's delicious.

"You have powdered sugar on your mouth," Christopher informs me.

Frantically I wipe away at it, but he chuckles.

"You just smeared it everywhere."

He slips his hand under my chin, turning my head in his direction. Following suit, I shift in my spot until my upper body faces him too. Christopher dusts his fingers over my mouth, rubbing with his thumb on the left corner. Then he drags it down to the center of my lower lip and desire spears me instantly. A low moan tumbles out of me, and we both suck in our breath, the space between us suddenly feeling too small. He peers behind me, and it takes me a second to realize he must be checking whether there are guests in the booth opposite us. There aren't. I already checked earlier.

Christopher closes the distance between us, sealing his lips over mine. His kiss is like a breath of fresh air on a warm spring morning. Crisp and invigorating, taking over all of my senses. I succumb to it all, entwining my tongue with his, probing and tasting. He explores me like a man determined to uncover my deepest secrets. His hand cups the back of my neck, his fingers digging into my hair. The gesture sends a jolt right through my center, all my nerve endings zipping to life.

His mouth is a thing of wonder. I could drown in him like this for hours.

When we pull apart for air, we rest our foreheads against one another's, the tension between us so thick I could bite into it. Christopher's hand is still at the back of my neck, and he tilts my head slightly to one side, trailing his mouth down my cheek until he reaches my ear.

"I've been fantasizing about this for weeks," he whispers in a low, delicious voice. "I'm so hard right now, I can barely see straight. But I can imagine all the ways I could love you right here on this table."

"Christopher!"

"Don't say my name like that or I'll kiss you again,

and this time I might forget we're in a public place."

Knowing I can make this man lose control without even trying gives me immense satisfaction. As we hear the unmistakable sound of Ms. Winters's heels approaching, we pull apart, trying to compose ourselves.

"Here is your bill," she informs me, placing it on the table. Christopher's hand shoots toward it, but I block him.

"Absolutely not. I invited you." I pay Ms. Winters before he has the chance to fight me. As the elder woman chats me up, asking me about my business, I rise from the table, slipping into my coat.

"Are you coming?" I ask Christopher, who hasn't moved from his spot.

He cocks a brow, gesturing with his chin down below. My cheeks instantly heat as I remember what he told me after the kiss.

"I'll talk to you on the phone, then," I say, attempting to gather my wits and not allow the image of Christopher's predicament to hijack my thoughts. No such luck. "About your keys, and...."

"Other things," Christopher finishes for me, the corner of his mouth lifting up. "You should probably go to the kids, in the car."

That snaps me out of my haze, and I check the old grandfather clock on the wall. The kids have only been gone a few minutes, though it feels like an hour has passed since they left.

After a curt good-bye, Ms. Winters walks me out of the coffee shop. As I hurry to the car, one thing becomes clear. Next time Christopher and I are alone, I'm going to be in big trouble.

***

Sleep evades me that night. I go to bed early because I have an early meeting with a potential client, but I end up staring at the ceiling for what feels like hours, replaying the kiss in my mind, touching my lips as if I can barely believe it happened. I wonder if Christopher is awake too.

Almost unwillingly, I reach out in the direction of the nightstand, curling my fingers around my phone. A small voice in my mind tells me it wouldn't be appropriate to text Christopher right now, but I brush it off. We crossed to inappropriate a few hours ago. Hovering with my fingers over the screen of my phone, I begin to type a message, then delete it. After repeating the process a few times, I sigh in frustration. That's when the brilliant idea strikes me of replicating one of his own icebreakers.

Victoria: I have a problem.

Only after pressing Send do I realize that it's much later than I thought—it's past midnight. Christopher must be asleep. Still, I hold onto the sliver of hope that maybe he's awake. My breath catches when my screen lights up with an incoming message.

Christopher: And what's that?

Victoria: A certain someone gave me the most amazing kiss a few hours ago, and I can't stop thinking about it.

This time when my screen lights up, it's not with a message, but with a call. I don't even think twice before answering.

"Excuse the late call, but this requires more assistance than a text message." Just the sound of his voice is enough to send my pulse into overdrive. I easily slip into his game.

"Thank you for taking your time to help me with this serious matter."

"You know what the real problem is?"

"What?"

"That you rate that as 'the most amazing kiss.'"

My stomach plummets and I pull my covers up to my chin, insecurity gripping me. "You didn't like it?"

"I loved it, Victoria. But we were in public."

I try hard not to acknowledge the flutter in my stomach at hearing the words "loved" and "Victoria" in the same sentence. Those damn butterflies again.

"What's that supposed to mean?" I ask.

"That I was holding back."

"Oh." *Ohohoh!* Now I understand, and my mind conjures up images of Christopher and me in a private place, of his mouth covering mine, of him not holding back anymore. I search for a safe topic, something to take my thoughts out of the gutter. "What are you doing up so late?"

"Unfortunately, work. Issues I didn't get to finish today at the office."

"Sorry for keeping you away from work today."

"Hey, I wouldn't have missed the chance to celebrate with all of you for anything in the world."

I melt a little under the covers, giddy with happiness that we rank on the *important* part on Christopher's scale.

"Do you like your job?"

"Yeah. Sure, there are days when I get fed up with it, but that's normal."

"Why did you choose the operations side of the business?" I inquire, remembering he's Head of Operations at Bennett Enterprises.

"Funny story. My first internship at the company was in finance. My brother Logan is the CFO, and he took me under his wing, showed me the ropes. During my internship, the head of operations quit, and then two other employees left. They promptly replaced the head with someone else, but the department was in need of more people. As an intern, I became a jack of all trades. Whenever there was something to be fixed, I'd jump in and do it. They gave me the nickname 'The Fixer.' I liked it. It was dynamic, always kept me on my toes. Did I bore you to tears yet?"

"Not at all. I love hearing you talk about your job. How did you end up in Hong Kong?"

"We expanded in Asia, and we wanted someone from the family there. Max was in London, and I wanted an adventure so I relocated there."

"Why did you come back?"

He chuckles softly. "I missed my family. I love traveling, but it loses the appeal when you have no one to return home to. My family is big and meddling, and I missed them like crazy."

"That is the sweetest thing I've heard in a long time."

"And you are the first person outside of my family who didn't balk at it. People usually look at me like I've grown a second head when I say it."

"Possibly because I grew up in a big meddling family too. Though I'm starting to think mine isn't half as meddling as yours."

I understand where he's coming from. In college, I was one of the few who was actually ecstatic whenever parents came to visit, and I talked to them on the phone often. Even now in my day-to-day life, I'm always surprised when people seem to go out of their way to avoid their families, or to minimize contact as if the mere existence of an extended family is a chore. I'd give a limb to have my parents back.

"You're one hundred percent right, and to tell you the truth, when I was away, I even missed the meddling," he says.

"As you should. Sometimes it can be very helpful. Sometimes you can end up on a blind date with a douche."

"What?"

"Mom thought I didn't date enough, and that was her attempt to set me up."

"Your mother would have liked my sister Pippa."

"She dabbles in setting people up?"

"Not only dabbles, but she's also successful. She had a hand in Sebastian's and Logan's love lives, and Max's too. She's calmed down a notch now, even though I think that's the result of her kids keeping her busy. Every time Pippa questions me about my love life, I'm half expecting to walk into my apartment and find a naked woman in my bed."

"From one to ten, how likely is that to happen?" I ask before I can stop myself, a pit forming inside me as unease coils in my stomach. With a jolt, I recognize this feeling—jealousy. That's when I realize how deep into this I am.

"If I say eleven, does it increase my chances of finding *you* in my bed?"

"Christopher!" His name comes out of my mouth on a moan, and I hear him suck in a breath at the other end. Instinctively I press my thighs together, a familiar ache already forming between them.

"That came out wrong. I don't just want you in my bed. I want you in my life, Victoria. You're constantly on my mind."

"I don't know what to say."

"Here's a hint. If I'm not constantly on your

mind, for the sake of this conversation, pretend I am. There's only so much heartbreak a man can take over the phone."

His self-deprecating humor paints a smile on my face. He's more *man* than anyone I've dated, and infinitely kinder. Sure, it could all be an act. Men have faked interest in more than getting me in their bed before, and I've fallen for it, but Christopher is different. I can't be that far off base.

"You are on my mind, and I'm not pretending. It's just that after you left my house following your first training session with Lucas, I talked to the kids. Lucas and Chloe are afraid that I'll leave them if I fall in love and… I mean, in their world, dating automatically leads to marriage and children, and they're afraid I'll abandon them if I have my own children."

"Shit, those poor kids," Christopher mutters. "How can I help?"

This unexpected offer warms my heart, and when I speak next, my voice catches. "I don't know that you can. I talked to our therapist, and she says it's an expected reaction in kids after they lose their parents, more so because Lucas and Chloe know they were adopted. They're afraid of being abandoned. But she also said that I'm doing a great job providing them with a safe environment, and that it's important to carry on with my life."

"I didn't know you all see a therapist," he says gently. His voice is like a balm, slipping through the cracks dug by my fears and insecurities.

"We started going right after the funeral, and it's helping. I'm trying to do the right thing, but how do I do that when I don't even know what the right thing is?" I take a deep breath, and that's when I realize how much I shared with him. "Sorry, I didn't mean to dump all this on you."

"I'm glad you did. Listen, let's not overthink this. Let's just let the pieces fall in their place."

"You don't strike me as the kind of man who lets things happen. You're the kind who *makes* them happen."

"It's true. But I hadn't planned on you entering my life, and so far, I've been pleasantly surprised. Besides, who said I won't have a hand in how those chips will fall?"

"What's that hand entailing, Bennett?" I can't help the grin spreading on my face.

"Hot looks, shameless flirting."

Oh my. Considering this man can set my body ablaze even with a regular look, there's nothing safe in store for me.

"Still with me?"

"Yeah," I whisper.

"Proper kissing and showcasing some of my other seduction techniques. Just giving you a heads-up."

I am officially a bundle of desire, waiting to be unwrapped. A shiver runs through me as I imagine Christopher doing just that. Racking my mind, I attempt a witty comeback, but all I come up with is "How generous of you."

"Have a *good* night Victoria. I certainly will."

Chapter Thirteen

Victoria

Over the next week, I don't meet Christopher again, but we do text a few times a day, and the man is constantly on my mind. I ordered the furniture for all his rooms except the kitchen. Since that one is custom made, it's best to measure it. I have the blueprint of the apartment, of course, but I always like to see the space. For one, because nothing is as inspiring as seeing a new place and imagining all the ways I can transform it into a home. And second, because actual measurements sometimes differ from the plan, and in some spaces, such as the kitchen, I can't run that risk. Christopher will receive the keys to his apartment on Monday afternoon at four o'clock. My goal is to be there at ten past four to measure the kitchen and then call the store to place the order.

On Monday morning, I find out there's a hitch in Christopher's moving plans. The builders discovered a problem on the fourth and the ninth floors, and consequently, they're delaying the key handover for a week. What that means is I can go only to take measurements in one week, then place the order for the kitchen furniture. Well, this simply won't do. I gave my word to Christopher that he'll be able to move in on a certain date, and I will make sure all of his furniture is in the apartment by then.

"It's not such a big deal," he assures me. "I can move in even if the kitchen isn't there yet."

"Moving into an unfinished apartment is like eating a cake without sugar," I argue. "It tarnishes the entire experience."

"I can move in later, then."

But I know how much he dislikes the rental he lives in now, and I want him to be happy.

"I'll handle this. It's a promise."

And handle I do. Over the years, I've learned there is a back door to everything, from convincing suppliers to speed up an order, to gaining access to a building which is technically still under construction. The back door to the latter is the construction site superintendent. He has a copy of the keys for each of the apartments for the entire duration of the construction process.

A quick research tells me who the superintendent is in this case, and after half a dozen phone calls, I finally reach him. After a short conversation, I convince him to let me in for no more than fifteen minutes so I can do measurements, and then I call Christopher.

"Guess who's going to your apartment to take measurements today?"

"How did you do that? I tried to bribe, threaten, and blackmail the guy I talked to and he wouldn't budge."

"I have my tactics," I say proudly, hurrying to my car. I'm downtown, having just visited an antique shop for one of my clients. The sound of cars, horn blares, and the usual city noise fills the air, so I press the phone to my ear as I hurry to cross the street. "Which include none of the above. It's called being nice to people. You should try it sometime. I'll call you to report everything once I'm done."

"You're kidding, right? I'm coming too. I want to see the place."

"Err… I negotiated entrance for one. It's a sneaky operation."

"Then it'll be a *sneaky* operation involving both of us. I'll meet you there. What time?"

"One o'clock."

"Okay."

I arrive in front of his high-rise two hours later, overcome by the usual giddiness that grips me when I'm about to enter a new residential building. I'd put this up to being some sort of decorator quirk, but the truth is, new homes have fascinated me since I was a kid.

This time though, my stomach is in knots too, and Christopher himself is the reason for that. This will be the first time we've seen each other since the kiss. When we talked on the phone earlier, we were professional, and I resolve to do the same while I take the measurements.

When Christopher joins me, it's obvious he has something very different in mind.

He greets me by kissing my cheek, which he's never done before. The second his mouth touch my skin, my entire body buzzes with life. When he places one hand on my waist, the innocent kiss suddenly becomes an intimate experience. Even the air between us seems to crackle with tension. I become acutely aware of the fact that his lips are only a fraction of an inch away from mine.

Stepping back, I put some much-needed distance between us. "Hi."

In response, he offers me one of his trademark drop-your-clothes smiles.

He hands me a paper cup I hadn't noticed before, his fingers lingering a second too long on mine. The brief touch is enough to send my senses into a tailspin. *Oh boy.*

"One eggnog with extra whipped cream and caramel topping. Your favorite," he informs me, and I melt even more than I did when he kissed my cheek. This is something I shared with him in a text almost three weeks ago. The fact that he remembers this little tidbit is beyond endearing.

"Thank you. Ahh, this is like a holiday in a cup for me, but it has alcohol. That's why I only drink it outside office hours."

"I know." He wiggles his brows. "I was counting on that leading to some inappropriate behavior during this sneaky operation."

"You're impossible." A white-hot current runs through me, watching the twinkle of mischief in his gaze. Holding my chin high, I decide to take charge. *He wants to challenge me? Fine. Two can play at this game.* Taking a sip, I enjoy the exquisite taste in my mouth, purposely letting out a small sound of pleasure. Christopher's expression of shock is the best damn reward.

Game on, Bennett.

"Follow me," I say.

My mole, Frank, waits for me in front of the construction container placed at the corner of the building.

"Hi, Frank! I'm Victoria. We spoke on the phone," I greet him, holding out my hand. He's in his fifties, with a bushy mustache and a beer belly. Frank bears an uncanny resemblance to Santa Claus.

"Victoria! Nice to meet you." He casts an

uncertain glance to Christopher.

"Christopher's the owner of the apartment," I explain as the two men shake hands.

"I see. Let's get the two of you up, then. My lunch break begins in two minutes, and no one stops by the trailer at that time."

"You can just give me the key if you want to and enjoy your lunch, you don't have to show us up."

"Nah, it's best if I come with you. If some of the boys see you, they'll get smart with questions." The implication is clear: no one will question us if we're with him. Frank strikes me as someone who has the kind of quiet authority that people seldom question.

"Thank you for sacrificing your lunch break for us," I tell him sincerely.

"You made a very convincing case."

Frank disappears inside the trailer, marching back out a minute later holding a set of keys. He leads us straight through the front doors of the building.

The smell of paint greets us in the hallway. It bothers most people, but I like it. To our right is a sleek reception area, which will have twenty-four-hour service. Two construction workers walk in through the door behind the reception, eyeing Christopher and me curiously, but as Frank predicted, they don't say a word.

Everything about this building speaks of elegance and efficiency. Frank leads us to one of the six elevators, and while we speed up to the seventh floor, I sip from my cup of eggnog. I can't help a squeal when we step inside the apartment a few minutes later.

"There's so much light," I exclaim, walking directly to the large window that stretches out onto the terrace. "I saw the size of the windows on the plan, but this is truly beautiful."

I resist the temptation to walk on the balcony and soak in a few rays of sun. I'm here for measurements.

"I'll leave the two of you to do your business," Frank announces. "I need to check some wiring at an apartment two floors above. Since I'm here, I'll do it now. I'll be back in half an hour. It's unlikely that any of the boys will bother you up here."

Oh, so much for the buffer. But as he leaves, I notice Christopher inspecting the place without enthusiasm. "This looks so—"

"Don't say another word," I interrupt. "I know this looks like an empty shell right now, but it'll look welcome and warm when I'm done with it. I promise I'll even bake cookies in your brand new kitchen the day you move in, so it smells like home."

He blinks, clearly taken aback by my offer. To be honest, I'm surprised myself. It's not like I'm going around offering to bake for my clients. But recalling his boyish enthusiasm when he stepped into my kitchen after training Lucas, I know this will make him happy.

"You're very sweet, Victoria," he says simply while I down the last drops of my eggnog.

"I'll start taking measurements now."

"I'll help."

"No, you can enjoy your apartment. I'm going to do my job." Placing the now empty eggnog cup next to the front door, I fish out the measuring tape from my bag and get to work. Out of the corner of my eye, I see him heading out to the balcony. Since I'm here anyway, I'll measure the entire apartment, just so I can rest assured that there are no unpleasant surprises. I finish measuring most of the rooms in the apartment in a record time, leaving the kitchen for last.

Christopher's pacing around in the living room.

It's obvious he's not used to just sitting around, doing nothing.

"If you're bored, help me measure the kitchen."

"Sure. What do you need me to do?"

I hand him one end of the tape, instructing him to walk to the end of the wall we're measuring. As he does what I say, I can't help noticing the way the fabric of his pants molds to his ass. Those are some great pants and an even better ass. Damn, that suit he's wearing should be illegal. Or maybe his ass should be.

"That's about nine feet and two inches," he says.

"Not about. I need the exact number. Every inch matters."

"Really?"

"Yeah," I reply, head bent down to my phone while I wait for him to tell me the correct number to type in my notes. "All your kitchen furniture will be custom made, and if the counter is even half an inch too large, we're going to have a problem. So even a fraction of an inch matters."

Belatedly I realize how I sound. When I look up at him, he's grinning from ear to ear. I can't even pin this one on him; I laid my trap and stepped right into it. I begin to wonder if my subconscious is trying to sabotage me.

"Nine feet and two and a half inches," Christopher says. To his credit, he keeps a straight face.

"Thank you."

"Is there something you want to tell me?"

I'm surprised he picked up on this. New spaces inspire me, which shouldn't be a problem in my profession, but in my case, it is. On countless occasions similar to this one, in which I only saw the location after my client got the key, I couldn't stop talking about all the shiny new ideas inspiring me. That brought me more than one accusation of trying to upsell. I honestly wasn't, but I can never stop the influx of ideas when I step into a virgin space. I try to contain the avalanche of ideas that threaten to burst out of me. To no avail.

"Well…," I start, then talk his ear off for the next little while until I'm out of breath.

"Victoria? No offense, but that all sounds like pig latin to me. If there's anything you know will make this place look like a home, go ahead. I'm giving you carte blanche." Evidently, I was so immersed in my proposal, I didn't take notice of him advancing toward me, or me backing into the wall opposite the kitchen. One of his hands is propped against the wall near my ear, and with the other one, he twirls a strand of my hair in his fingers.

"Really? I don't want you to think I'm trying to upsell you things. I want you to love your new home." The words tumble out of my mouth at an alarming speed, but Christopher's proximity is setting me on edge. Drawing in a deep breath, I attempt to calm myself, but my heart rate ratchets up. Feeling his fingers move from my hair to my temple and then descend to my jaw isn't helping.

"I was hoping it was just an excuse to spend more time with me," he says gently. The space between us seems to become increasingly smaller, even though neither of us moves. "You smell like eggnog." Something in his voice has changed. I can't pinpoint what; maybe his timbre is lower, but it sounds more intimate than it did seconds ago. It sends desire coursing through me, and I become aware of the fact that my breasts are squished against his chest. His hot breath lands on my cheek, like a forbidden whisper. "I am going to kiss you, Victoria." His words unleash a hunger inside me, so deep and so powerful that I have no hope of resisting it. I nod slightly, and then his mouth covers mine. I part my lips invitingly, and when he coaxes my tongue with his, I'm on fire.

Oh, this man knows how to *kiss*. He is demanding and in control, and I love every second of it. Before long, we're a tangle of limbs because I need to feel so much more, and I'm not alone in my desperation. One of his hands finds the hem of my sweater, and I shudder. Pressing his knee between my legs, he opens my thighs. Driven by a will of their own, my hips roll forward, and I find myself pressing my center against his thigh. A rough groan reverberates from his chest, and his hand slides up, stopping where the fabric of my bra meets my skin. All movement stops for a few interminable seconds, and I realize he's seeking permission.

I nod almost imperceptibly, and our control snaps. Christopher cups my breast over the fabric of the bra, and my nipples turn hard within seconds. His mouth descends to my neck.

"I am going to make you come, Victoria," he whispers against my skin. Heat pools between my thighs at his words, and when he undoes the button of my jeans, I become putty in his hands, driven by a blind desire.

"I want to touch you too," I complain, groping shamelessly at his shirt, reaching down to his belt.

"No. I want to focus on you."

He doesn't give me the chance to protest, sealing his mouth over mine again while sliding a hand inside my panties. I'm drenched, of course, and when his fingers move up and down the rim of my entrance, I all but break out of my skin. I need something to support myself, but there's nothing except a wall behind me, so I lace my arms around Christopher's neck, deepening the kiss. I can't get enough of this man. When he slides one finger inside me, pressing his palm against my clit, I lose all sense of time and space. Right now there's nothing in my world except this beautiful man and all the sinful sensations he awakens in me. He ignites me from deep inside, and before long, my hips move against his hand, driven by a will of their own as my entire body tightens with pressure.

We come up for breath, and I hold on to him for dear life.

"Do you want me to slide a second finger inside you?"

"Yes," I answer through heavy breaths, my hand yearning to touch him intimately. Dropping one hand between us, I cup his erection over his pants. The groan reverberating from deep inside his chest is music to my ears.

"Victoria, I said no touching me."

"I can't help it."

"If you don't do as I say, I'll stop what I'm doing."

"Not fair," I mumble, but quickly obey because I have a hunch he'd carry out his threat in no time. Closing my eyelids, I rest my head against the wall as he slides a second finger inside, stretching me.

"You're so tight."

Heat singes me like a lightning bolt as he increases the rhythm of his movements, and the pressure of his palm on my bundle of nerves is pure perfection.

"Open your eyes," he commands in a low, seductive tone. I blink them open and find him gazing intensely at me. "I want you to look at me right until the end."

Nodding, I ride the wave of pleasure. Losing myself in his dark gaze only makes this moment more intimate. Needing to feel closer to him, I hitch a leg up his thigh, practically straddling him. I curl my fingers around his hair, desperation coursing through me. My climax shatters me into a million flaming pieces, and I cling to Christopher for dear life, moaning, and whimpering but never looking away.

"You're so beautiful when you come." He rests his forehead against mine for the briefest of seconds, and he blows heated, short breaths against my lips.

This moment is pure magic. I don't know why or how, but I'm not ready for it to end.

When he pulls his hand out of my jeans, his fingers are coated in my wetness. The sight turns me on.

Then, with a jolt, I realize where we are, and that Frank is about to return. Oh God. Frank. What if he'd walked in on us?

Christopher seems to be thinking along the same lines.

"Frank will be back," he says.

"The sink in the bathroom is already connected to the water supply."

Christopher takes off without another word while I try to compose myself, waiting for Frank to arrive. Checking the time on my phone, I note there are still five minutes left until the half hour Frank gave us expires.

Drawing in a lungful of air, I try to calm myself and wrap my mind around what just happened. Before I have time to gather my wits, the door opens, and Frank walks in.

"Done?" he inquires.

"Yes. All measurements taken. As soon as Christopher comes back from the bathroom, we can go. Did you check the… wiring?"

Frank takes my bait and starts rattling about how he needed to fix it, and that no one takes their job seriously anymore these days. Christopher returns in the meantime, winking at me. The three of us leave the apartment, Frank walking in front of us.

***

Christopher places his hand at the small of my back as we exit the elevator on the ground floor, kissing my temple. This unexpected display of affection warms me on the inside, and I lean into his touch without much thought. We share an accomplice glance, and in his molten dark eyes, I see honesty, kindness, and a dash of mischief. Raising his hand up to the nape of my neck, Christopher brings his lips to my ear.

"You're gorgeous," he whispers only for me to hear just as Frank pushes the door to the building open and we step onto the bustling street.

Pulling myself out of Christopher's grasp, I square my shoulders and hold out my hand to Frank, who turned around to face us.

"Thank you for letting us in." I shake his hand, and then Christopher does the same.

"We took inappropriate to a whole new level," Christopher comments the moment we're alone. Swirling around, I take in his body language. Feet planted wide, arms hanging at his side, shit-eating grin stretching on his handsome face. He couldn't be happier if I told him Christmas is coming earlier.

"If it had been any more inappropriate, I would have climbed you."

"I believe you straddling my leg counts as climbing. Let's talk—"

A loud ringing interrupts him, and it takes a second for both of us to realize it's coming from his phone, which is tucked in a chest pocket on the inside of his suit. Pulling it out, he frowns at the screen.

"Have to take this."

I nod, stepping away to give him space, but he speaks so loud that it's impossible not to listen.

"That's a serious situation."

He's not shouting, but his tone is so cutting he might as well do it. Whoever is at the other end of the line has my sympathy.

"It's not going to cut it," Christopher thunders. "We need to solve the packaging issues in two weeks maximum if we want to be in good shape for the Christmas season."

Wow. It's barely mid-October, and they're already preparing for Christmas. As Christopher spells out strategies and potential problem-solving activities, his voice grows calmer. I take note of the use of "we." Bosses tend to do this, but what they usually mean is *you* do the job, *I* take all the credit, and *we* will call it teamwork. Christopher's intent is the opposite, taking responsibility for all the mishaps. I like this very much about him.

"Okay. Here's what's going to happen," Christopher continues. "I will fly out to Seattle and stay there for two weeks, or however long it takes for everything to run smoothly."

And just like that, I lose all sympathy for the person he's talking to. The news that Christopher will be gone for who knows how many weeks hits me like a punch in the gut. I already miss him. How silly is that?

"Call my assistant and have her sort out the flight and accommodation details," he instructs before hanging up. Rubbing his forehead, he tilts his head to one side and then the other, as if wanting to shake off tension.

"'The Fixer's' problem-solving skills are needed," I say lightly, attempting to cheer him up.

"Yeah. It'll be best if I'm on location to see things through."

"When do you leave?"

"I'll fly out today."

"Oh!" I try to hide my disappointment, but I'm not fooling him. Stepping right in front of me, he pushes a loose strand of hair behind my ear, resting his fingers on a spot at the base of my neck.

"I didn't plan what happened today," he says softly.

My skin prickles at the point of contact, and I lean in like a kitten searching for affection. I feel more vulnerable and exposed than I have in a long time. With no idea how to handle this, I try to cover it up with humor.

"So all that talk about seduction techniques was just that? Talk?"

Christopher chuckles lightly. "I think we have different ideas about what seduction means, Victoria."

"Enlighten me."

"I meant flowers and gifts and dates. All of that culminating with a night in which I take my time to explore you for hours."

With every word he utters, blood rushes to my cheeks. "You can't say those things to me out on the street."

"Why?"

"I'll start swooning." *Not to mention there's a real danger I might spontaneously combust.*

"Exactly what I'm after."

"You're a romantic," I whisper, the realization slipping into every cell of my body. He hides it well behind his self-deprecating humor and shameless flirting. *Why yes, I am already swooning, thank you very much.*

"Of the worst kind." Here's that innocent smile again. I swear my heart just doubled in size. "But I rarely unleash this terrible trait."

"So I'm special?"

"Yeah." Cupping my cheeks, he pulls me close to him, brushing his lips on my forehead. "You're special, and a bad influence. What happened upstairs is proof."

I'm on the verge of pointing out he's the one who corrupted me, but instead, I choose to lay my head against his chest, inhaling his masculine scent. Instantly, he lowers his hands, wrapping his arms around me, holding me, as if there's nothing more natural in the world. It feels so good and safe, and perfect. I love everything about this: listening to his rhythmic heartbeats, feeling the heat of his body seep into mine.

"Victoria," he says in a low voice. "Up there, we had a moment."

"We did."

"While I'm gone, don't forget that." He talks as if he has plans for us. For the first time, I allow myself to entertain that thought, pushing away any worry. What would it be like to let this man sweep me off my feet? To indulge in his kisses and his touch?

"Stop making me swoon, Bennett."

He hugs me tighter and I bury my nose in his neck—or try to, as he towers over me despite my heels. I want us to stay like this forever. But of course, his phone starts ringing again, forcing us apart. I hate this pesky reality taking me away from this wonderful man.

Glancing at the screen, Christopher sets his jaw.

"Answer the phone," I encourage him. "My car is just around the corner. I'm heading there."

"I'll talk to you soon." His features relax as one corner of his mouth lifts in a smile. "And don't forget the moment."

Chapter Fourteen

Victoria

I spend the entire day in a frenzy, replaying the time I spent with Christopher in my mind again and again, smiling more brightly each time. I have two more appointments. One of them is an expectant mother wishing to decorate the baby's room; the other is a middle-aged couple looking to do something with their poolhouse, which they've used as a shed for years. All of them watch me dubiously as I pitch ideas, clearly thinking I'm high on my own Kool-Aid. Even to my own ears, I sound a little too eager. I can't help myself though. It turns out being kissed by Christopher unleashes my creativity. I'm sure the orgasm helped too.

Though I know Christopher must be en route to Seattle, or already in the process of putting out fires, I can't help glancing at my phone from time to time, hoping to see a text from him. No such luck. I wrote him one message, asking if he landed already, but he didn't reply. Not that it did anything to dampen my mood.

I'm downright grinning when I step inside my house that afternoon, an hour before dinnertime. My good mood continues while I prepare chicken enchiladas, and during dinner, the kids notice.

"Any reason you've been smiling since you arrived home?" Sienna inquires, biting into her enchilada.

"Just had a good day. How was yours?"

She clearly sees through my poor attempt at deflecting the topic from me, but doesn't call me out. We chitchat lightly for the next hour, and after Lucas and Chloe go to sleep, Sienna curls with a book on the ottoman in the living room, glancing curiously at me.

"Have you been to your room?" she asks.

"No, why?"

"You received some flowers today. I put them on your desk."

I dash out of the room so fast you'd think there was someone chasing me. On the desk in my room, I find beautiful red roses in a vase. There's a note too.

To many more moments.

Christopher

I press the note to my chest, leaning down to smell the roses. My first instinct is to call Christopher, but I left the phone in the living room. Upon my return, I find Sienna with her nose buried in her book, blushing suspiciously.

"Sienna?"

"Hmm?"

"Did you read the note?"

"No," she answers a little too quickly, tucking her legs under her. Eventually, she lowers her book. "Fine, I admit. I read the note. What did he mean by 'moments'?"

"Something romantic."

"I figured that much out. Care to elaborate?"

I'm tempted to say no for several reasons, one being that she deserves to be teased for being nosy. The chief reason though, is that the experience was of a sexual nature. Sienna is seventeen; she's not a kid anymore, and we've always been close. If I censor my story enough….

"Well—" I begin, but Sienna holds out her hand,

jumping down from the ottoman.

"Hold it."

"What?"

"This is girl talk. Girl talk requires nail painting."

Without disputing her claim, I follow her to the bathroom where we keep our collection of nail polish. It's been our tradition for years. Even before we lost our parents, I made it a point to spend quality time with my siblings. I used to stop by my parents' house once a week for dinner, and Sienna and I often did our nails after dessert while talking. When she's old enough, we'll upgrade to wine.

Back in the living room, armed with two shades of nail polish, I throw a large towel over the floor, so we don't accidentally stain the carpet. I type on my phone quickly, thanking Christopher for the flowers, and keep the phone nearby in case he answers.

Between doing our toes, I recount today's events—omitting the orgasm and the preceding sexy time, reducing the experience to a kiss—and everything he made me feel.

"Wow, he knows how to lay on the romance," Sienna says with appreciation. "Guys at my school think it's romantic if they don't ignore you while they're with their buddies."

"To be fair, guys are pretty dumb when they're your age," I comfort her.

"Yeah, somehow I doubt all of them reach Christopher's level of swoonworthiness even when they're older."

I merely smile because I can't contradict her. My dating experience for the past ten years confirms her doubt.

"So, does Christopher have a younger brother? Like way younger?"

"He does—Hang on. Why do you ask?"

"If any of them is looking to date, I volunteer."

"They're not that young," I explain. "Let's finish here. I have to go to bed. Long day tomorrow. I'm going to the store to buy some baking supplies. Do you want me to buy you anything?"

"Nah, I'm good."

We focus on each other's toes for the next few minutes. We're both pros at this, but it still requires concentration; otherwise we'll look as if Chloe "helped" us. After we finish applying the second layer, we stretch our legs, wiggling our toes before leaving them to dry.

"Victoria?"

"Yeah."

"You're doing a great job taking care of us."

"Thank you."

"I never told Mom and Dad that. I took it for granted." Her voice wavers, but she shakes her head, as if the gesture is enough to push the sad thoughts away. "So I wanted to tell you. If you want to date Christopher, I think that's a great idea. I'm sure Lucas and Chloe think so too."

Shifting next to her, I cover her hand with mine, squeezing it reassuringly. I once asked Mom why she wanted so many kids. She said she'd been an only child and often wished she'd had at least a sister, and that she felt having one would've been like living with your best friend. As Sienna and I admire our toes, proud of our workmanship, I can't help thinking how right Mom was.

Later on, just as I climb in my bed, my phone beeps.

Christopher: Are you asleep?

Instead of replying, I call him.

"Hey!"

"It's good to hear your voice. I feel like it's been a month since I saw you." He sounds impossibly tired. Checking the screen, I realize it's almost midnight.

"You've been working until now?"

"Yeah, I just got out of the cab and am about to enter my hotel." Straining my ears, I pick up the street noise in his background, which promptly turns to silence as he presumably steps inside the hotel. "It's going to be that kind of week too."

"So you'll be back in a week?" Turning on one side, I curl my knees up to my chest, trying to reign in my excitement.

"Miss me already?"

"Just a little," I tease him.

"I need to send more flowers next time, then."

"I love the ones you sent. They're perfect. Back to what we were saying. You'll be back in a week?"

"Probably two. I don't see us wrapping this up in just one week, even if we work throughout the weekend."

"What happened?"

"We bought a packaging company here. Before that, the packaging was done externally, but we wanted to integrate that part of the process in Bennett Enterprises, so we purchased this company in Seattle. From the preliminary meetings and analysis, it looked like the integration would run smoother than it actually has. Today was insane."

"And you still made time to send me flowers," I say softly. "You're amazing."

"I took care of that before getting on the plane. I figured if I only do one thing right today, it was going to be sending you flowers."

I simply sigh in response, my heart doubling in size. "You're so good with words."

"I can't wait to be back home to show you my other talents too. I need to go to bed now though. I'm dead tired."

"Good night, Christopher."

Over the next few days, I learn that the quicker you want time to pass, the slower it moves. Christopher and I send each other text messages throughout the day, but we don't get the chance to talk. Still, those messages are enough to keep my ecstatic mood—and slightly manic grin—in place. "Girl, you're going to pull a muscle from so much smiling," Isabelle says during our weekly catch-up lunch. "Any chance it has something to do with one Christopher Bennett?"

"It does," I admit, feasting on my turkey salad, trying to school my expression. "It turns out I am falling for his charms."

"I'd be surprised if you didn't. Besides, once you're done having his furniture delivered and installed, he's no longer our client." Winking at me, she adds, "I think we should change that rule anyway to 'We can't date asshole clients.'"

"Yeah, but it's hard to tell the assholes from the good guys in the beginning," I remark. "Hence the rule."

"You know what? Helen and I should drop by your house sometime this week so the three of us can catch up."

"True, I haven't seen her in a long while."

Isabelle leans slightly over the table, dropping her voice to a conspiratorial whisper, "Feels exciting to break the rules though, doesn't it?"

My grin is so wide I think I might actually pull a

muscle.

On Friday afternoon, while enjoying a well-deserved eggnog and inspecting a Halloween display in a shop I pass by downtown, my phone rings. *Christopher.*

"Well, well, well," I greet. "I was just thinking about you while enjoying my first after-hours eggnog today."

"The first one? How many do you intend to have? Do I need to worry about your climbing tendencies?"

Blushing furiously, I fix my gaze on a zombie mask, sipping from my cup. "No worry, you're the only one I want to climb."

Christopher groans, a sounds that travels right through me, heating a certain area of my body. "You're killing me, Victoria. I'm tempted to fly back to see you."

"Why don't you?" I brainstorm for ways to persuade him because I miss him terribly. It's a little ridiculous because it's not as if I saw him daily before he left for Seattle. But something changed between us when we were in his apartment, spurring feelings that are somewhat outlandish and entirely new to me. It scares me out of my wits.

"Because I plan to do more than just see you, and I'll need more than a few hours for what I have in mind."

"Which is?"

"Kissing every inch of your body and making love to you until you ache are high on my priority list."

I clutch my cup so tightly that it crumbles in my fist. Luckily I'd already drank it up. "Christopher," I admonish, glancing to my left and then my right, irrationally afraid that passersby might have heard him. They didn't, of course, but that doesn't stop the heat from crawling up my cheeks.

"You asked." He has a point, of course, and I need to remember not to ask questions if I can't handle the answers. Judging by the way my entire body has heated up and my mind trips for a way to continue the conversation, I clearly can't. As if sensing my ordeal, Christopher adds, "Where are you?"

"Downtown. Brainstorming a few things for a client I'm meeting Monday."

"I wish you'd decorated this hotel. Everything's gray, I swear. It's like the decorator went out of the way to ensure the place has zero warmth to it."

"You can always buy a pumpkin," I tease him. "Or a skeleton. I'm sure they're everywhere."

"Huh?"

"I'm staring at a Halloween display in a store."

"Ah yeah, it's mid-October. The city will be full of Halloween displays for the next two weeks."

"In some households, this used to be the month of pranks."

"Huh?"

"Lucas used to start with the pranks at the beginning of October. He'd routinely scare the crap out of my parents. They never got used to it." I scan the display, which showcases every imaginable Halloween scare from masks to spiders and fake teeth. I'm more of a Christmas girl, but even so, I can appreciate their range. I'm tempted to buy Lucas some supplies, but I'm almost certain he already owns half of what's inside this store. There is a box in our basement labeled *Lucas's Halloween Box*.

"And no prank so far?"

"None," I confirm. "I used to hate them, because no matter how often he'd put spiders in my hair, it would shock and annoy the hell out of me. I have three gray hairs, and they all sprouted last year in October after his prank. I'd gladly welcome white hair if it meant Lucas was his old self again."

"These things take time, Victoria," Christopher says gently. "But I swear to God, that kid could be my own. When I was his age, it was my mission in life to give everyone a heart attack around Halloween. I thought it was the height of fun, and I always hoped they'd start to prank me back, but only Max ever did."

Conjuring up the image of two mini Christophers in my mind, running around and terrorizing their poor families, I can't help beaming.

"I have to go," Christopher says unexpectedly. "My next meeting is starting earlier. Don't drink too many eggnogs."

"Afraid I'll show off my climbing skills to some other man?"

"Any prospectives?"

"Oh yeah. Several new clients I'd rank somewhere between extremely handsome and utterly climbworthy. I'm meeting one in twenty minutes, just in time for the eggnog to be effective."

I was hoping to get a few laughs out of him, but in the silence that follows, I realize my joke might have had the opposite effect.

"I don't share, Victoria." His voice is low, tinged with unease and—I realize with a rush of guilt—hurt.

"You.... It was supposed to be a joke, which should give you an idea of why I never prank people. I suck at it. I.... There are no prospectives."

"Right, sorry. I overreacted."

"Who knew there was a caveman inside you?"

"Oh, there is."

"Another family trait?"

"You bet. I keep him well hidden, but he's definitely here." Someone in his background clearly asks if they can start the meeting already. "I really have to go now."

"Go get them, Bennett."

After clicking off, I glance at my phone, grinning like a lunatic. Caveman, romantic, and reformed prankster. The different sides of Christopher come to me like pieces of a puzzle, and I can't wait to discover more.

Chapter Fifteen

Victoria

On Friday afternoon, Isabelle keeps her promise and shows up with Helen at my house.

"Girl, there's only so long we can go without seeing each other before the best friend tag won't fit anymore," Helen exclaims, pulling me into a hug. Rich blonde hair cascades over her shoulders, framing her beautiful features.

"Sorry, things have just been—"

"I know," she says as I lead her and Isabelle in the living room. "Isabelle says you have dirty news."

"Shh, the kids will hear you." Chloe and Lucas are in the living room, bickering. Sienna's out with her friends Emma and Ben.

"Oh no, we have to censor our conversation?" Helen complains under her breath. I give her a strained smile, and Isabelle elbows her gently. Yeah, some friendships adapt to changes better than others. We spend the next two hours catching up with each other, and when the kids move to the backyard, I dish out details about Christopher. The girls are excited, trying to lure every dirty detail out of me, but our conversation comes to an abrupt halt when Chloe stomps back in, jumping into my arms and seeking reassurance from Lucas's relentless teasing. Helen and Isabelle leave shortly afterward, abruptly ending our girls night. Yeah. . .I bet it will take a while before Helen will be up for one again. Kids aren't her thing.

Over the weekend, the kids and I decorate the house properly for fall with strings of dry leaves and whatnot. Aunt Christina, Uncle Bill, and their three children come over on Saturday, and we have a blast carving pumpkins, placing them on the porch, which now has a distinct Halloween feel, and baking apples with cinnamon. The entire house smells like heaven.

When our guests prepare to leave, the usual bargaining begins. The cousins would like to sleep over, but the house is too tiny for five kids plus Sienna and me. Sleepovers always happen at Aunt Christina's house, and we agree to have one next Friday. That also happens to be Halloween night, and the kids will do some quality trick-or-treating together at Christina's. With a jolt, I remember that's the day Christopher returns from Seattle. Sienna usually skips sleepovers because she's older than everyone else, but now she winks at me wickedly and casually adds that she'd like to pop over for the sleepover as well.

On Sunday afternoon, Sienna's friend Ben comes by at the house because the two of them have to work on a science project.

"Hi, Ben!"

He waves, nodding before he and Sienna head up the stairs to her room. I've always liked Ben, and having known him for years, it's hard to forget he's a teenager. I trust them both, and Sienna always insists they're just friends, but it won't hurt to remind them about the golden rule.

"If you're going to work upstairs—" I begin, but

they interrupt me.

"We'll keep the door open," Sienna and Ben say at the same time. I bet they're rolling their eyes in unison too, but better safe than sorry.

While they work, I check Lucas's math homework. Hunched over his desk, I run the numbers in my mind, double-checking them. I'm about to congratulate him on getting everything right, when I feel something crawling at the back of my neck. My hair is swept to one side, so my neck is bared to the nasty creature. Freezing in my seat, I splay my fingers on Lucas's notebook, attempting to draw in a lungful of breath to calm myself down. It can only be an insect. I hope it's an insect. If there are rodents in this house, I'm moving us out. Immediately. Clenching my teeth, I slap my palm so hard against the back of my neck that I nearly buckle.

A shriek followed by a snort of laughter startles me. Jumping out of the seat, I do a one-eighty twirl, only to find Lucas holding his belly with his left hand. With his other hand, he holds a rope, which has a rubber spider at the other end.

"I scared you again," Lucas says between shrieks of laughter while I'm massaging the spot I slapped. Snapping out of my post-fake-spider terror, recognition sets in. My limbs instantly become as light as air. Lucas just pulled a prank on me. Stepping forward, I hug the hell out of my little brother, squishing him against me, ruffling his hair and kissing the top of his head.

"This is weird. Why aren't you yelling? Victoria, please stop hugging me."

"There's no one here to see, and this is the least you can do to make up for scaring me."

A few seconds later, he wiggles out of my

embrace, clutching the damned spider to his chest. That's when I notice the huge box behind him. Lucas's Halloween Box.

"When did you bring this up? I didn't hear you."

"While you were checking my homework, I went to the basement all by myself," he exclaims proudly. "Every man worth his salt must prank the women in his house, especially during the month of Halloween."

Something in his posture and the stiffness in his words alerts me that these aren't *his* words. I have a hunch I know who they belong to, and my heart grows in size.

After informing him that his math homework was correct, I take refuge in my room, dialing Christopher's number. He doesn't pick up, and after a few rings, I give up. I debate sending him a message, but he said he'll be working over the weekend, and if he's still at the office, I don't want to disturb him.

***

Christopher

It's almost midnight when I leave the company building, heading straight for the cab the doorman called for me. My neck is stiff, and no amount of flexing it will release the tension. When I first joined Bennett Enterprises, I used to make fun of my brothers for practically never leaving the office. I insisted that the human body wasn't built for sitting in a chair all day, with bathroom trips and pacing around the office making up the sole physical activity. I should heed my own advice more often these days. But the truth is, as I learned over the years, some things can't be helped. When there's work to be done, there's work to be done. I can't just pretend it doesn't exist. What I didn't know then was that *work* doesn't just equal *money*. It equals people too.

For example, when we bought the packaging company here in Seattle, the previous owner had nearly brought it to bankruptcy with some bad decisions. During the initial assessment, it became clear that if we didn't fire half the employees, we'd incur huge losses for the first year. Most of them had worked at the company all their lives. What were they supposed to do, find a new job at one of the other non-packaging companies in the area? Train for a new career when they were nearing their sixties? The thought of practically putting people out on the street kept me up at night. I chose not to fire anyone. Bennett Enterprises could absorb that loss for a while, and my family agreed with me. It's just one of the benefits of keeping the shares in the family. The bank, on the other hand, wasn't a fan of the plan.

"Mr. Bennett, I'll be frank. This is not a smart business move," Regis Johnson, our bank advisor, said.

"No, but it's the right human move to make," I replied calmly. I'd called him into my office to relay the news, knowing that being on our premises would give me the upper hand.

"Bennett Enterprises is not a charity."

I rose from my seat and placed my knuckles on the desk, leaning slightly over it. I could practically see Regis cowering. I don't often resort to intimidation, but when I do, it's for a good cause.

"We can change banks at any time, Regis. Your competitors are banging on our doors, begging us to work with them."

That was the end of the conversation, but the decision not to fire anyone also meant that I, and the entire operations department, had to put in double the work to turn the newly acquired packaging division around. Hence this trip to Seattle and the late nights.

Bone-tired as I am, I'm happy we've been making progress. So why do I have an unpleasant feeling in my gut? I can't place it, and it bothers me.

Five short minutes later, I place that feeling when I step inside the hotel. That's it. I don't hate the work, just coming "home" to an impersonal hotel room and a cold bed.

"Evening, Mr. Bennett," the receptionist greets me, smiling a little too brightly, leaning over the reception desk to display her cleavage. She's been hitting on me since I arrived, making it plenty clear she'd love to warm my bed. I just nod, considering some rude one-liners to make it clear I'm not interested since she's not a hint taker. In the end, I decide against it because I'm far too tired to come up with anything smart.

"I have a package for you," she says. At first I think she means it as an innuendo, but then she places an actual package on the reception desk. "It arrived yesterday, but the other shift manager forgot about it."

"Thanks."

Surprised, I pick it up, inspecting it on the way to the elevator. There are no details on the sender, which makes me think my family's up to something. I wait until I'm inside my room to open it.

"What the…?"

I find a red, midsized blanket inside and a note.

Red warms up the surrounding colors, even gray. Try putting it on the couch in your room.

Victoria

Heading straight to the couch, I crumple the blanket and toss it in one corner. It looks as if someone recently sat there. I imagine it was Victoria, curled up with a book, drinking eggnog. She's right; the room instantly looks less like a cave. It looks warmer. The corners of my mouth lift up, and I have the sudden urge to hear her voice. She called earlier, but I was in a meeting. I almost call her but then I remember the time, so I settle for sending her a text message instead.

Christopher: Thanks for the blanket. You're right. It does warm the room up.

I type a few more things, then delete them. I wasn't expecting her to do this, mostly because I've come to expect nothing from the women I date. I'm used to being the one with the surprise gifts. The dating I've done over the past years never ran deeper than physical attraction and having a good time together, but I still wanted my partners to be happy. Happiness usually translated to presents, not of a romantic nature because I'd left those behind until recently. The gifts were of the truckload-of-money nature. The more expensive, the brighter their smile. When things eventually ended, they missed the gifts more than they missed me. The sound of my ringtone jolts me to the here and now. Victoria is calling.

Putting the phone to my ear, I say, "I thought you'd be sleeping."

"Nah, I've been reading. I couldn't fall asleep."

"Admit it. You were waiting for me to call back. Sorry for not answering. I was in a meeting."

"I will admit to nothing. All you will get is a *maybe*."

That's more than enough for me. "Thanks for the blanket again."

"It's not much of a redo, but hopefully it'll make your room more welcoming."

"You know what I'd really like to have in my room?"

"What?"

"You. I'd never leave this room again."

"That would be very bad for your Seattle business," she says.

"True, but it would be very good for both of us."

I realize at this moment how much I miss her. Her and the kiss police. Chloe and Lucas arguing about which tone of gray in this room is shittier, with Sienna telling them "shitty" is a bad word would definitely liven things up.

"How was your weekend?" I ask.

"Well, something happened, and I called you earlier to ask if you talked to Lucas recently."

"During lunch yesterday. Why?"

"Because he just scared the wits out of me. Pranking Lucas is back in business. He brought up his Halloween box and everything."

"I'm so proud of that kid."

"What did you tell him?"

Lucas called me yesterday at lunch, eager to talk about the big soccer game from Friday night. He was very disappointed I hadn't watched it. I can't blame him though; when I was nine, if someone had told me they worked on Friday evening instead of watching a soccer game, I would've dropped them from my "cool people" list. I took advantage of the opportunity to prod him, sniffing for information.

"I tested the waters, trying to understand why he stopped. Turns out, he thought being the man of the house meant being a grown-up, and grown-ups don't prank people. I used myself as an example to prove the opposite," I say.

"You're a genius. I never get him to tell me these things."

I stay silent for a while, mulling over a thought

that occurred a while back. "I think it's easier for him to talk about these things with outsiders."

"Christopher?"

"Yeah?"

"Thank you for talking to Lucas. This is the most romantic thing you could have done."

"Happy I helped. In all honesty, I was dying to have someone to pass on the pranking skills to. My nieces are sadly still too young. Anyway, I always said a prank is the best way to lighten up any day."

She snorts. "Please explain."

"What did Lucas do?"

"He put a spider on my neck."

"Still hasn't moved past the spider phase? I have to teach that kid better pranks."

"Should I be afraid?"

"Terrified. Anyway, before you realized the spider was just rubber, I bet you almost had a panic attack, thinking over all the worst-case scenarios."

"Yeah."

"So after learning it was a prank, you realized all your real problems are nothing compared to the scenarios. See, your day is better."

"You have a unique view of the world," she informs me as politely as possible. I never understood why people didn't get my point of view on this. It makes perfect sense.

"If I had a nickel every time I heard that from my family. They were more direct though. I believed they use the word 'crazy,' and sometimes 'twisted.'"

"I can't imagine why. I'm sure I'll have some nightmares tonight. That'll be a change in dreams."

Something in the way she says "dreams," as if it's a dirty secret, shoots adrenaline through my veins. I rise from the couch, stretching my legs before heading toward the bed, shrugging off the jacket of my suit and kicking off my shoes on the way.

"Did you have dirty dreams?"

She gasps lightly, and I imagine her covering her mouth. "How do you know?"

"You whispered the word."

"Oh."

"Are you alone?"

"Yes. I'm in my room."

"Tell me your dreams."

"Um… well, we were in a room, and you were doing wicked things to me."

I cling to her words like a desperate man, her silence feeling like a punishment.

"With my fingers? My mouth? My cock?"

Lying on my back on the cold bed, I imagine her blushing, getting turned on.

"All of them," she whispers. "And you were really good."

I close my eyes, imagining I'm next to her right this minute, only inches away from her soft skin. The things I'd do to her if she were within my reach. Wicked wouldn't even come close to describing it.

"I want to kiss you right now," I say. "I'd start with your mouth, continue with your neck. You have that sweet spot, right above the collarbone. I want to lick you there."

"Christopher!"

Her voice is a little hushed, a lot aroused. Energy strums through me, and my pants tighten uncomfortably.

"Touch yourself, Victoria. I want to hear you. I *need* this."

"I need it too. I… *oh*!"

A white-hot current jolts through me. In a flash of a second, I undo my belt, push my shirt up, and lower my hand into my pants.

"Are you wet?" I ask, gripping my erection tightly. I imagine touching her breasts, worshiping them the way they deserve.

"Yes," she pants, letting out small delicious moans. I increase the pressure with my hand, imagining it's her mouth. Just visualizing those pink, plump lips around my crown, I almost blow.

"Imagine my tongue where your fingers are."

Her sharp exhale travels straight to my groin. I increase the rhythm of my strokes, listening to her moans growing more desperate. In my mind, I worship every inch of her body, learning what she loves and what makes her come apart. But I'm too far gone to be able to coherently tease her. When I imagine sinking into her, I nearly explode. Warm and soft, she'd fit me to perfection.

"Fuck, Victoria. I want you."

Her response? A low primal groan that sends a white-hot flash from my base right to the crown. I inhale deeply, aware that every vein in my body is catching fire. Pacing myself, I loosen my grip a notch, wanting to wait so she finishes first.

She comes apart beautifully, crying out my name. I almost black out as warm liquid shoots onto my stomach.

"I.... This was...," she whispers, her breath still ragged.

"I know. And Victoria? I will make those dreams of yours a reality. And it will be a million times more intense than this."

Chapter Sixteen

Victoria

On Thursday, Isabelle and I visit an interior design fair downtown. Furniture designers show off their creations, and the venue will be buzzing with vendors and buyers alike. Hello, potential clients. The chances of convincing someone to hire us merely by pitching to them at a fair are much slimmer than in the case of people coming from recommendations, but it's still a source. We try to attend as many local fairs as possible.

By the time Isabelle and I reach the venue, it's raining cats and dogs. We both have umbrellas, but it's not helping much. The strong wind carries the raindrops everywhere, drenching my coat.

"Damn," Isabelle exclaims as we enter the venue.

"Yeah."

The place is packed, of course, as I expected it to be.

"Divide and conquer?" I suggest.

"You're on," she replies. The venue has been split into four areas, and we each take on two.

"Let's meet up at the coffee shop area at the end of the hall afterward to talk about our findings," I suggest.

"Perfect."

I fish the notebook I brought out of my bag and start writing down trends that strike me as innovative, aesthetically pleasant, or just practical. My clients' needs and requirements vary considerably, which is good; it keeps me on my toes, makes things more interesting. I jot down items that might be a good fit for my current clients, and I also hand out business cards to people looking for decorators.

When I arrive in front of a classic living room display, I bump into the one person I was hoping to avoid: my former employer, Natasha Jenkins. I haven't seen her since she fired me. Isabelle said Natasha was furious when she left the company to join me.

"Hi, Natasha!" I extend my hand to her, which she shakes stiffly.

"Victoria! How's business going?"

"It's good," I say with a smile. "Finding clients isn't easy, but it's better than I expected."

Natasha scrutinizes me, pursing her lips. I know the gesture too well. It means she's carefully considering her words.

"I've been at Alice Bennett's newest restaurant. Imagine my surprise when she said you decorated it."

"Why are you surprised? I decorated the first one too."

"My company decorated it." Ah yes, Natasha is definitely one of those bosses who loves to take all of the credit. "She was our client. I wasn't aware your business model is stealing our clients."

I freeze as if someone doused a bucket with ice over my head. "I didn't steal anyone. Alice was my account when I worked for you. I decorated her entire restaurant. She was happy with my work and wanted me to help her with the second one too."

"The correct thing would have been to ask her to find another decorator within my company."

Crossing my arms over my chest, I tap my fingers on the opposite elbow. "I told her I'm no longer employed by you. It was her choice to go with me."

Natasha smiles tightly. "If I find out that any other clients of mine will *choose* to go with you, you're going to have a lawsuit on your hands."

When did she become so catty? I found out how unfair she was when she fired me at the first sign I had a personal life with new responsibilities, but even then she was diplomatic.

"I'm in no mood to listen to your unfounded accusations. Have a good day, Natasha."

I'm fuming as I walk over to the next display, and several minutes pass before I'm calm enough to concentrate on my task again. After finishing my rounds, I join Isabelle at the standing coffee shop at the back of the venue.

"What goodies did you find?" I inquire as she hands me a cup of tea. We exchange information and opinions for half an hour before I bring up the topic of our former employer.

"I bumped into Natasha," I tell her.

Isabelle jerks her head back in surprise.

"How did it go?"

"She basically accused us of stealing Alice Bennett from her."

Isabelle snorts, looking through some of my notes. "I spoke to some girls from the office, and apparently business isn't going too well. I guess now that the bees have left the nest, the queen actually has to do some work herself."

I know what she means. Natasha never came to fairs, only her employees. She still has about seven girls in the office, but the fact that she came here herself means she's desperate for clients.

"Can she really sue us?" I ask. "We've done nothing wrong."

"Absolutely not. She was just trying to intimidate you."

Still, I can't help the uneasy feeling forming in the pit of my stomach.

***

The next week is hell. Half of my clients seem to want to change their setup, and the other half seem to go out of their way to complain about something. Among all the mayhem, I pick up the keys to Christopher's apartment and make sure to prioritize it.

I encounter a few hitches along the way. Nothing more than the usual back and forth with delivery services trying to move me around for their convenience, but I ride anyone's ass who tries to wiggle their way out of my time frame.

I want everything to be perfect when Christopher returns.

On Friday afternoon, as I help the kids pack for their overnight stay at Aunt Christina's, I mull over the idea of talking to them about Christopher, telling them there's more than friendship between us. Sienna already knows, of course, but Lucas and Chloe see him as a family friend.

There's a healthy dose of hero-worshipping involved too, especially on Lucas's part. After running the pros and cons in my mind, I decide to keep quiet on this topic, mostly because I can't answer the questions Lucas would surely ask. I don't have answers. I just know I can't wait to see Christopher tonight. I miss him so much it scares me.

Part of me also can't help drowning in guilt, remembering Lucas and Chloe's apprehensive expressions when they asked if I'm still going to look after them when I have my own kids. My heart squeezes, their little faces appearing clearly in my mind. I wonder if I shouldn't press pause on things with Christopher. Then our therapist's words replay in my mind, that it's important to carry on as normal, not put my life on hold. That the kids, even Chloe, are old enough to understand certain issues if properly explained. Drawing in a deep breath, I hold on to those words, but I have a hard time ignoring the suspicion that I'm being selfish.

"Victoria," Chloe says, snapping me out of my mental drama. "Can I take Mr. Cuddles with me to Aunt Christina's?"

"Sure thing. Let's pack him too."

My phone vibrates just as I finish zipping up Chloe's backpack.

Christopher: Can't wait to see you tonight. So happy this trip is over.

The plan is as follows. I'll drive to the airport with the kids in the car and pick up Christopher. We'll drop them off at Aunt Christina's, and then I'll drive him to his fully furnished apartment. Since I have his keys, it makes sense for me to drive him there. In addition, I had his car brought to the garage underneath his building. Also, I have a surprise for him. Initially, I wanted to first drop the kids off and then pick up Christopher, but they wouldn't hear of it. Chloe says she must tell him about the new superhero cape she made for her doll. Lucas insists he tells him about some soccer techniques he learned at school.

"Can I take my prank box to Aunt Christina's?"

Lucas asks as we load the backpacks in the car.

"That's not such a good idea, champ."

He sticks out his bottom lip, frowning. "But Chloe's allowed to take her teddy bear."

"The bear is smaller than your box." The second I say it out loud, I know I chose the wrong words.

"Then I can just take my spider or my skeleton mask. It's Halloween."

"You already have your costumes with you for trick-or-treating. And Aunt Christina doesn't like getting scared much." With a stroke of genius, I add, "But you know who does? Christopher! Why don't you take something to scare him?"

"Really?"

"Yeah. He'll love it." He's the one who said there's nothing like a prank to make his day better, and from his message, I can tell he needs cheering up. "But maybe not the spider or the skeleton mask. Something more creative?"

Lucas practically flies back inside the house.

Half an hour later, I'm speeding on toward the airport. The kids are in the back, suspiciously silent. Lucas refuses to tell me what he has in store for Christopher, though I have a hunch the girls know. My stomach twists and turns with anticipation the closer we get to the airport. I took an inordinate amount of time dressing, second-guessing every choice. I ended up wearing jeans and a figure-hugging sweater, which shows enough cleavage to entice. Now I'm second-guessing the choice *again*, feeling silly. We didn't make plans for the evening beyond me driving him to his apartment. Oh, there was plenty of banter and insinuations, but nothing more substantial.

For all I know, he could have plans with his family for tonight. I mean, he was gone for two weeks. What are the chances of him wanting to spend his first night back at home with me?

"Seems like we're here a bit early," I say, pulling into the airport parking lot.

"Half an hour. Someone was eager," Sienna comments with a knowing smile.

"I didn't know how bad the traffic would be at this time," I mumble.

"That would be more believable if you wouldn't actually spend half of your working time driving through the city."

We spend the spare time talking about their plans for tonight at Aunt Christina's, and when Christopher texts, letting me know he's landed, we climb out of the car and wait for him in front of the parking lot. When he joins us, my heart all but leaps out of my chest. Chloe jumps straight in his arms, while Lucas talks his ear off about soccer. Sienna just glances between Christopher and me, suppressing a grin.

"Come on, let's go back to the car," I say loudly. Sienna walks away with Chloe, Lucas tagging after them.

"Welcome back," I tell Christopher, suddenly feeling shy.

"Thanks for picking me up. You—"

A sound pierces the crisp air, a sharp wail that sounds almost inhuman. Except it is human, because I know the voice, even distorted by pain as it is. It belongs to Lucas. Whipping around, I see my brother a few feet behind, his left arm covered in blood. There is so much blood; he must have cut an artery, but how? A shard of glass lies at his feet, one of its edges dipped in blood.

Panic numbs my reflexes, freezes my breath in my

lungs. Christopher is already halfway to Lucas by the time my legs move, carrying me forward.

"Call an ambulance," Christopher barks at me over his shoulder. His voice reaches me even through the haze of horror, and with trembling hands, I take the phone out of my pocket. The tremor grows so intense that I drop my phone.

"Where did you hurt yourself?" Christopher asks Lucas. "Where is the cut?"

Lucas's answer is another scream. I almost faint while ducking to pick up my phone from the concrete.

"Lucas, I know it hurts," Christopher says calmly, "but I need you to tell me where the cut is so I can try to stop the bleeding."

I'm dialing the emergency number when the screaming stops, laughter replacing it. Sienna and Chloe are holding their bellies, guffawing like I've never seen them. Lucas is jumping up and down, wiping tears of laughter with both hands. Both *uninjured* hands.

Christopher looks from Lucas to me and then back at Lucas, raising his arms in bewilderment.

"What is going on?" he asks.

I have no answer, shock still gripping my body.

"That was a prank," Sienna says between guffaws. Turning to Lucas, she adds, "Told you it might be a bit too much."

Christopher recovers first. "Fake blood?"

"Yes," Lucas confirms, drawing in deep breaths to calm himself down. "And fake glass." He picks up the shard at his feet, holding it out proudly. "It comes in a kit. It's the first time I used it. Victoria, you said I should be creative."

"Without giving anyone a heart attack," I say. Thank God no one else was around us, or they would've had a heart attack too.

Christopher is grinning now, shaking his head at Lucas. "Kid, you've got me there. And you have a weird sense of humor."

Sienna rolls her eyes. "You're such adults. I was expecting better of you, Christopher."

"Okay, why don't we get in the car and drive to Aunt Christina's?" I ask, still shaking a little. "We're going to be late otherwise, and that's not polite."

Chapter Seventeen

Victoria

After dropping off the kids at Aunt Christina's, we walk back to the car side by side, Christopher chuckling to himself. God, I love that sound. I missed it while he was gone. He laughed often enough when we talked on the phone, but being next to him turns it into a whole new experience because Christopher laughs with his whole body. It's contagious; the grin on my face can attest to that. We recovered from the shock completely somewhere on the road.

The air between us is light and playful, right until he places his hand at the small of my back. Energy strums through me at the contact, spreading everywhere, making my heart somersault and my toes curl. *Damn, damn, damn....* This man lights up my body without even trying. Out of the corner of my eye, I peek at him, trying to gauge whether he's aware of the sudden change between us or if I'm the only one feeling naughty.

His mouth has curled into a smirk that indicates he's very pleased with himself. *Aha! I'm definitely not the only one with X-rated thoughts.*

"I still can't get over Lucas's sense of humor," he remarks just as we reach the car. He opens the door for me, but I don't climb inside just yet. "Too much on the morbid side, I have to say. I'm sure if I look closely, I'll find some white hair. Those were some of the most terrible seconds of my life." His smile falters, his gaze clouding with worry. I want to kiss that worry away, to hug and thank him for being so strong in a moment of—fake—need. He was so composed, where I was so lost and scared. Usually, I rise up to any challenge, and I can count on myself to react swiftly, but all I could think at that moment was that I couldn't lose Lucas like I lost my parents. Christopher was calm and in charge, and it felt so good to have someone to count on.

Chewing the inside of my cheek, I decide to keep all this to myself instead of thanking him. Since none of that danger was real, I'd sound silly.

"Should have made him tell me what he was planning," is all I say.

"You put him up to it?"

"Yes. You seemed down when you messaged me, and you did say pranks cheer you up. So, I thought…." I shrug, licking my lower lip, acutely aware of the short distance between us. Christopher reaches out to me, dragging his knuckles across my cheek. I barely hold back from turning his palm up and burying my cheek in it.

"You're one hell of a woman, Victoria." He scrutinizes me in a way he never has before. The intensity in his gaze smolders. Without another word, I lower myself into the driver's seat. The second he climbs in the car as well, the air thickens with tension.

"Excited to see your apartment?" I ask, gunning the engine, rolling my shoulders when the car lurches forward.

"If you come up with me, yeah."

"Of course I'll come upstairs." I focus on the road, my voice even. "I need to give you a tour."

"Of my own apartment?"

"Yeah," I continue undeterred. "I need to show you how to use the appliances and—"

"Make sure I really know how to open and close the drawers? Sit on the couch?"

"You woke up with an extra dose of smartass," I remark, enjoying this immensely.

"Nah, I stocked up on it on the plane. Come to think of it, you're right. You absolutely have to give me a tour."

"Why the sudden change of heart?"

"There're some things I definitely need your help testing." He leans closer to me, dropping his voice to a whisper. "The bed, the shower."

"Personally, I was hoping we could test the kitchen counter. Always been a fantasy of mine."

My words are met with silence, and out of the corner of my eye, I notice his lips part open in shock.

"It's good to have you back, Christopher."

He grunts something I can't quite make out, and I'm so proud I managed to unhinge *him* for once that it's almost silly.

When we arrive, I park on the side street adjacent to his building. He takes his large suitcase from the back, and I lead the way inside. The concierge, Tom, greets me from behind the reception desk, flashing me a conspiratorial smile.

"I see you and Tom are friends already," Christopher says once we're in the elevator, and I think I detect a hint of jealousy in his tone. It delights me.

"I found out early on that the fastest way to get things done quickly is to have the people you work with like you. Also, I genuinely like people."

Butterflies roam in my stomach once we step out of the elevator on his floor, and telling myself I'm being ridiculous is futile. I'm not usually nervous when I show clients the outcome because I'm confident in my work. I am now too, but this is important to Christopher, and he's important to me. Also, I have a surprise waiting for him.

The first inkling that things won't go as planned is the smell of burned pastry assaulting my nostrils when we step inside the apartment.

"What the—" Christopher begins, but I hurry to the kitchen before he has the chance to finish the sentence. Sure enough, smoke comes out of the oven. I turn it off, opening the window and then, after a brief hesitation, open the oven too. A thick cloud of smoke comes out, and I duck away from it, hoping it'll go out the window and won't trigger the fire alarm. Yeah, my cookies are burned to a crisp. I almost want to cry in frustration.

Resigned that I have to throw them away, I turn around to face Christopher, who's standing in the middle of the kitchen, watching me with an expression somewhere between amused and incredulous. He dropped his suitcase next to the pile of boxes containing all his belongings, which still have to be unpacked.

"Victoria?"

"You said you'd like for your apartment to smell like cookies, so I thought I'd surprise you. It was physically impossible for me to actually be here while they baked, and I didn't want to bake them before because they'd be cold. So I asked Tom to start the oven half an hour before and gave him instructions, but he set the temperature far too high. Not to be sexist or anything, but I'm never letting a man anywhere near my cookies ever again."

Christopher is silent, but I think if he fights the

laughter much longer, he'll crack a rib.

"Go on, laugh," I encourage. "I'd do the same if I weren't so disappointed."

Taking my hand, he leads me away from the smelly kitchen, which is probably a good thing. Except that the smell's spread to the whole living room, and I know it'll take days for him to get it out. Just the perfect welcome gift. Opening the doors to the balcony, we step outside into the crisp, fresh air. Even with my jacket on, I feel a little cold.

"Why are you so upset about this?" Christopher asks as I lean against the wall, watching the city lights. He's not inspecting the balcony or admiring the view. He's watching me, and I feel sillier by the second.

"Because I wanted the first night in your new home to be perfect."

"It is."

"Your living room smells like someone set it on fire."

"But you're here. That more than balances it out."

Ah, I thought I'd seen every single type of smile this man has to offer until now, but I was wrong. His entire expression lights up, and he gives off a kind of exuberance I want to bottle and carry with me everywhere.

"I thought about you constantly this week." He caresses my jaw with his thumb, a slow, deliberate movement. "All I could think about every night was seeing you when I got back. Whatever this is between us, I don't want to let it go, not before we try and see where it leads."

This is a night of many firsts. At the airport, I saw the strong and take-charge side of him. Now all I see is a raw vulnerability. He doesn't put himself out there often, and at this moment, he's going out on a limb. His vulnerability coaxes me out of my shell.

"That…." Suddenly, I'm breathless. "Yeah."

"Which part?"

"All of it."

His thumb inches up to the corner of my mouth, where it lingers for a split second before gliding over my lower lip, resting exactly in the center of it. He trains his eyes on my mouth, then snaps them back up, focusing on me.

"I admit I'm not great at trying. Actually, I'm not even good at it. I haven't tried in a long time. The list of women who'd like to have my balls removed is quite long. I once had a shoe thrown at my head during a break-up conversation. If you look closely, you'll see the mark of the heel here." He presses his forefinger to the side of his head.

He places one hand on my waist, leaning toward me until our bodies almost touch. Almost, but not quite. He tilts his head down and to the side as if wanting to rest it in the crook of my neck.

"Do you want to stay the night?" he whispers against my skin, while his thumb rubs little circles on my waist, driving me insane with need.

"Yes."

Our control snaps at the same time. Christopher kisses the base of my neck, and I lift my hand, digging my fingers into his hair, needing him closer. Needing all of him. Feeling his hot mouth on my skin while the cold autumn breeze surrounds us is exquisite.

"I want you, Victoria. Let's go inside."

"Why?"

He presses his hips against me, and that's when I feel how hard he is for me. "Because I'm one second away from taking you against this wall."

Oh my.

He covers my mouth with his and we tumble inside, a tangle of limbs, lost in the kiss. His hands are at the side of my face, cradling my head as his tongue probes and tastes, driving me insane with need.

Pulling apart, we both draw in deep breaths, then start laughing. With no small surprise, I realize I'm shaking, and so is he. We both unzip and drop our jackets on the couch.

"I feel like I'm sixteen," he confesses, then seals his lips over mine again.

He might feel like a teenager, but he kisses and touches like a man. His hands slide down my back, grabbing my ass and lifting me up, and I wrap my legs around his waist. When I press my center against him, he releases a deep, primal groan. It sounds like a promise: that he'll make love to me, and he's going to make me feel things I never have before.

***

Christopher

She melts in my arms, pressing her soft curves against me. Damn. The way she gives herself to me without restraint nearly has me exploding. I carry her in my arms, only putting her feet back on the floor when we reach the bedroom. After switching on the light, I feast on her delicate skin, kissing her neck, licking the hollow at the base of her throat. She rewards me with a moan, pushing her hips against me.

"I'm going to make you feel so good, you're not going to want to leave my bed."

She chuckles, though her breath catches. "It's a good bed."

"Lie on it," I demand, and she does as I say.

"Are you going to join me, or what?"

Lowering myself on the bed, I grab the hem of her sweater and push it up, my mouth trailing along every inch of skin I expose.

"You're beautiful," I whisper to her, discarding her sweater next to the bed. Drinking in the swell of her breasts and the curve of her waist, I cup one of her breasts over her bra and Victoria arches against me, inviting me. It's all I can do not to do away with her jeans and bury myself inside her. No, I want to taste her first. I place my mouth on her collarbone, descending until the fabric of her bra meets the skin, licking her there. The effect is instantaneous. Her hips arch up, colliding with my groin.

"Christopher."

Hearing my name come out of her mouth is as much a turn-on as seeing her come undone before me. Like a man possessed, I unclasp her bra, needing her bare before me. Her nipples are puckered, begging for my attention, and damn, I plan to lavish them with attention. Worship them, along with every other part of her. When I cover one nipple with my mouth, she fists my hair, tugging at it. My woman's feisty, and I love it. I flick my tongue against the hardened nub, while my hands work on unzipping her jeans.

Unhitching my mouth from her sensitive skin, I pull back to make enough space to tug her pants down her thighs and toss them away. One glance at her soaked thong and my control falters. Victoria lifts her hips off the bed, giving me a peek of the perfect roundness of her ass. She pushes her panties down to her ankles, kicking them off. Then she opens her thighs, inviting me.

I lower myself until my mouth hovers directly above her center. I trail my finger up and down the rim of her opening, enjoying the way she writhes against the sheets, eager for more. I slide one finger inside her with ease.

"More. I want more," she whispers.

"You're a feisty little thing," I reply, but oblige, sliding in a second finger and curling both of them, touching a sensitive spot inside her.

"Oh, God. That feels—Oh!"

I'm so hard I can barely stand it, but I want to make sure she's ready first. I could spend days pleasuring her and wouldn't get enough. Her eyelids flutter shut as I slide my fingers in and out of her. When I press my thumb on her clit, she clenches around my fingers. Energy zips down my spine, and my cock throbs painfully against the waistband of my jeans.

"What are you doing?" she complains as I pull out my fingers.

"I want to taste you."

Slipping my hands under her ass, I lift her until my mouth is directly in front of her center. I swipe my tongue along the length of her ripe flesh once, and then again. With every swipe, Victoria shudders, the muscles in her ass cheeks tightening. Then I slip my tongue inside her, driving her crazy. Driving myself crazy. Hearing her whimpers and moans of pleasure is the best aphrodisiac in the world.

"Christopher, I want you inside me. *Please.*"

My plan is to torture her some more, but her next words undo me.

"I *need* you."

The next minutes are a blur. I descend from the bed, retrieving a condom from the back pocket of my jeans. No, I don't usually walk around with a condom in my back pocket, but I brought one tonight. What can I say? I'm an optimistic guy. I lose my clothes with lightning speed, and when I look at her again, a shadow crosses her features. I lie next to her, cupping her jaw, watching her chest rise up and down with quick breaths, which further betray her nervousness.

As I move over her, I interlace my fingers with hers, kissing her neck. I want her to feel that this isn't just quick fun for me. I don't know what it is, but it's not that. The tension bleeds away from her, and she relaxes underneath me. I enter her slowly. Damn it, I was planning to be gentle with her tonight, but feeling her inner walls clench around me makes that impossible.

Blind with need for her, I pull out, grasping each of her ankles and placing them on my shoulders. Then I bury myself inside her. Victoria gasps, biting down on her plump lip. I ease in and out of her, the sound of skin slapping against skin filling the room, intermingling with our groans.

"You feel so good," I tell her. "So good."

My thumb rests on her sensitive spot, applying a slight pressure while my hips slam against her more ferociously. Her breasts move in sync, and fuck, what a sight she is. I could watch her forever. Pausing, I take a deep breath, trying to keep in check the white-hot current that shoots right through my groin. Pushing her legs to the side, I lean forward until my lips are level with hers.

We move in unison, gazes interlocked. Gripping a few strands of her hair, I tug her head gently to one side, baring her neck to me. She lets out the softest moan when I bite gently at her earlobe. The sound fuels my desire, and I drive into her hard.

"Touch your clit," I command in her ear. She lets out a delicious gasp. "Touch yourself."

She slips her delicate hand between our bodies and lowers it. Red splotches appear on her cheeks and her neck when she gasps. "Oh. This is…. I'm going to…."

"I need to kiss you when you come." I want to own her sounds of pleasure. I want to own *her*. My mouth captures hers as she explodes, clenches around me, and drives me to a ravaging orgasm.

Once we both calm down, I pull out, already wanting her again. After discarding the condom, I lie next to her, losing myself in her sweet scent and the warmth of her skin. As I place my hand on her chest, feeling her labored breaths, the only coherent thought I can form is that she belongs here, in my bed.

Chapter Eighteen

Victoria

I wake up to blinding light the next morning, and it takes a few seconds for my eyes to adjust and focus. Next to me, Christopher sleeps soundly, lying on his back. Rays of sunlight fall directly on his face, but that doesn't seem to disturb him in the slightest. I turn to one side, propping myself up on an elbow, inspecting him.

His features appear softer in sleep, but one thing hasn't changed. His lips have that curl to them as if they're about to break into a smile at any second. I barely restrain myself from leaning to kiss him.

When he shifts slightly, the sheet covering him slides away, leaving him in all his naked glory before me. This is getting worse. Now I just want to lick him everywhere. His body is toned and demands my attention.

That mouth calls to me, but it would be selfish of me to wake him up. He works long hours during the week, so I suspect he likes to sleep in on the weekends. Not to mention he's been working the past few weekends. He needs his rest.

I check my phone on the bedside table. It's eight o'clock, which means I have an hour and a half to go home, change, and then head to Aunt Christina's to pick up the kids. I have plenty of time, enough for a morning cuddling session, but he is soundly asleep. Waking him up would be selfish.

Terribly selfish.

Mmm... but one tiny, tiny kiss won't wake him up. There's no way anyone could expect me to leave his bed without a good-bye kiss, right? Ever so carefully, I lean in, feathering my lips over his. Christopher shifts underneath me, opening his eyes. *Damn it.* I pull back, hanging my head in shame.

"Sorry for waking you up," I mutter, even though now that he's awake, I can't help imagining all the... possibilities for this morning. Christopher runs a hand through his hair, his expression still groggy with sleep. Feeling like I need to explain myself some more, I add, "I just couldn't leave without kissing you."

"That irresistible, huh? I'm glad you didn't leave while I was sleeping. I would've felt a little used."

"Oh, that hadn't even crossed my mind."

"Well, now that we're awake, you're welcome to use me some more," he says with a grin, scooting closer to me on the bed and tracing the contour of my jaw. "I won't mind it *too* much."

My heart swells with joy at the ease of our interactions, and my relief manifests in a chuckle.

"What?" Christopher inquires.

"I'm happy there's no awkwardness between us," I say honestly.

"Were you expecting some?"

"Sometimes things get awkward *after.*"

"Yeah, when you barely know the other person." He kisses my forehead softly. I melt against him, his words reaching somewhere deep inside me. I have zero regrets for waking him now.

"What's with that smile?" he asks. "I haven't seen it before."

I don't miss a beat. "It's my 'Christopher gave me the most amazing orgasm' smile."

He tilts his head to the side.

"What?" I ask, a little defensive.

"I'm trying to picture your 'Christopher gave me the most amazing multiple orgasms' smile."

"Want to get started on that project right away?"

Christopher opens his mouth, but before he has a chance to answer, a beep from the nightstand startles both of us.

"That was my phone. A reminder I have to pick up the kids in about seventy-five minutes." Pouting, I add, "No time for your project right now."

"Not to brag, but I can do *a lot* in that time."

"I want to go home and change first. If they see me in these clothes, they'll realize I haven't slept at home."

Christopher pulls away. "You don't want to tell them about us?"

My stomach drops as I try to explain my conundrum. I push myself into a sitting position and cover my naked body with the bedsheet.

"I do. It's just that I… I don't know what to tell them. I don't want them to think we're going to start popping out babies soon. They like you a lot, but Lucas and Chloe think about you like a family friend of sorts. I don't want to confuse them, and I also don't want to get their hopes up." I groan, dropping my head in my hands. "I sound like a crazy person right now."

"No, you don't." Christopher runs his palm up and down my back, and the gesture relaxes me tremendously. "You sound like someone who's parenting her siblings and trying to do the best for them. That's one of the things I love about you."

His words fill me with a warm, fuzzy feeling, and I dive right back in the bed, cocooning at his side.

"You say all the right things. How do you always do that?"

"Special talent."

"Inherited?"

"Nope, all mine." He spoons against me, kissing the back of my neck.

"Say, why do you blame all the bad traits on your DNA but take full credit for the good ones? I can't help but be a little suspicious."

"Trust is the base of any healthy relationship," he says seriously, kissing that spot some more, luring a giggle out of me. "By the way, we can tell the kids together if you want. Your call."

"I think it's best if I do it alone."

"Okay. But I want to make one thing clear. When I made that commitment last night, it wasn't just to you. It was to them too."

"No disrespect to your seduction skills, but I wouldn't be in your bed if I didn't think you cared for my siblings." Last night with him was... I don't even know how to describe it. It's as if my world had been spinning for months, and last night I found my balance in his solid, strong arms. "I want to make you the happiest man."

"I aim to make all four of you happy."

As he pulls me into a hug, I can't help the sense of unease taking residence inside my chest. With a jolt, I realize it's November, almost two months since I met Christopher. In the short time I've known him, he's become important to me. Too important. If I had to let him go, I'd be devastated.

"You really do give the best cuddles," I inform him as I cocoon against him. Christopher instantly curls an arm around me, pulling me into a half embrace.

When I hear him yawn, I cringe, looking up at him. "Again, sorry for kissing you while you were sleeping. I didn't mean to wake you up."

"If there's one thing you never have to apologize for, it's kissing me." He surveys me, his gaze lingering on my mouth. "Actually, I've changed my mind. How do you plan to make it up to me for waking me up?"

"Letting you go back to sleep?"

"Wrong answer."

"So you're mad at me now?" I ask, grinning.

"Very." Wiggling his eyebrows, he leans into me, placing a gentle kiss on the hollow of my neck, then whispering against my skin, "I require a thorough apology."

"Define thorough."

Christopher pulls back, furrowing his brow as if this requires his utmost concentration.

"You can kiss me *everywhere*. I'll leave you the choice of where to start."

"You are so generous." I place my lips above his navel, peppering his torso with kisses, tracing the sinewy lines highlighting his muscles with my tongue. Christopher rewards me with delicious groans, his hand gripping my hair gently. As I continue with my ministrations up to his neck, I climb over him, and I can't help smiling against his skin when I feel how hard he is for me.

"I think there's a situation requiring your attention further south," Christopher says on a groan.

"Is that so?" I tease, then begin my descent, trailing kisses along the way. I stop at his navel, nuzzling it while palming his erection. Moving my hand up and down, I enjoy the way his breath becomes more labored.

It pleases me immensely to know I have this effect on him. Deciding to be a naughty tease, I swipe my tongue over the tip of his hard-on exactly once before climbing off him and lounging on the bed next to him on one side, propping myself up on an elbow.

He raises an eyebrow, to which I respond with a playful shrug of my shoulder.

"I can't put out again so soon after last night. I wouldn't want you to get the wrong impression."

"I see." His tone holds a silent challenge, one that I meet with my chin held high. "You were all in for the multi-orgasm project earlier."

"Hormones were clouding my mind. Now I'm one hundred percent sober."

Abruptly, Christopher pushes me on by back, leveling himself over me.

"What are you doing?" I inquire.

"Changing that. And getting my revenge."

With those revelatory words, Christopher pins my hands above my head against the mattress. His mouth finds its way to the sweet spot on my neck, just below my earlobe. I arch my back involuntarily as he lights up every nerve ending in my body until my intimate spot pulses for him. Releasing my hands, he lowers himself until his mouth is level with my breasts, and holy sweet Sunday. His tongue is doing sinful things to my nipples, but that's nothing compared to the sweet torture of his thumb rubbing against my clit.

"Ah! Christopher. Don't stop."

He does exactly that, of course, pulling away from me and sitting up on the bed with a devilish smile. Teasing suddenly feels like the worst idea in the world because he's much better at it than I am.

Note to self: must up my teasing game.

"Those hormone clouds back?"

"Nope, not at all. How about I give you a tour of the apartment before leaving?" My entire body is burning, and my skin is yearning for him to touch me, but I'm not about to give him the satisfaction of knowing that.

I crawl out of bed, stretching my arms in an attempt to shake off the last vestiges of sleep. I make sure to stand right in front of Christopher as I do it, tempting the hell out of him.

"You don't mind if it's a *naked* tour, do you?" I ask. The glimpse of shock and desire in his eyes? *Priceless.*

I start by showing him the walk-in closet adjacent to his bedroom, and then as I tiptoe out of the room, I'm overcome by a sense of giddiness. Christopher walks a few feet behind me, which I suspect is so he can gaze unabashedly at my ass. I add an extra sway to my hips to test my theory. His sharp intake of breath is my answer.

I've never seen myself as a vixen or a seductress, but Christopher is bringing that side out of me. The tour takes less than ten minutes, during which I do all the talking, and Christopher does all the gawking. Well, that last part isn't exactly true; I admire him too when he isn't looking. This man is a piece of art. Every muscle is sculpted beautifully, and I commit every inch of him to memory.

Because the smell of burned cookies still lingers in the kitchen and living room, we open the door to the balcony but close it quickly. The weather has clearly received the wrong memo. It's November, not December! Even though we closed the door within seconds, I swear the cold has seeped into my bones. On the bright side, my nipples have turned to pebbles, something Christopher is appreciating greatly.

***

"I had all your boxes brought over," I inform him on a more serious tone once we're both dressed, and I'm about to leave.

I collaborated with his sister Alice on that one. When Christopher abruptly took off to Seattle, he hadn't packed up the things at his old apartment, so she did it for him. "But I didn't unpack them. I thought you'd prefer to do it yourself."

"Not really looking forward to that, but I'll start on it today. One question though. Why did you put sheets on my bed?"

I grin. "For the same reason you had a condom in your back pocket."

"You little feisty thing."

"You wake up a wild side in me."

He rests his hands on my waist, peppering my temple with kisses. "Back at you."

From the bedroom, the alarm on my phone blares again. "I have to hurry to pick up the kids." Tipping my head upward, I look at him expectantly, nearly burning with anticipation.

"No good-bye kiss for you today as punishment for teasing me since we woke up."

"Is that your last word?"

"Yeah, and I'm sticking to it come hell or high water."

"Famous last words, Bennett. Famous last words."

Chapter Nineteen

Christopher

At six o'clock, I finish throwing away the last of my boxes, and the apartment finally looks like it's lived in. Looking around the living room, I can proudly say Victoria did a great job making this place look like a home. There's just one problem. It's huge, and I am one person. What the hell was I thinking when I bought this place?

I wanted to live in this building, and I wanted the top floor. The three penthouses were all huge, so it's not as if I had much of a choice, but standing inside now, it seems like a dumb choice. Demolishing the walls of the five bedrooms to merge them into two hasn't chipped away at the square feet. The space feels empty, especially after having had Victoria here, and it's too quiet. Lucas would have a field day. The living room alone is so huge, he could play soccer, which is an excellent reason to invite them over. Reaching for my phone, I'm about to message Victoria when I see she's already sent me one.

Victoria: Talked to the kids! It went well.

"Well" wasn't exactly the word I was hoping for, but it'll do for now. I call her right away, pacing the living room.

"Hey, handsome," she answers.

"You never called me that before."

"Hmm, after recent events, an upgrade was in order."

"Recent events? Is this code for 'I'm not alone'?"

"Exactly."

"I have an idea. Why don't you and the kids come over? We could watch a movie or something."

"Ah, we were about to ask you to come over here, if you don't have plans."

"Tell him to bring ice cream too," Chloe yells in the background.

"I don't have plans. I can be at your house in about forty minutes. With ice cream."

"That's great, but no ice cream because we're eating enough junk food tonight as it is." Her background goes quiet, and I assume she went into another room. "I'm alone now."

"So how *well* did telling them go?"

"They like you a lot, so that helped. Sienna was already on top of things. Chloe asked what the specific difference between a friend and a boyfriend is. I.... Is it okay I said you're my boyfriend? I mean, we haven't officially—"

"Yes, Victoria. It's perfectly okay. I am your *handsome* boyfriend."

She laughs softly in response. "Yeah, so I explained the difference, and then she asked if it means she'll have a sister/cousin. So I had to give her and Lucas the birds and bees talk."

"It required giving them the birds and bees talk? Jesus!" I stop pacing, dragging my hand down my face.

"Yep. Pretty sure Lucas knew I was bullshitting."

"He's nine. Of course, he did."

"Anyway, all in all, I think neither of them should ask you about a wedding or something. And they can't wait to have you over. You can sleep here too, if you want."

Grabbing my car keys and a jacket, I head out the door. "Are you kidding? Of course, I want to. I'm on my way."

"I have to get back to them now. I left the three of them alone in the kitchen. Last time I did that, Lucas snuck chili peppers in the cookie dough when Sienna wasn't looking. She needs backup. Drive safe, handsome."

"What's it take to be upgraded to the next level?"

"Huh?"

"I'm not really happy with the handsome moniker. I have a few suggestions. They're far better."

"You suck at negotiating. Get your ass over here, Bennett."

***

I walk up Victoria's front steps a while later. Sienna opens the door before I even ring the bell.

"Come in." She gives me a solid "I approve of you" smile.

When I sent the flowers two weeks ago, I was hoping Victoria wouldn't be home when they arrived, so Sienna would have time to inspect them. I knew she'd read the card. I'm not often sneaky, but when I am, it's for a good cause, such as winning Sienna to my side.

"Victoria had to run to the store, but she'll be home in a few minutes."

I follow her into the living room, where Lucas and Chloe are sitting on the couch. Both are silent, which is my first clue that something's up. Growing up, the only time our house was silent was when some serious shit went down, and we wanted to keep it from Mom and Dad. Not that we ever managed to; Mom had a sixth sense when it came to those things.

"What are we watching?" I ask them, breaking the weird silence.

"We haven't decided yet," Lucas answers. "Chloe, take your position."

Huh? Chloe half walks, half crawls to the armrest. Kneeling on it, she props her tiny hands on the windowsill, peering outside. Lucas mouths to Sienna, "You first."

"Okay, what's going on?" I ask, sitting on the ottoman opposite the couch. "I feel like I'm missing something. What's Chloe doing at the window?"

"Sounding the alarm when I see Victoria," the girl responds, which only further confuses me.

"If we don't hurry up, she'll be home soon," Lucas tells his older sister. "Cheese-flavored popcorn is easy to find."

"Nah, I told her to buy nachos with guacamole instead," Sienna says thoughtfully. "Those are never where they're supposed to be. I always have to ask the clerk to bring it from the back."

"What's going on?" I repeat.

"We wanted to talk to you," Lucas says.

"When Victoria's not around," Sienna adds.

Ah, and now it becomes crystal clear. I'm being ambushed.

"Let's hear it."

"Victoria told us today you guys are dating," Sienna begins, and the "I approve of you" smile is gone. "And we like you."

"Okay…," I say cautiously, not feeling very liked right now.

"We want to know if you're serious about her," Sienna says.

Well, I'll be damned. Over the years, I've heard

variations of the talk from a lot of people, including my own family. I usually dismissed their questioning with a variation of "It's none of your business," but seeing these kids look up at me with hope… this is a whole new set of expectations. And I don't want to let them down.

"I am," I answer without hesitation.

"How serious?" Lucas presses.

"Are we getting a new sister?" Chloe asks, snapping her gaze from the window to me.

"It wouldn't be a sister," Lucas corrects instantly. "It would be a niece. Victoria already explained."

"Whatever." Chloe darts her tongue at her brother. "Are we getting a new baby? I don't want to be the baby forever." She practically winces at the word "baby," and she's downright adorable. But I'd be a liar not to admit that hearing that word made my entire stomach coil with panic.

"You're not a baby anymore," Lucas says. "You're a midget now."

"I am not." Chloe balls her little hands into fists.

"Lucas, stop being mean to Chloe," Sienna hisses. "Chloe, you're our lookout. Lucas and I are asking the questions."

"Okay, listen up. Relationships between adults are complicated, but Victoria and I want to make this work," I tell them.

"That sounds like bullshit," Lucas affirms.

"Language," Sienna, Chloe, and I say at the same time.

"He's right, Lucas," Sienna explains patiently. "Relationships are complicated."

I grimace, trying not to give too much thought to how much she knows about relationships firsthand. She's only seventeen. I make a mental note to do some digging on this topic later on when I'm back in Sienna's good graces.

"But you're going to take care of Victoria and spoil her, right?" Sienna presses.

"I give you my word."

"If you make her cry, don't forget I have my sisters' backs. I protect them. That's what brothers do." Lucas frowns in a very un-Lucas way, crossing his arms over his chest. I have déjà vu, remembering the day I told him that. Talking to these kids is like talking to the police. Everything you say can and will be used against you.

"You'd better, buddy," I encourage. "That's what siblings are for. Kicking any guy's ass who messes with his sister."

Sienna smiles, and Lucas gives me a thumbs-up, and I know the grilling is over. Just in time too, because Chloe squeaks, "Victoria's here."

"You two sit on the couch, bickering as usual." Sienna points her siblings to the couch. "I'll bring the cookies."

"I'll help," I offer, following her to the kitchen.

"Err… I think Lucas got into his character a little too much," Sienna says once we're out of earshot. "He wasn't nearly as menacing when we rehearsed."

"You rehearsed this?" I ask in amazement.

Sienna gives me a sheepish look while opening the oven and taking out the cookies. "After the airport incident, I thought it was for the best. Victoria already talked to us today, but we wanted to hear your version too. I'm glad you and Victoria are dating. It's been hardest for her. We all miss our parents." Her eyes become glassy, but then she takes a deep breath, smiling again. "But Victoria also had to take care of us on top of it all, and she's kind of put her personal life on hold. Just take care of her, okay?"

"Will do."

We carry the cookies in bowls to the living room, where Victoria awaits.

"Nachos with guacamole," Victoria barks. "Sienna, I'm murdering you. I had to wait forever for the vendor to bring it from the back."

Sienna's cheeks turn pink as she relieves Victoria of the bags.

"Hope you survived this bunch on your own," Victoria says when she sees me. "How long have you been here?"

Sienna shoots me a panicked look from behind Victoria, shaking her head, and it doesn't take a genius to know what she means. *Don't tell her.*

"I just arrived," I tell Victoria, winking at Sienna, who lets out a breath of relief. It'll be our secret. We unpack all the goodies she bought, laying them out on the coffee table, loading it down.

"What are we watching?" I ask.

"We want to watch the first Percy Jackson movie again," Sienna says, backed up by an eager Chloe and Lucas.

"I want to see that romantic comedy with doctors that came out last year," Victoria says, making me wince. The woman truly has dreadful taste in movies.

"You're outnumbered," Lucas points out.

"Christopher hasn't cast his vote," Victoria retaliates. "And his vote counts twice."

"Why?" the kids ask in unison.

"Because I need someone on my side." She looks at me expectantly. The wheels start turning in my head, measuring my chances of being denied the pleasure of sinking into her tonight if I don't side with her.

Fuck this. I'm not putting myself and the kids—but mostly myself because I'm a selfish bastard—through two hours of hell just to get laid. Besides, I'm confident enough in my seductive abilities to *persuade* Victoria in case I have to.

"I vote Percy Jackson."

Victoria gasps. The kids burst out laughing at the same time.

"I'm sorry, but you have terrible taste," I inform her.

"I keep telling her that," Sienna says.

"I can't believe you're siding with them." Victoria folds her arms over her chest, shaking her head. "Fine, you all win. Let's watch Percy Jackson for the tenth time," she says with a huff, sitting at the far corner of the couch. When I attempt to sit next to her, she gives me the evil eye, plopping her bowl of cookies there.

"My cookies need their own seat," she states.

Right. I foresee a lot of seductive work being required tonight. But I'm more than up to the task.

Within a few minutes, the room is dark, the TV is on, and we're watching in silence.

I sit next to Victoria's *bowl.* Lucas sits next to me. Chloe and Sienna are at the other end of the couch, wolfing down nachos with guacamole. Midway through the movie, Chloe changes places, wiggling herself between Victoria and me while holding the bowl in her lap. As Chloe rests her little head against my arm, it dawns on me how trusting these kids are. Yeah, their almost-intimidating attempt at grilling me was a surprise, but they've been accepting and welcome all-around. I make myself a promise. I won't let them down.

I peek at Victoria, who is watching Chloe with a bright smile. She snaps her gaze up, sending me an air kiss, and I know I'm forgiven. But that doesn't mean I won't employ some of my world-class seduction techniques. It'd be a shame to waste them.

After the movie ends, Victoria informs Chloe that it's her bedtime, and it's non-negotiable. Chloe pouts for a few good minutes, but by the frequency of her yawns, even she knows she'll fall asleep soon.

"I'm going up with Chloe to make sure she goes through her routine," Sienna tells Victoria, in an obvious attempt to give us some alone time.

"Lucas, are you coming upstairs too?" Sienna inquires, but Lucas is too busy rattling about his latest soccer game to do anything more than shake his head. Sienna glares at him but doesn't insist.

Some ten minutes later, we move from talking about soccer moves to soccer players when Chloe pops into the living room wearing neon green pajamas and clutching a book against her chest.

"I'm coming right away to read your story, Chloe," Victoria says. "Lucas, you should really go to bed too."

"But Christopher is still telling me about the players."

"Let's make a deal," I chime in. "Lucas and I will clean up while talking, and when we're done, he'll go to bed."

Lucas nods eagerly and pumps his fist in the air when Victoria agrees.

Chapter Twenty

Victoria

After Chloe falls asleep, I tiptoe out of her room. Soft music comes from Sienna's room, and I'm about to check if Lucas is up too when I see him climbing the staircase, smiling before disappearing in the bathroom. Descending the stairs, I find Christopher in the kitchen, looking sexy as sin.

"Hey!"

Snapping his head up, he glances my way, offering me a sly smile. "You're a quick reader."

"Chloe fell asleep when I reached the part where Cinderella sneaks away to go to the ball."

I lean against the counter and Christopher encircles me in his arms. His presence fills the room, and I can't help thinking how effortlessly he's slipped into our routine. It scares me. He drags the back of his hand down my cheek in a gesture so tender, I all but melt in his arms.

"I don't get why Cinderella is considered a story fit for kids," he says with a smirk.

"Huh? What are you talking about?"

"She snuck out of her house, trusted a completely random woman to give her clothes—by the way, I think that was code for she got high and imagined a fairy godmother—and then made out with a guy she barely knew."

For all of two seconds, I'm convinced he's pulling my leg, but nope. My man is serious.

"She didn't actually make out with the prince. And her family was evil."

"That's beside the point. What kind of example is that for young, impressionable girls?" He pinches his brows together, frowning as if concentrating on solving a mystery.

"You win the trophy for the world's most adorabilicious man."

"That's not a word," he deadpans.

"I just made it one. Relax, they're just stories."

"Hmm...."

"You know, we've been alone for almost a minute, and you haven't even tried to kiss me."

"Counting the seconds, were you?"

I shrug one shoulder, trying to play it cool.

"After the whole movie debate, I was sure I had to work hard to get back in your good graces."

"I admit I was going to grill you pretty hard, but your adorabiliciousness changed my mind."

"Stop repeating that word."

"Why? Is it assaulting your masculinity?"

"Ah, no, thanks for the concern. My masculinity is just fine, thank you. My ego on the other hand—"

I silence him by popping open the top button of his shirt and placing a kiss on the patch of skin I revealed. He sucks in a deep breath as I lick the hollow at the base of his neck.

Christopher backs me against the kitchen counter, rocking his hips into me. I swallow when I realize he's hard as steel. Pushing a strand of hair behind my ear, he tilts my head up.

"I love that you can't get enough of me."

"Pride is a sin, you know that?" My voice comes out as a strangled whisper because Christopher's mouth is at the base of my neck, nipping and biting gently.

"So is tempting me."

"I'm not doing anything," I point out, holding my hands up to prove my point. Christopher is too busy doing delicious things to my neck to pay me any attention.

"Oh, you tempt me all the time. Everything about you is a temptation."

"You're a bad man, seducing me like this," I say weakly. "Do you want to go to my room?"

"I thought you'd never ask."

In silence, I lead him out of the kitchen, toward my office/bedroom. He keeps his hand on my lower back the entire way. There's something deeply intimate and protective about the gesture, and I love it.

Once inside the office, I lead him through the narrow space separating the office from the bedroom. It was masked by a tall ficus tree last time he was here.

"Smart way to separate spaces. I hadn't even realized there was a room here," he remarks as I activate the twinkle lights I laid across my headboard.

"This is it," I announce, gesturing around the small space.

"What's wrong?" he asks. "You sound off." When I don't offer an explanation, he tilts my head up so I have no choice but to make eye contact. "Victoria, if you don't want me to stay overnight, say it. I promise I won't mind."

"I… just…. This is the first time I've brought a man into this room. This house, actually." I shrug, not really sure what my jitters are about.

Christopher kisses my forehead, resting his hands

on my shoulders. "It's an honor, Victoria. I promise I appreciate it."

"It feels so weird to have you here now that we're dating. Good weird," I add at his puzzled expression. "It's just a giant step… exposing the kids to someone new to love. If they lose you too…."

"Are you talking just about the kids or about you too?" His voice is soft, but the words pierce through me.

"Me too," I admit, feeling as if I've put my heart in his hands. His lips cover mine, gentle, reassuring, and passionate at the same time. I lose myself in his kiss, tugging at his hair, lightly grazing his scalp. With my other hand, I explore his torso, slipping under his shirt. His taut muscles feel amazing under the pads of my fingers.

"Thank you for being open with me," he whispers, descending to kiss my neck. I move my hips, pressing myself against him. "I love discovering this feisty side of you."

"And I love discovering your protective side." Protective is code for adorabilicious, but I needn't have bothered protecting his ego. He's too busy turning me on. "We have to be silent."

"Sweetheart, I can do silent and loud and everything in between. I will rock your world either way."

A sassy reply sits on the tip of my lip, but it melts away as Christopher sets me ablaze with one dark, meaningful look. He backs me against the wall, parting my legs with his knees. Leaning his forehead against mine, he breathes in deeply, smoothing his hands down my hair before descending to my cheeks, cupping them in a tender gesture.

There is something different about this moment. The whole evening has been beautiful, but this, right here, goes beyond beautiful. It's perfect and so intense that I swear the air between us crackles. This moment belongs to us alone, and I never want it to end.

"You feel it?" he asks.

"Yeah."

Pulling back, he places the pad of his thumb on a corner of my mouth, dragging it ever so slowly across my lower lip to the other corner.

"Since the first time I was here, I fantasized about bending you over your desk and fucking you silly."

His words travel straight to my intimate spot. His appearance turns almost feral. Stepping back, he pries me away from the wall, interlacing his fingers with mine. The contact is gentle and reassuring, and once again, I marvel at how fast he can go from passionate to gentle and caring.

"Since we're exchanging fantasies, I was hoping for some wall sex too."

"There's always later." He wiggles his eyebrows as we move into my office area.

I walk up to him next to the desk, feeling oddly naked in front of him, even though my dress isn't provocative in the slightest. It's homey and comfortable. But the way he looks at me, it's as if he can see what's underneath the deep blue fabric. With a simple, quick movement, he pulls the zipper down, pushing the dress off my shoulders. It falls to my feet, revealing my newest acquisitions, a matching set of red lace panties and bra. I might have put on a casual, homey dress, but underneath I dressed to impress, and my man seems very impressed.

"You're killing me," he whispers, cupping my breast over the fabric. My nipples turn to pebbles under the fabric, already yearning. "Your body is so responsive."

Looping an arm around my waist, he hoists me up on the desk. I want to lick the bit of skin visible through the opened top button of his shirt.

"How did I end up naked faster than you *again*?" I wonder out loud.

"You're not naked," he points out. In one swift move, he unclasps my bra, prying it away. My breasts spill free and Christopher groans. Pushing me back slightly, he lowers his head, taking one nipple between his lips.

Oh, damn damn damn!

My back arches involuntarily, and when he lightly twists the other nipple with his thumb and forefinger, I nearly lose it.

"Christopher!"

He pulls away, straightening up. The hunger in his expression is more intense than before.

"Lie back, rest on your elbows," he commands. His voice, so full of confidence and authority, turns me on as much as seeing his desire for me.

I decide to tease him first. I undo the button of his jeans and lower his zipper, pushing his pants and boxers down. Wrapping my hand around his hard-on, I move it up and down, watching him slowly come undone. His breath quickens, coming out in sharp exhales. When I drag my thumb across the tip of his length, he rewards me with a groan.

"Lie back," he repeats, his voice even more authoritative than before. I do as he says, perching my heels on the table, opening myself for him.

He touches my center over my panties, which are soaked. My thighs quiver slightly as he peels the thong off me, leaving me completely exposed.

Lowering himself a tad, he cups each of my ass cheeks in a hand, lifting my butt up until my center is level with his mouth. And then he licks me once, from my entrance up to my clit. My body becomes a slave to his mouth as he continues to pleasure me, and when he dips his tongue inside me, mimicking the act of making love, I feel like I'm about to rip out of my skin.

"I need…." My voice fades because my already sensitive nerve endings explode, heat radiating through me, making my toes curl.

Christopher pulls back, damn him.

"What do you need?"

"To touch you," I say with bated breath.

"Whatever the lady says." With a rueful smile, he holds out his hand, helping me hop down from the table. We're both shaking with desire as my fingers grope at his chest, a fumbled attempt to undo his buttons. Eventually I rid him of his shirt, tracing the lines and muscles of his chest with my fingers.

Lowering my hand, I palm his thick and hot length and I can feel his composure melting away. And then I feel his fingers gliding up and down my folds before dipping slightly inside me. Touching him while he touches me arouses me to no end.

"I'll bring a condom." I hurry to the nightstand next to my bed, returning quickly with a condom, ripping the package open and sliding it over him.

"Fuck," he growls. "I want to feel that sweet ass of yours against my thighs while I'm buried deep inside you."

"Do it," I challenge.

He turns me around, bending me slightly. I rest my palms against the wooden surface. He trails his mouth up my back, lavishing me with kisses.

Pushing my hair to the side, he kisses the back of my neck while he settles the tip of his erection against my ripe flesh. A shiver travels down my spine. When he rubs his tip around my entrance, teasing me, I suck in a deep breath. I've never been so aroused in my life.

He enters me in one swift move, and office sex might just become one of my favorite things. Sweet heavens, he's so deep inside me.

"Oh! This…." Dropping my voice to a whisper, I admit, "It's so deep."

He stills. "Does it hurt?"

"No, I love it. I…. It never felt like this."

"I will be rough."

Goose bumps rise on my skin.

"I want you to," I say confidently. He pulls out only to slam into me, filling me. My knees become weak as he repeats the movement, faster, deeper. He places one hand on my shoulder, the other on my hipbone, gripping me tightly as if needing to ground himself. Then his hand descends from my hip to my center, and he circles my sensitive spot with his fingers. I nearly explode, meeting his thrusts with equal fervor and desperation, wanting my climax but at the same time not wanting this to end.

"I love seeing you this wild," he murmurs between groans. "You feel so perfect." His words spur something deep inside me. My orgasm builds slowly, with every thrust and every touch of his fingers on my bundle of nerves, but my release hits me with a mind-blowing intensity, fast and exhilarating.

Moments later, I feel him widening inside me, and he cries out his own release. Pulling me to him until my back is flat against his chest, he cradles me, his head resting in the crook of my neck. I sigh, safe and happy in his arms.

Chapter Twenty-One

Victoria

Over the next week, Christopher stops by the house every other night, sometimes eating dinner with us, sometimes only arriving after dinner if he had a late meeting. On Thursday, Sienna puts her foot down after dessert, saying Christopher and I need time alone for a proper date. She announces that the three of them will spend the weekend at Aunt Christina's.

Christopher grins at her appreciatively, turning to me. "Since we're being bossed into a day-long date, I'm going to make plans."

"Weekend-long date," Sienna corrects. "Aunt Christina said we can stay overnight."

"By the way, I have an invitation," Christopher says. "My parents have invited all of you for Thanksgiving dinner at their house."

"We'd love to join you," I reply honestly, though my stomach is in knots at the thought of meeting his parents.

"Excellent," Sienna says. "So you two are going on a weekend-long date this week, and in two weeks we'll be meeting your parents. I like how things are progressing."

Once Sienna leaves us alone, Christopher says, "There's something on your mind."

"How do you know?"

"Just a hunch."

We're sitting on the couch in the living room, and all the kids are upstairs. There is no chance of anyone overhearing us.

"I'm worried," I say.

"Has the guy from social services bugged you again?"

"No! I mean, I've talked to him on the phone for the monthly updates, but I'm worried about something else. A while ago I bumped into my former employer, Natasha, and she accused me of stealing her clients. When I decorated Alice's first restaurant, I was working for Natasha. She was pissed that Alice didn't use her company for the second restaurant. This week I met with a potential client who said he had a meeting with Natasha but didn't like what she pitched him. Then he saw my work. It's still in the company's portfolio since I was with Natasha while completing it, and he decided to contact me directly. I don't want to give her grounds to sue me or anything. I don't know if I should take him on as a client."

Christopher frowns, rubbing his jaw. "I don't see why you shouldn't, but I'm no lawyer. However, I have contact with very good lawyers. Would you like to talk to one?"

"Yes! Wait—What's he charging per hour?"

"He won't charge you."

"Hey, that's not fair. I don't want a free ride."

"You can pay me instead." He wiggles his eyebrows suggestively.

"Christopher!"

"He won't charge you for one question, Victoria. But I want you to know one thing. You can count on me, no matter what." He pulls me onto his lap so that I'm straddling him. "Anything you or the kids need, just tell me. Anything, and I'll make it happen."

"You're awfully sweet," I say quietly.

"Your wish is my command. And your trouble is my trouble."

Christopher has slipped into my life so deeply I can't imagine it without him. I swear my heart skips a beat. "That's the most romantic thing you've said."

"Really?" He flashes my favorite grin. "I wasn't even trying. But since I just earned some points, can I spend the night here?"

"You don't have to ask. Of course you can. Don't you miss that beautiful apartment of yours?" We've been there with the kids one evening this week, giving them a tour. They loved it and wanted to sleep over, but since Christopher's second bedroom is an office and the couch is not a sleeper, that wasn't possible. Though I have the sneaking suspicion the kids would have happily slept on the floor just to stay there.

"Nah. I don't like being there on my own. It's empty without you and the kids."

I am simply in awe. That is until Christopher smirks.

"Now I *was* trying to be romantic. But it's true. In case you want to swoon, I've got you."

The mischievous bastard. I hold my ground, but I'm secretly swooning, of course.

***

The next day, I talk to Christopher's lawyer on the phone. He puts my mind at ease, assuring me Natasha has no grounds for suing, and it's absolutely my right to take on the client.

On Saturday morning, I drop the kids at Christina's house at ten o'clock and then return to my place to get ready for my date. The weekend with Christopher officially starts in two hours. He had a family thing this morning, but that worked for me. We made great plans for today. Going through our schedule in my mind, I realize it seems more like a marathon tour of San Francisco than a date, but we have a very logical explanation. We want to show each other the parts we love most about our city. He and I agree that no two people look at a city and see the same. On Sunday, we'll stay in at his apartment for a lazy day. I'm delighted at the possibilities brought by an entire day indoors with him alone. Yes, Christopher definitely woke my feisty side, and I'm enjoying the hell out of it.

I'm halfway dressed when my phone rings, Christopher's name appearing on the screen.

"Thinking of the devil," I say instead of hello upon answering. "I was trying to decide what would drive you crazier. Option one is a deep V-neck sweater, so deep you could see my navel if I bend forward and you really focus. Option two is a regular sweater with a decent neckline that I can wear without a bra. Thoughts?"

"Jesus. Are you trying to kill me here?"

"No, I merely like it when you look at me as if I walk on water."

"I always look at you that way."

It's true. With just one look, this man has the uncanny ability to make me feel like I'm the most important person in the world for him. But teasing him is too much fun to let this go.

"Well, it tends to happen more often when I wear

something provocative."

"I can't help but feel a little insulted."

"Please do. Can you keep feeling insulted until you pick me up? I love your 'I have to prove something' kisses the most."

"That is adding injury to insult."

"I think it's the other way around."

"Possibly. Listen, I can't make it in time."

My stomach drops. "What happened?"

"This thing we're building is more complicated than we thought. It'll take another few hours."

"Who is we? What are you building?"

"My brothers Sebastian, Logan, Blake, and me. My parents wanted an outdoor gazebo in time for Thanksgiving, and Mom ordered one online. The thing arrived earlier. My parents are out of town, and I thought we'd surprise them by building it for them. I thought it would be a piece of cake." In the background, male voices are arguing. I almost laugh as I imagine the four brothers flexing their macho streak, declaring it would be child's play to build the gazebo only to realize they were in over their heads. "I should be done by dinnertime. We'd need to skip the city tour, but I promise I'll make it up to you. Sorry."

"You have nothing to be sorry about," I assure him. "How about I come by and keep you company?"

"You'd do that?"

"Of course. My other options for today are staying home and reading, going for a run, or going out with Isabelle and our other girlfriends if any of them doesn't have plans already, which is a slim chance. That only leaves you," I tease.

"I feel really special right now." Sarcasm drips from his voice. "But seriously, it would be very boring for you."

"I assure you it won't. I want to spend the day with you."

"Ah yeah, me and my brothers."

"Perfect. I get to meet them too. That way I'll already know a few people next week." I didn't tell him this, but the prospect of meeting his entire family is giving me jitters. At least if I meet some of his brothers today, I'll have a head start. I'm good at one-on-one conversations or entertaining a small group, but working a crowd, not so much. I want his family's approval. I want them to like me.

"Should I bring some cookies? We have a ton left from this morning."

"Did Lucas sneak chili peppers in them again or something?"

"No, I just made too many."

"Sure. We can do with some sustenance. Write the address down."

Ten minutes later, I'm speeding along the highway, grinning like I'm going on some big adventure. I keep switching radio channels, finally settling on the only one that seems to play happy, upbeat songs. Drumming my fingers on the wheel to the rhythm, I start singing along, fully aware that I'm as off-key as I can be. But what the hell; there's no one here to hear or judge me. Some people like to sing in the shower, but my need to express my vocally creative side seems to only kick in while I'm in motion.

Sometime along the way, doubt creeps in. What if Christopher didn't really want me to come over? We've been spending a lot of time together lately. What if he wanted some space? My heart squeezes as I weigh the merits of that theory. The truth is I've always been rather bad at catching on when a man needs his space, or not. I've had dates who threw in my face that I was *too* all over them, and others who claimed I wasn't all over them *enough*. What am I supposed to make of that?

The problem when it comes to Christopher is that I can't get enough of him no matter how often I see him. He seemed excited back when we made plans for the weekend, but what if he's not on the same page as me? My stomach constricts as I rewind our earlier conversation in my mind, searching for signs that he didn't want my company until dinner. I can't find any. He seemed genuinely excited when I told him I wanted to spend the day with him.

I'm being silly and overthinking things. Christopher has been very upfront with me until now. There's no reason to mistrust him.

Chapter Twenty-Two

Victoria

When I arrive at the address Christopher gave me, the double gates at the front of the property are open. Behind them is a thick patch of trees, almost a small forest. I drive along until the woods spill into a large clearing. The Bennett home stands at the other end of the clearing, a proud three-story house. It's simple, yet beautiful. The facade is the color of vanilla, but the red roof gives it a vibrant appearance.

I pull my car next to the four others. After climbing out, I head to the four men surrounded by construction tools and materials near the house. I'll be damned, but the Bennett men are a sight for sore eyes. They're all over six feet, with a robust build, strong but lean, not bulky. They also share the same dark shade of hair. Christopher is the best-looking one, of course, but I dearly hope all of them will go on and have as many kids as possible. Such good genes must be spread around.

"Here's your girl, Christopher," one of them says, stretching out his hand to me. "I'm Blake."

"And these are my older brothers, Sebastian and Logan," Christopher explains.

I shake hands with Sebastian and Logan next.

"I brought everyone cookies," I announce, fishing the Tupperware container out of my bag. Blake relieves me of it immediately. I peer behind them at the gazebo they're building. They don't seem to have gotten very far.

"What's the trouble with the gazebo?"

Sebastian picks up an instruction notebook from the floor, handing it to me.

"These instructions are a deathtrap."

I scan them with attention, and while they're not straightforward, they aren't overly complex either.

"Are you sure you followed these?" I ask carefully. The four men exchange glances.

"Not in the beginning," Logan answers. "I mean, we've built enough stuff before."

Ooooh, I recognize this. Mom dubbed it the caveman syndrome, in which a man relies on his gut and refuses to follow instructions, whether it's for building something or finding an address, as if that somehow diminishes his masculinity. Dad did it all the time. We got lost on more trips than I can count because of his *infallible* orientation sense.

"Right," I say. "Well, from now on, you'll follow the instructions."

"You can translate them?" Blake asks.

"Yep."

Blake positively glows, munching on a cookie. "You make great cookies, and you know how to read instructions? Darling, if Christopher won't do, you can always marry me."

"Oh my. If I knew I'd get proposed to today, I would have dressed up for the occasion." I let out an exaggerated giggle, and Christopher instantly steps next to me, curling an arm around my waist.

"This one's very territorial." I point with my thumb to Christopher.

"Blake, you seem a little desperate of late,"

Sebastian remarks. "Why don't you find a girl for yourself?"

"We should put Pippa on your case," Logan says solemnly. "Looking at Christopher and Victoria here, it's clear our sister hasn't lost her touch."

Christopher gives an almost imperceptible wince.

"What do you mean?" I ask. Sebastian, Logan, and Blake exchange glances, all three men on the verge of laughter.

"Someone's got to fess up," Sebastian says. "I'll give you the cliff notes. Our dearest sister likes to think of herself as the family's matchmaker. She gave us a much-needed push."

"You too? You never told me that." I take a step back, focusing on my man. He stares at his brothers as if he's considering what the most painful torture method would be. When he notices me watching him, his murderous expression morphs into a sheepish smile. Sheepish! I didn't think Christopher could even do sheepish.

"Yeah… well… when you worked for Pippa, she thought we'd be a good match."

"I see. Did she give you any pointers?"

"No."

"You're lying."

"Well, Alice did. She told me your favorite ice cream flavor."

"Ah!" I open my mouth theatrically. "And I thought that was a sign that we're meant for each other. Damn!"

"I like her," Logan whispers to Sebastian. I wink at Christopher's brothers.

"Anything else to confess?" I inquire.

Christopher doesn't miss a beat. "No."

"Is your name really Christopher Bennett? Just checking."

"You know, a few years ago that would have been a legitimate question," Blake says. "Max did steal his girl once when they were sixteen."

It takes me a split second to understand what he means. Max and Christopher are identical twins.

"Why didn't I know this?" I ask in amazement.

"I was hoping to keep my last shreds of pride," Christopher says.

"I'm here to kill that hope any time," Blake says. "You just have to ask."

"I wasn't asking," Christopher retorts.

"Blake!" I clap his shoulder, or rather his upper arm because he's so tall. "I think you're my new best friend."

He nods. "I have a favor to ask. For the sake of our friendship and out of consideration for the single people around here—"

"You mean yourself," Sebastian says with a grin. Blake cocks a brow.

"You will refrain from making puppy dog eyes at each other and kissing noises. Yeah?"

I tap my chin as if considering this. "So we can kiss if we don't make noises?"

Logan, Sebastian, and Christopher burst out laughing.

"Welcome to the family, Victoria," Logan declares.

We start working on the gazebo, and after a while, Christopher says in a low voice,

"Are you sure you want to stick around for this?"

"Your trouble is my trouble," I say, repeating what he said to me a few nights ago. "Except your trouble is more fun."

"You do have some original romantic lines, don't you?" Christopher asks.

"No, but I'm an excellent copycat."

"Wouldn't have expected this from someone who claims to love mushy stuff like *Gone with the Wind*."

"Oy," Blake exclaims from behind us. "I forgot to say. Too much cutesy is just as insulting as noisy kissing."

"We should definitely talk to Pippa," I whisper to Christopher.

***

After about an hour, I make a quick trip to my car to bring the second Tupperware container of cookies. When I return, Christopher is alone. Peering past him, I see his brothers entering the house. I observe him in silence. Wearing rugged jeans and a simple shirt, he's a damn sight to behold. Strong hands grip the hammer, expertly maneuvering it. As he turns his head slightly to the side, I admire his three-day beard, perfectly groomed, as always. There's something distinctly manly about him today, and his occasional grunt reminds me of the delicious sounds he makes when loving me. Almost involuntarily, my mind slides toward dangerous—or shall I say dirty—territory, wondering if jumping his bones here is a possibility. Then I remember his brothers are around. *The inside of the house later, though…?*

"Hey, beautiful," he says, snapping me out of my dirty dream. "What are you doing over there?"

I shrug, interlacing my fingers behind my back. "I wanted to admire you in silence. And then my thoughts spiraled into dirty territory, and I ended up weighing the pros and cons of trying to seduce you here or in the house."

Christopher nods, then he turns back to his work as if I wasn't here at all.

"What are you doing?" I ask, confused.

"Waiting for you to finish weighing those pros and cons and decide. Personally, I'd add my car as an option too. Plenty of space."

We both burst out laughing, and then I close the distance between us, walking with quick steps until I'm a breath away from him.

"You're unbelievable," I inform him.

"You started it." His grin stretches wider. "I was just trying to be helpful."

Hooking an arm around my waist, he pulls me in for a kiss. His lips move over mine gently, his tongue exploring my mouth expertly until he coaxes a whimper of pleasure out of me. I cup his face with my hands, his rough stubble grazing lightly against the sensitive skin of my palms. He makes it so easy for me to lose myself in him. By the time we pull apart to breathe, my entire body is humming.

"In all fairness," he says in a low, gruff voice, "I'll have to ask you to wait with those dirty plans until we leave."

Disentangling myself from his arms, I take a step back, putting some distance between us, and also assessing the amount of work still necessary. My guess is we'll be here for dinner too.

"Did you grow up here? It's a beautiful house."

"Nah. We grew up on a ranch. My parents sold it and gave the capital to Sebastian to start Bennett Enterprises. Three years ago, it came up for sale, and Sebastian bought it back for them. They turned it into a B&B and spend a lot of time there."

"Wow. You all have a nice relationship with your parents. It reminds me of mine, though my surprises were on the low-end variety. I miss them so much," I find myself saying, and realize I haven't said those words out loud to anyone since they passed away. I was afraid I'd break down if I did, but right now, I just feel an immense sadness engulfing me.

"They'd be really proud of you," he murmurs against my hair, pulling me into his arms again. He simply holds me, and it's perfect, his strength and warmth chasing away the sadness. I love this about him. How strong and stable he is, as if nothing could uproot him.

When I step back, I decide it's time to lighten the mood. "So are you going to work on this, or are you waiting for your brothers to do all the work?"

"I could build the whole thing by myself. At the risk of sounding cocky—"

"No risk. You do sound cocky very often," I state.

He pinches my ass, which has the unexpected effect of turning me on. *To hell with it all.* Is there anything this man can do that wouldn't set my hormones haywire? I school my features, trying to hide the slightly dubious side effect of his pinching.

"Well, I know what I'm doing."

"I want to help. I can do more than explain the instructions to you guys."

"Are you any good with a hammer and a nail?" He wiggles his eyebrows.

"Are you dirty talking to me right now?" I inquire, just to be sure. His smirk is my answer. I rehearse my reply in my mind, shooting for sexy vixen. "I can learn to use any tools of yours if you show me what to do, *Mr. Bennett.*"

Christopher exhales sharply. Holy bejeezus. My

attempt at sexy vixen actually worked.

"I know how to assemble furniture, Christopher. I've had to do it for my clients on countless occasions when the people who were supposed to do it botched their job."

He clears his throat, clearly still thrown off by my sexy vixen moment. "Okay."

As we work together for the next few minutes, the clouds of doubt gather in my mind again. I toy with the idea of not saying anything about it, but I just know I'll drive myself crazy.

"Christopher, it's okay I came by, right?"

He stops midtask, snapping his gaze up to me. By the playful set of his mouth, I can tell he was planning to shoot back a sarcastic answer, but something in my features must alert him that I'm serious because he changes gears, straightening up.

"Of course. Why are you asking?"

I shrug, trying to backpedal, feeling a little foolish. Okay, a lot. "It's just that we've been spending a lot of time together lately, and I was wondering if you need some time for yourself."

Christopher puts his tools down, closing the distance to me. When he's right in front of me, he places a hand on my waist, cupping my cheek with the other one.

"I don't need space."

"Sorry, I'm being silly," I say quickly.

"No, you're not. I want you to talk to me whenever there's something on your mind."

I laugh nervously, biting my lower lip. "Okay."

A gust of wind ruffles my hair and Christopher brushes it away from my face, resting his forehead against mine. "I have a problem, Victoria."

"Hmm?"

"I can't get enough of you."

"Funny, we have the same problem." Butterflies flutter around in my belly, filling me with a giddy happiness.

"I think about you all the time when I'm not with you."

I flatten myself against him, needing to feel him nearer.

"You're an amazing woman. You're funny, loving, loyal. Sometimes I smile to myself like an idiot in my office thinking about you. Once, I completely blanked out during a meeting, but I made it pass as weighing the benefits of Max's proposal. By the way, if my brother mentions it, don't tell him the truth. I'll never live that down."

"I'll keep your secret," I assure him, unable to withhold a smile. The thought of Christopher, wearing his business face and matching cufflinks, losing the thread of his thoughts because of me is delightful.

The air between us is loaded with emotions as we both become aware we're headed toward unchartered territory, with no certainty as to where this will lead.

"I love every minute we spend together. Even when you're against me and make me watch a terrible, awful movie," I begin.

"We really need to work on your taste in movies."

"Shush, you're interrupting my speech."

"Please continue."

"You make me laugh, and you're adorable with my siblings. And you're just strong and big… and I totally didn't mean that in a sexual way," I finish lamely. Completely flustered, I make myself small, resting my head in the crook of his neck. Feeling his pulse against my chin has the unexpected effect of calming me.

"I wouldn't take offense if you did," he says with a chuckle.

"Of course not."

"Look at me, Victoria."

I pull away from him, straightening up so I can see him better. Those eyes, the color of chocolate that I adore so much.

"I've never laid myself bare this way, to anyone," I say honestly.

"Neither have I." He caresses my cheek with the back of his hand, pressing his thumb gently at the corner of my lip. "It never felt right before, but it does now."

A rush of euphoria fills me at his confession, and I rise on my tiptoes to press my lips against his in what is definitely an "I adore you forever' kiss. The boys return shortly afterward, and there are no more kisses.

Chapter Twenty-Three

Victoria

As I predicted, dinnertime comes and goes, and we're still at his parents' house. We all hoped that by forgoing a dinner break, we'd finish sooner, but we're all starving. Blake caves in first, threatening to go on a hunger strike if we don't order food. Twenty minutes later, we're wolfing down tacos. Another two hours later, the gazebo is completely done.

Christopher and I drive to his apartment separately since we're both here with our cars. The new plan is for both of us to shower and then go out to explore the city, because we had some after-dinner places we wanted to visit. But once we've showered and changed—I have an overnight bag with me—it's clear we're both bone-tired.

"We can just stay in," I suggest.

"Well, I did have an indoor, nocturnal activity planned."

"You don't say. And what might that be?"

"You'll see. Follow me."

To my surprise, he leads me out of his apartment. We walk down the corridor in the opposite direction to the elevator. I've never been this way. He pushes open a door that leads to a staircase. We climb a flight of stairs and arrive in paradise.

"I completely forgot you had one of those fancy

rooftops."

Christopher's building has a veritable garden on top, with several lounge chairs and cozy sitting areas. There is also a possibility to grill up here. But the pièce de résistance, in my opinion, is the indoor heated pool, surrounded by glass walls so you can swim *and* have an amazing view at the same time.

"How do you already have access?" I inquire as he lets us in the pool house. When I picked up Christopher's keys, the building management said that it would be another sixty days before the residents would have access to the rooftop.

"I called in some favors for tonight." He offers me a cheeky smile.

"Of course you did. Can we use the pool?"

"Absolutely."

"Why didn't you tell me to bring a swimming suit?"

"That would've ruined the surprise."

Tiptoeing around the edge of the pool, I start taking off my clothes. "Underwear it is, then."

“No skinny-dipping?”

“Sorry, not gonna happen. My wild days are behind me.”

Christopher lifts an eyebrow in a silent challenge. Once we're in our underwear only, we lower ourselves in the water.

"This is amazing," I tell him honestly, walking around in the pool. The water is pleasantly warm and covers me up to my neck. The glass walls around the pool area offer an amazing view. "I can't believe they actually build these things on top of a residential building."

"Why not?" he asks, swimming away.

"Well, it's more difficult. Sorry, just nerdy stuff. I

don't want to bore you."

He smiles, swimming to back to me. "Nothing you ever say bores me."

"Aren't you a charmer," I say softly, drinking him in. Taut skin covers his torso, with shapely muscles—lean and strong—showing off just how much he likes to work out. I can barely believe this is my life now. I'm in a heated, indoor pool on a rooftop, with a gorgeous and kind man. What did I do to deserve this?

"I'm actually serious. Intelligent conversation turns me on. It also helps that your bra shifted, so your boobs are practically in my face."

I look down and groan, quickly rearranging my bra. "Just my luck, having a wardrobe mishap in front of you."

He shrugs. "Possibly your clothes have a sixth sense. 'Hey, Christopher is here. We'd better disappear.'"

Narrowing my eyes at him, I cross my arms over my chest. "Are you trying to sweet talk me to do the nasty with you here in the pool?"

"It's not me, I swear." Pointing with his forefingers to his boxers, he adds, "It's him."

"Christopher Bennett, this is the most shameless idea you've had. And I'm totally on board with it."

"Ah, I knew your wild side was still there, waiting to resurface."

"Wait, no one's gonna come, right?"

"Oh, we both will, Victoria."

My cheeks heat up. "You know what I mean. Don't mess with me."

"No one will come up here. The doorman told me no one else has been notified the pool is already open."

I relax a tad. "How is it that you make me want to

be reckless?"

"I'm a known bad influence on those around me. I should've warned you before."

"Too late," I whisper. "You've already corrupted me."

He smiles ruefully. "Sweeter words were never spoken."

He advances toward me with determined strides, his grin stretching even more. His entire face lights up when he smiles, which he does often. "What are you thinking?"

"That you look beautiful when you smile." I wince, realizing what I just said. "Sorry, that sounded dopey."

"It sounded like a compliment. I happen to like those."

When he's close enough to me, I run my hands up and down his arms and over his chest.

Christopher tilts my head up, covering my mouth with his. Warm, soft and inviting. One of his hands rests on my hips as the other cups my cheek. His tongue probes and explores my mouth like I'm a dessert he intends to savor for as longs as possible. Damn, this man knows how to kiss.

His kiss has the power to turn me to putty in his hands, drive me blind with desire. When he pulls away, I'm left panting and needing more.

"Your lips are puffy. It suits you."

"Less talking," I admonish. "Kiss me some more."

"Someone's feisty tonight." He contours my mouth with his thumb, resting briefly on my lower lip. On a whim, I suck it in my mouth. "Feisty *and* naughty," he remarks.

"Very. What are you going to do about it?"

"First, I'm going to kiss you some more." He gently grazes my earlobe with his teeth before descending to my neck, continuing to my shoulders. Energy zaps through me, and it's as if a torch was lit inside me. Desire consumes me, red-hot and blazing. Feeling his breath against my skin while he tortures me with kisses is exquisite.

Lowering my hand between us, I reach into his boxers. He's so hard for me already. Christopher pauses in the act of kissing my shoulder as I drag my palm across the tip of his erection.

"Open your legs for me," he rasps.

I do as he says, and he slides closer to me, lowering his hand between us.

"My thong—"

In response, he just moves the portion of the thong covering my center to the side. "Problem solved," he whispers, sliding his fingers up and down my folds. Every nerve ending zips to life, ripe for pleasure, hungry for him.

"I want you to come like this." He circles my clit with his thumb, sliding two fingers inside, luring moans out of me. Maybe being around him the entire day has been foreplay, but I'm so close to falling over the edge, I'm almost embarrassed. His mouth leaves a trail of scorching hot kisses on my neck as he descends to my breasts, which are just above the water level. When he unclasps my bra, pushing it aside and sealing his lips over the peak of my breasts, I come so hard, I nearly black out.

"Fuck, I love how you clench around my fingers."

Still riding the wave of my release, I reach out for him, wanting to give him the same pleasure, but he blocks my hand.

"Let's go back to the apartment. I didn't bring any

condoms."

We dress up in a matter of minutes. Since we didn't bring any towels, we try to wipe away the water as best as we can. Without putting the wet underwear on, we slip into our clothes, which will be damp soon, but neither of us really cares. I'm overcome with an almost girlish giddiness.

"What?"

"I haven't done anything this wild in a long time," I confess. My drenched underwear is in one hand, my shoes in the other. "Well, actually since we came to take measurements in your apartment. You're a bad, bad influence on me."

"I'll have you know, my wild side was in hibernation until you stumbled in my life."

"Are you saying I'm the bad influence?"

"Maybe." Kissing my forehead, he adds, "Years from now, we'll look back on this moment and have no idea which one of us was the bad influence."

I swoon all the way to the apartment.

Chapter Twenty-Four

Christopher

"You're a genius," Alice exclaims, looking over the spreadsheet model I have for her on my laptop. I rub my stiff neck, stretching on my seat, glancing around the buzzing restaurant. We're sitting at a table at the very back. When Alice and I met up months ago to look into streamlining her operations, she mentioned she'd like to add a bar area to a third restaurant she plans to open. Recently, Blake said he is looking into opening a second bar, and I mentioned to them that joining forces would be smart. The idea has been nagging at me ever since. So even though I have a million things to do at the office, I drew up a cost model, showing the economies of scale they could achieve among some other operational benefits. Uniting their branding will be tricky, and marketing is not my area of expertise, but Sebastian should arrive any minute now so Alice can pick his brain. Ava, Sebastian's wife and the company's marketing manager, was supposed to join us too, but she had to fly out to Washington on short notice.

"You're a genius," she repeats, murmuring as she inspects the numbers closer. "I can't wait to show Blake all this. Pity he couldn't join us tonight."

"Does your genius brother deserve a second serving of roast duck?" I ask.

"An extra large one." Alice instructs one of the waitresses to bring me a second serving, and by the time she arrives with it, Sebastian steps into the restaurant, heading toward us.

When he's in front of us, I can tell something's happened, because Sebastian is grinning ear to ear.

"Is Christmas coming early?" Alice asks, obviously noting our brother seems a little high.

"Better. I'm going to be a father."

Alice springs from her chair instantly, throwing her arms around our brother's neck, kissing his cheek. I choose a less invasive—and more manly—approach and shake hands with him, then pat his back.

"Ava called me literally the second I arrived in front of the restaurant. She took a test today and at first wanted to wait until she's back to tell me in person, but she couldn't help herself."

"So, this begs the question, why aren't you on a plane to Washington?" I ask as the three of us sit at the table.

"Next flight is tomorrow morning," Sebastian answers.

I smile triumphantly. "You forget Bennett Enterprises owns a private jet?"

Judging by his expression, he did forget.

"Do you have the pilot's number?"

"Yeah. Here." I hand him my phone and can't help feeling smug. It was Max's idea for the company to buy a small private jet, and I was for it from the first moment. Sebastian and Logan, ever the responsible brothers in the family, felt it was an unnecessary luxury. Max and I wore them down eventually; what's the point of having so much money if we can't even travel in style? Until now, our older brothers didn't seem one hundred percent convinced it was the right decision, hence why I'm feeling smug.

"He'll have the plane ready in two hours," Sebastian says after handing me the phone back.

"We'll talk about this another time." Alice points to the laptop, waving her hand. "I can't believe it. You'll be a dad."

"Yeah." After a few beats of silence, he adds, "Here's to hoping I'll be a good one."

Alice and I exchange a startled glance. I don't remember Sebastian ever sounding uncertain about anything. Even when there are crises at the office or when my father had surgery, he was calm, in control.

"Of course you'll be a great dad," Alice says.

Far from calming down, Sebastian drums his fingers on the table, his smile faltering. "I don't know what to expect."

"You saw us growing up," I remind him.

"That was different."

"Yeah, but it'll help," I insist. "All kids resemble each other in some things. At least in the developmental stages. When they're four years old, they want you to read fairy tales to them. When they're nine, they need your help to make the soccer team."

I stop when Alice glances at me curiously, the corner of her mouth lifting in a smirk. Somewhere at the back of my mind, I realize I've been talking as if Victoria's siblings are my kids. They're not, of course, but in some ways, it feels like they are.

"Sebastian," Alice says gently, "You were as much a father figure to us as you were a brother, and you were great."

"Yeah. If there's one person who can pull off this parenting thing, it's you," I add.

"I'm going to be a father," Sebastian repeats, still stunned but smiling, his hands clasped in front of him.

"I know," Alice whispers, reaching for Sebastian's hand over the table.

"I have to go," Sebastian says eventually, a tad less tense, though not completely relaxed, "to make it to the airport in time."

"What just happened?" Alice asks once he's out of earshot. "Was that Sebastian freaking out, or did I imagine things?"

"Not imagining them, nope."

"And you've been holding out on us. Mom told me you're bringing Victoria and the kids to Thanksgiving dinner on Thursday, but I didn't know you're that close." She elbows me hard in the ribs.

"Now you know."

"So you're not going to give me and Pippa any credit at all?"

"None whatsoever." I shrug, knowing how much this will annoy her. To my surprise, she doesn't insist. Instead, she looks at the seat Sebastian just vacated, sighing.

"Things have changed so much, haven't they? All our older siblings are married, I bet Max and Emilia will set the date soon, and we're getting a new niece or nephew. Wow."

I'll be the first to admit I don't notice these kinds of things, but something in Alice's tone tips me off.

"Are you seeing anyone?" I ask with caution.

Alice huffs, focusing on the spreadsheet again. "When would I have time to meet someone new?"

"Someone you already know, then?"

My sister turns her head in my direction so quickly I'm surprised it doesn't snap. "Max told you!"

I give up. When my sisters sniff out information from me, it's only after a few tries that I catch on, if at all. When I try it, Alice sniffs me out from the first question. Max told me some time ago that Alice has a crush on a close family friend, and we've been trying to guess who the bastard is ever since with no luck. If the lines on Alice's forehead are any indication, I'm not about to receive a name tonight, so I raise my hands in surrender.

"It was just a question. How about we go back to the spreadsheet? There's some stuff I haven't shown you, and I have to leave in an hour."

"Going to Victoria and the kids? I'm still taking credit for that. You don't need to award it to me."

Chapter Twenty-Five

Victoria

"Sienna, am I going to have any eyebrows left?" I ask nervously. We're in our living room on Thanksgiving afternoon. Lucas and Chloe are in the kitchen, bickering. Usually, I trust my sister to groom my eyebrows blindly, but today I have second thoughts. "You've been plucking for an hour."

"No, I haven't. You're just very jumpy today."

Yeah, the prospect of meeting Christopher's parents in about an hour and forty minutes—not that I'm counting—has turned me into a ball of unease. It started during the night when I woke up with a start. At first, I didn't know what woke me up, but then I acknowledged the stomach cramps. I haven't had cramps since college when I used to regularly get them before exams. That's exactly how I feel about today, like I'm about to face my most important exam.

"The jumpiness aside, I've never seen you this happy," my sister comments after she announces she's done torturing my eyebrows.

This has the unexpected effect of melting some of the tension I accumulated between my shoulder blades. My stomach is still in knots though. Sienna and I switch places. She lies on the couch with her head on the armrest, and I sit on the ottoman, focusing on her eyebrows.

"I am very happy," I say shyly.

"So, at the risk of sounding like Chloe—"

"I swear if you're going to bring up the baby topic, I will leave you with no eyebrows."

Sienna grins, laying it on thick. "I wasn't going to bring up babies."

"Good."

"But you're meeting his parents today. That's a pretty big deal. So…."

"Sienna, I have the upper hand here." I wiggle the tweezers in front of her eyes to drive my point home. "One wrong word and your eyebrows will pay for it."

She tells me about her chemistry project for the rest of the routine. Christopher is picking us up at five, and we're all set at four fifty. I don't recall Lucas and Chloe ever being ready on time for anything, but today they've been surprisingly cooperative.

Christopher pulls his car in front of the house at four fifty-seven. Chloe rushes forward, jumping straight into his arms the second he walks inside. He scoops her up without hesitation. I think Chloe has adored Christopher from that first day they met. Seeing him reciprocate her affection warms me on the inside.

"I see you're all ready," he says with surprise.

Sienna rubs her hands in excitement. "Yes, we are."

"We just have to move Chloe's car seat from my car to yours."

"I can do that," Sienna exclaims, giving me a significant look. "Lucas, Chloe, help me. We're going to need about ten minutes."

"Sienna's a subtle one," Christopher remarks as my siblings leave the house. He surveys me from my feet up to the top of my head, lingering lavishly on my hips and the swell of my breasts. "You look beautiful."

"Thank you."

I'm wearing a figure-hugging red cotton dress, paired with black tights and ankle boots. The outfit is a little too optimistic for the end of November, but we're going to spend most of the time indoors. The foyer grows smaller the longer Christopher gazes at me, desire lacing the air. I avert my gaze, my cheeks feeling flush. Whenever the kids are around, we keep our kisses chaste and our touching spare. The restrained display of affection usually means that the second we're alone, we can't keep our hands off each other.

Stepping forward, he pushes me against the door, brushing a strand of hair out of my face.

"I'm going to kiss you thoroughly now, Victoria. I need to get my fill of you before we arrive at my parents'."

"So this kiss has to last for the entire evening?" I tease as he places his palms against the door at my sides, trapping me in between. As if I'd go anywhere.

"Yeah."

"Then you'd better make it count."

He feathers his lips over my cheek first, descending to my jaw before sealing them over my mouth. His kiss is gentle and desperate at the same time, nipping and exploring—and above all, demanding. There is nothing halfhearted about this. He kisses like a man determined to light up every single nerve in my body. One of his hands soon drops to my waist, the other to my hip, tugging at my sweater dress, more and more until his fingers reach my… tights. Christopher groans, pushing my dress back down.

"The person who invented tights must have hated

men." He trails his kisses down my neck, breathing in and out deeply as if trying to calm himself. His thumb moves in little circles on my hip, and the simple gesture lures a moan out of me. I feel him smile against my neck before he descends to my collarbone.

"Or was concerned about women's privates freezing in the cold season."

"Makes sense, but there was still a definite man-hating streak somewhere there. I mean, the damn things don't even have a zipper somewhere for *quick* and *easy* access." He kisses the sweet spot at the base of my neck once, drawing himself up to his full height, wiggling his eyebrows.

"Don't you even think about it," I warn. "I'm not easy, and I don't like it quick." Not to mention, there are few things less sexy than getting rid of tights, especially since I bought them a size too big, and the elastic band is practically under my boobs. My hope is that when the sexy time comes around, I'll ditch them when he isn't looking.

"Oh, but I am so very easy," he teases. "And I can do a lot in a few minutes."

"How about kissing me some more, then?"

***

"Christopher," Sienna says once we're on our way, "is there anyone in your family who won't be there?"

"Just my baby sister Summer and Daniel. Summer is in Italy. She's working at a museum, and they extended her contract, and Daniel had to go to New York and couldn't make it back in time."

"I hope I won't mix up anyone's names," Sienna

continues. "There are so many of you."

"If you do forget, just smile and improvise," Christopher says. "It always works."

Chloe and Lucas are loud and excited on the ride to the Bennett house. I, on the other hand, am quiet and nervous.

"Kids," I tell them for the hundredth time. "Please be polite when we arrive. Always say please and thank you—"

"Also feel free to break windows or bang doors," Christopher adds helpfully. I nudge him with my elbow—hard. "Ouch. What was that for?"

I give him a meaningful look, but he shrugs.

"Mom always says she misses the time when we were kids, and that she wants grandkids. We used to break at least a window a week. I'm sure she misses it now that her windows are in pristine condition.

"Christopher logic," I mutter to myself, then realize the kids have gone quiet—radio silent. I look at them in the rearview mirror. Sienna has her headset on, moving her lips to the lyrics she's hearing and gazing out the window. Chloe's and Lucas's gazes are glued to Christopher's headrest, and I swear they seem to be holding their breaths. The man in question also notices the unnatural silence, shooting me an alarmed look.

"Chloe, Lucas, anything wrong?" I ask, my heart clenching.

"Can we be grandkids?" Chloe asks quietly.

"Don't they have to be like Mom and Dad's parents?" Lucas continues.

"Wh-huh…." I draw blank, taken aback by their questions.

"Of course you can be their grandkids," Christopher answers for me.

"But we're not related," Lucas insists.

"You don't have to be related by blood to be family," Christopher says.

"Are you just saying that because Chloe and I are adopted?" Lucas asks boldly, and my chest tightens.

"No, I'm saying it because it's true. For the record, my family always referred to close friends as adopted Bennetts. But you'd be grandkids. That means you can do as many pranks and shenanigans as you want."

Several seconds of silence follow, and then Lucas and Chloe start talking at the same time.

"We'll have grandparents?"

"We never had grandparents before."

"Do you think they'll let us eat sweets before dinner?"

I sink in my seat, smiling broadly. Christopher grins as he slows down, coming to a halt at a gas station.

"Pit stop. Tank is almost empty," he explains before getting out. Seizing my last chance to talk to him alone before we make it to his parents' house, I tell the kids, "Stay inside. I'm just going to be at the back of the car for a few minutes."

With that, I climb out of the car and join Christopher, who's filling the tank.

"You were very sweet in there. But why are you encouraging the kids to do shenanigans?" I inquire.

He looks up from the pump. "Because that's what kids do. Mom always said to worry if kids are silent, not if they're loud. I was a loud kid who couldn't stand still for more than ten minutes at a time, and look how smart and charming I turned out."

"But that doesn't mean you should encourage them to—"

He cups my cheek with one hand. "I don't want any of you to stress out. You're already all tied up in knots. Why?"

"I'm nervous about all this. Meeting your parents. Can you give me pointers? I really want them to like me."

Kissing my forehead, he says, "I know they'll like you. But here are a few pointers regarding my siblings. Don't trust Blake. For that matter, Max either. And whatever you do, don't let Pippa rope you into a conversation if the two of you are alone. She'll make you spill all your secrets."

"You make it sound like Pippa has some kind of truth serum."

"She does." Though his expression is serious, I know he's barely suppressing laughter. Why my jitters amuse him so much, I have no idea.

"I know Pippa, remember? I decorated her house."

"And she never asked you personal questions? You never had the feeling you're saying more than you should, but you couldn't stop yourself?"

"Hmm… a few times."

"Aha!" He points his forefinger at me, raising his shoulders. "And that was nothing. She was still assessing your potential at that point, so she wasn't grilling you too hard. Now however…."

"You're confusing me. Lots of don'ts here. Anything I *should* do?"

Christopher takes his time placing the nozzle back in its socket and closing the lid to the gas tank before focusing his attention on me. "Now that you mention it, it might be a good idea to profess your undying love for me. That'll win everyone over instantly."

"If I didn't know better, I'd say you're fishing for

a love declaration."

"Nah! Just giving you pointers, as you asked. On second thought, don't do that. Then they'll start nagging me about proposing and babies."

"Your family sounds suspiciously like Chloe."

"In many ways, they are."

"Can I ask you something?"

"Anything."

"Why do you almost choke every time you say 'proposing'? For the record, I'm not fishing for a ring."

"Just like I'm not fishing for a love declaration." He chuckles, but as I shift from one leg to the other, I take in the subtle way his expression changes. "I proposed once."

Oh crap. "It didn't go well?"

"Exactly. She said no, explaining she needed to find herself and couldn't do that with me. I was blindsided. She'd never said anything like that before."

Unzipping his jacket, I sneak my arms around his waist, resting my head against his chest, seeking to comfort him. My heart hurts for him, even as a pang of jealousy shoots through me.

"Does it make me a bad person that I'm glad she said no? I wouldn't have met you otherwise."

"It makes you a terrible person." His chest rumbles with laughter, and it's damn contagious. With the greatest regret, I peel myself off him, zipping his jacket back up. We really should get going, but I can't help asking one more thing.

"Did you love her?"

"I used to think so." He levels his gaze at me, emotions warring in his eyes. "Now that I've met you, I think I didn't know what love was. All these feelings I have for you… I didn't even know they existed."

"Back at you." I bounce up on my toes, planting a quick kiss on his chin, then step back to get a better view of him. "How do you always find new ways to make me swoon?"

"Special talent." One corner of his mouth lifts. "Possibly inherited."

Chapter Twenty-Six

Victoria

Lucas and Chloe are unusually quiet once we arrive at the Bennett house. Christopher parks the car in the driveway, and then all of us are on the way to the house. Christopher leads the way, Lucas walking quietly beside him. I take Chloe in my arms, rubbing my palm up and down her back. She sighs loudly, her nose scrunched.

"What is it, sweetie?" I whisper to her. She merely shrugs, shaking her head. Right. I'll get to the bottom of this later. Christopher pushes the door to the house open, and we all step inside. A whirlwind of voices resounds from deeper inside the home, mixed with laughter and colorful exclamations.

"Mom, Dad," Christopher calls out loudly. As if waiting for the signal, a couple steps into the corridor, hurrying toward us. Ah, and now I can see where Christopher gets his height and build. His father is just as tall as he is, with broad shoulders and an impressive physique. He is a giant with kind eyes and a friendly smile. Mrs. Bennett is petite, and warmth radiates from every pore of her face. Looking at Mr. and Mrs. Bennett, I can't help but be reminded of Mom and Dad. They have that closeness and care for each other that I've only seen in my parents before.

Sienna greets his parents first, and then Mrs.

Bennett steps in front of Lucas, who says, "Hi, Mrs. Bennett, I'm Lucas. Very pleased to meet you."

"Pleased to meet you too, Lucas."

I do a mental fist pump that my boy sounds all grown up.

"And you must be Chloe," Mrs. Bennett says.

Chloe, who is still in my arms, extends her small hand to Mrs. Bennett.

"Yes, ma'am. How do you do?"

What the heck. How do you do? That's so unlike her… or any four-year-old, for that matter. Mrs. Bennett shakes Chloe's hand.

Then she turns to me and says, "Nice to finally meet you in person, Victoria."

"Likewise, Mrs. Bennett."

"Call me Jenna." She kisses my cheek, and then I shake hands with Mr. Bennett. "Let's go to the living room so you can meet everyone."

"Wow," Chloe whispers when she sees the large group.

"Prepare for your head to spin as I introduce you to everyone," Christopher says. We do a round of introductions, after which my head truly spins. It helps that I already know Alice, and Pippa and her family, though this is the first time I'm meeting the two lovely additions, six-months-old Mia and Elena.

Things become even more blurry when we proceed to his brothers. I might have met Blake, Logan, and Sebastian, but I struggle to keep up with whose spouse is whose, and I hope I won't mix up the brothers' names. Speaking of mix-ups, the most memorable of the introductions is the one to his identical twin, Max. I just can't wrap my head around the idea of two Christophers running around.

"Ah," Max exclaims. "Your girl got all tongue-tied in front of me, brother. I still got game."

I grin at him, realizing I just got a partner in crime to give shit to Christopher. Besides Blake, of course. That one seems to be game for anything anytime.

"I heard all about you kissing his girl in high school," I inform Max. "Such bad form."

"Christopher's no saint," a beautiful blonde exclaims, appearing next to Max's side. "I'm Emilia. And that one"—she points to my man—"tried to pass himself off as Max with me."

Emilia winks at me, and at once I know that I have an ally. Sometime in the near future, she and I will plot against these two.

"Say, I heard a rumor that you and Daniel"—I point to Blake—"are the party brothers, while these two"—I turn my thumb in Max and Christopher's direction—"are the *serious* brothers. Care to enlighten me? They don't seem to understand the concept of serious."

Blake shakes his head. "I know. Blatant discrimination."

The next hour is somewhat of a blur. Sienna is entranced in a conversation with Logan's wife, Nadine, and Lucas is talking Blake's ear off about soccer. Chloe sticks to Jenna the entire time. When Mrs. Bennett announces dinner is ready, we all move into the dining room.

***

After Thanksgiving dinner, I finally seem to have lost some of my jitters. The delicious stuffed turkey helped, and the wine too. We eat dessert in the gazebo outside.

As we move the party back into the living room, Sienna accosts Nadine again, and Chloe and Lucas gravitate around Mr. and Mrs. Bennett. I finally inspect the place in detail. It's more spacious than a regular living room in a house this size. I suspect part of it used to be a separate room, and the Bennetts tore down a wall. Aside from the enormous couch on one wall, there are several groups of armchairs and ottomans spread around the room. The setup is perfect for large gatherings such as this one. Having everyone sit on or stand around the couch wouldn't be pleasant. It would result in too many simultaneous conversations, which would be hard to follow. As it is, one can choose to sit in one of the armchair or ottoman groups and carry on a conversation, while being able to cross over to the larger group in no time.

"Chloe is adorable," Pippa exclaims, appearing at my side. She sits on the nearest armchair, holding one of her daughters in her arms. I sit on the opposite chair, watching the large group from afar. Christopher is in his element with his siblings, winking at me from time to time.

"Yeah, and she's glued to your mother."

"Oh, don't you worry. Mom loves it." Pippa rocks her daughter in her arms, cooing at her.

"Motherhood suits you," I tell her.

"I love it, even though I do wonder if I'll feel less like a zombie anytime soon. The girls don't always sleep through the night, and I'm one of those people who takes ages to fall asleep. It's difficult to concentrate on work."

"Oh, you go into your office?" I inquire, worrying she's biting off more than she can chew.

"I mostly work from home, but a few times a week I do go into the office."

"Wow, I have no idea how you do it with two small children."

"It's all a bit of a mess, if I'm honest. I love my job, and I love my kids and my husband. But right now, I feel like I'm failing everywhere. Mom says I'm doing fine, and she helps me a lot, but...."

My heart squeezes, and I have the overwhelming urge to comfort her. I'm not exactly in her position, but I'm close. At the very least, I'm painfully familiar with the feeling of permanent failure. What surprises me is that even with her mother by her side, she still can't shake off that feeling. Talking to Mrs. Bennett on the phone all those months ago helped me a lot. Then I realize what Pippa needs: for someone outside the family to tell her she's doing just fine. After all, I never took Aunt Christina's assurances at face value. Sometimes you can't help feeling your own family is cutting you slack just because they love you.

"You're not failing, Pippa. It's normal to need a transitioning period. Be prepared for it to last a long time. You're doing a great job."

She smiles up at me, straightening her shoulders. "Thanks for the encouragement."

As if on cue, her husband steps in. "I just put Mia to sleep. I'll take Elena too."

"Best if they don't miss their nap time," she explains to me while placing her daughter in her husband's arms.

Once he's out of earshot, she says, "Watching my husband with a baby in his arms.... Maybe I'm still high on baby hormones, but I find him adorable and hot at the same time."

"It's not hormones," I assure her. "My heart somersaults every time Christopher carries Chloe in his arms."

"He does have a knack for kids, doesn't he?"

"Absolutely. They all worship him and love having him around. I love having him around too. Being with him is.... I've never felt for anyone what I feel for him. If I'm honest, it scares me."

"He's head over heels about you, and the kids. I've never seen him like this. And it's a good sign that you're afraid. You know it's real when it scares you."

It's only when I notice the twinkle of triumph in Pippa's eyes that I realize Christopher's warning has come to fruition. This woman definitely has a truth serum.

"I knew you'd be good for my brother since we worked together. That's why I recommended you to him."

"Ah, and I foolishly thought you were impressed with my decorating skills."

"Those too, don't worry. But my matchmaker sensor was in hyperalert when I met you. I had to do something about it."

"Completely understandable." We both start laughing until Sebastian and his wife, Ava, join us, and we slip into an easy conversation. Matchmaking isn't brought up again.

***

Hours later, as we're preparing to leave, I notice Chloe seems to be out of sorts.

"Everything okay, pumpkin?" I whisper, even though it's just the two of us in the foyer. Lucas, Sienna, and Christopher are already outside, and everyone else is still in the living room. She nods, huffing softly as I slide her jacket on.

"I can tell there's something up with you," I insist.

"Do you think Mr. and Mrs. Bennett like us?" she asks, surprising the hell out of me. I've been so busy fretting over my own anxiety at meeting the family, I haven't stopped to think about hers.

"I think they do."

"I really want them to like us," she insists. "Then it'll be like we're having a mom and dad again."

My throat constricts, words escaping me. I blink rapidly, trying to subdue the tears threatening to spill.

"I thought you wanted them to be your grandparents."

She frowns in concentration. "No, grandparents have white hair everywhere, but Mr. and Mrs. Bennett only have a little white hair, like Mom and Dad did. They can't be grandparents."

"I love you, pumpkin." I wrap my arms around Chloe, smothering her cheeks with kisses. "Mr. and Mrs. Bennett love you, and they can be whatever you want. Come on, let's go home."

"What are you two smiling about?" Christopher asks once we're in the car.

"We had a great time today," I answer.

"I love your family," Sienna chimes in from the backseat.

"Yeah," I add. "They're a great bunch. Now I see why you turned out okay."

"So my family is great, but I'm okay? I'm a little offended here."

Glancing in the rearview mirror, three large grins greet me. The kids love the banter between us.

I smack Christopher lightly with my elbow. "Can't help it if you're oversensitive."

***

Christopher

I spend the night at Victoria's house, which feels more natural than going home to my apartment. For years I was used to going home to an empty space, which often felt quiet and lonely. I had no pets because I was gone too long. I tried keeping plants, but they had a tendency to die—forgetting to water them would do that to a plant—and plants don't talk or bark, so they didn't really help with the issue of the deafening silence. Despite all those drawbacks, I grew accustomed to having my space. Now my space feels like an empty shell without Victoria and her siblings.

After the kids go to sleep, I plan to seduce Victoria, but she seems to have some plans of her own. Taking my hand, she walks us to her room. I drink in the way her hips sway in front of me, her dress clinging to her curves. She ditched the tights once we got home, which means I'll get easy access to nirvana.

"What are your plans, mighty temptress?" I ask her once we're inside.

"You're such a flirt, Christopher."

"It's my duty. You're mine."

"Yours, huh?" Turning around, she tilts her head to one side, a teasing smile making an appearance. "What gave you that idea?"

With my hands on her hips, I back her up against a wall, and she molds her sweet curves against me instantly.

"This. The way you look at me." I place one thumb on her cheek, dragging it down to the corner of her mouth. "The way you push yourself against me." Her hips are flush against mine, her breasts pressing against my chest. "The way your body responds to my touch." Victoria exhales sharply, tugging at her lower lip with her teeth, and then she pushes me to sit on the bed. She moves her fingers across my chest, heading downward. When she runs her palm over the bulge in my jeans, I groan.

That only fuels her further. She undoes the button of my jeans and then pulls at the zipper. I get rid of my jeans as she lowers herself to her knees, settling between my legs. After freeing my hard-on, she swipes her tongue over the tip. My balls tighten instantly. My fingers tug at her hair, anticipation zinging through my veins.

"Victoriaaaaa." My grip on her hair tightens, and she takes me in her mouth, closing her fist at the base while moving her mouth up and down. She's a wet dream come true. "You're so sexy. So good." With her other hand, she reaches farther down, cupping my balls. I thrust my hips up. When I feel my tip at the back of her throat, I nearly blow before pulling out completely. I'm a fucking jerk for losing control like this. I need to know if she's okay, if she wants it.

"Are you okay with this?"

Nodding, she moves her hand to the tip and down, repeating the movement over and over again. I'm pulsing in her hand, every muscle tightening. Slowly, she brings her mouth to the tip again. I hold my breath, waiting for her plump lips to touch me. When they do, I let out a deep groan, tipping my head back. Then she takes me in her mouth all the way to the base, cupping my balls in one hand, squeezing them gently.

"Are you trying to kill me?" I rasp. Pulling back, she swipes her tongue over the tip, tasting me before clamping her mouth tightly around it again. "Damn. You're so good at this." I grab her hair as I start moving in and out of her mouth with deep, measured strokes that grow less restrained by the second. I can tell she's never given anyone so much control over her, and I want her to feel safe. When I feel I'm about to snap, I pull out.

"Fuck, I'm sorry. I didn't—Are you okay?"

She looks up, nodding. In a fraction of a second, I pull her up to me, so she's sitting in my lap.

"I didn't mean to be so rough," I say, "but you made me lose control."

"I like it when you're rough," she replies.

"You're driving me crazy, Victoria." Without another word, I kiss her, deep and hungry. Pushing her dress up to her waist, I yank her closer, and her bare center slides against my groin.

"You're not wearing panties."

"No seductress worthy of her name does."

Pushing her dress further up until I relieve her of it, I kiss across her collarbone to her sweet spot. She moans against my mouth as I slide a hand between us, stroking her clit, coaxing more sounds of pleasure out of her.

"I need to be inside you. Now."

She reaches for the nightstand where the condoms are. After sliding one on me, she climbs back in my lap, her knees positioned at the sides of my thighs. We lock eyes for a brief moment, and then I nod, letting her know I'm up for the ride. Wanting to drive her crazy, I drag the tip of my erection up and down her folds.

"Christopher." Her thighs quiver violently when she lowers herself on me, taking me in.

"You look gorgeous like this."

I cup her cheek with one hand, and she turns her

head slightly, leaning into my touch. With the other hand, I grip her ass, guiding her moves, watching her reactions. I want to learn everything that gives this woman pleasure, everything that makes her happy, and I don't mind if that turns out to be one lifelong lesson. This is perfection.

She increases her pace, squeezing me good with her inner muscles. "I won't last long," I warn her before lowering my other thumb to her clit. The combined effect of feeling her ride me and seeing her come undone is violent. Energy shoots through me, my balls tightening.

I cover her mouth with mine, and we both moan our release. Afterward, I hold her tightly to me.

Chapter Twenty-Seven

Victoria

Mom used to say she always knew when something bad was going to happen, that she could feel it in her bones. The night before their accident, she called me and told me she loved me. I didn't inherit her talent for premonitions.

Today is a gorgeous Wednesday, seventy degrees with sun, a rarity in San Francisco for the beginning of December. Ah, how I love this month, even if it does rain a lot, and on some days the clouds are so dense, you can't see one speck of blue sky. The one thing I wish San Francisco had is snow. It would be considerably colder, but snow is just magic. Still, even without snow and the permanent presence of its much less magic sister rain, my birthday and Christmas are in December, which are reasons enough for it to be my favorite month. I'm a happy camper as I scour the city, searching for the perfect leather armchair for a client. When I can't find what I need through my usual suppliers, I start hunting.

San Francisco abounds in little thrift and antique shops. There is some serious crap in them, but there is the occasional gem to be found that makes the search worthwhile. Even the fact that I'm meeting Hervis Jackson today for the monthly update doesn't put a damper on my good mood.

Armed with a bucket-sized cup of cherry black tea, I search shops, finding just what I need in a quaint one with antiques. I take pictures and ask the vendor to put it on hold for me for two days so I can get my client's approval.

Afterward, I head to the coffee shop where I'm meeting Hervis. His schedule is so packed that he doesn't have time to drive all the way to our house, and he wanted more than a phone update. Suits me. I have nothing but good news to relay to him.

I arrive at the coffee shop a few minutes earlier than our scheduled meeting and head to a free table. I've barely reached it when my phone rings. Placing my huge bag on the table, I look through it until I find the phone. Isabelle is calling.

Holding the phone to my ear, I greet, "Hey!"

"Have you checked your e-mail?"

"Not in a few hours."

"Girl, you should sit on it for this news."

My heart soars in anticipation. I bet she's calling to tell me we nailed down the McLeod account. That would be our first business to business contract since I worked on Alice's restaurant, and it would be a nice extra income.

"I'm sitting," I lie, too excited to do so. Instead, I'm standing next to the table, grinning like a lunatic.

"Natasha is suing us. Her lawyer e-mailed us."

My stomach constricts, suddenly feeling nut-sized. Maybe I should have sat. Breathing in deeply and then releasing it out slowly, I try to calm myself down enough to think.

"What does the e-mail say?"

"A bunch of legal *blah blah*, but she basically wants the money we got from the Alice Bennett job and Julian

Humphrey."

Julian Humphrey was the client who first went to Natasha's office, then contacted me. But Christopher's lawyer assured me the guy was fair game. And how in the world did Natasha find out?

"We can't afford to pay her anything. I'll call the lawyer I talked to about Julian and ask him to see us today."

"Good." Isabelle falls silent but doesn't click off. "I'm scared," she says eventually. "We work so hard. What if we lose everything?"

The secret ingredient to our friendship has always been that when one of us is down, the other encourages her. This is excellent advice for times when problems are one-sided, but harder to follow through when we're potentially both in trouble up to our necks. Still, I find it in myself to sound strong and positive.

"We didn't do anything wrong, Isabelle. We'll go to the lawyer, and he'll set us straight. It's too soon to throw a pity party."

"You're right," she says at once, her no-nonsense tone back. "Let me know when the lawyer can see us."

I click the phone off but keep clutching it tightly.

First things first, I call the lawyer, asking if there's any chance we have to pay Natasha what Alice and Julian paid us, because there's no way in hell we can do that. He is ninety-nine percent certain we won't have to pay anything, and once he looks over the e-mail from Natasha, he'll be able to tell us more. Thankfully, he offers to squeeze us in his schedule in half an hour. If I leave the coffee shop right now, I should make it in time. I'll just have to find a good excuse for Hervis.

"We can reschedule for another time if you're busy," Hervis Jackson's voice booms from behind me the second I drop my phone in my bag. My insides clench instantly as I swirl on my heels to face him. Clearly, he'd been eavesdropping on my conversation with the lawyer.

"Yes. It's an urgent meeting—"

"Legal troubles, I heard."

Even though I'm dying on the inside, doubt and fear suffocating me, I pull myself straighter, rolling my shoulders. "My previous employer is completely out of line. I just talked to the lawyer, and he assured me I have nothing to worry about."

"You sounded *very* worried."

"It's unpleasant, but nothing I can't weather."

"Please keep me informed," Hervis says. "I sincerely hope it won't have any adverse effects on your business."

"It won't. Have a good day."

Once in my car, I call Isabelle and then drive to the lawyer's office. Isabelle's words roll back and forth in my mind. *What if we lose everything?*

She meant the business, the clients, but a deep fear takes roots in my mind, spreading like poison. *What if I lose the kids?* Minutes pass and everything around me blurs as scenario after scenario run through my head. Loud honking snaps me back to my senses. I didn't see the light turn green.

Isabelle is pacing around the lawyer's office when I arrive. Alan Smith is in his late fifties, but his hair is completely gray, which I find has a calming effect on me.

"Why don't you take a seat?" Sitting behind his large desk, he points to the two seats across him.

"I'm too nervous," Isabelle says.

"Same here."

"Very well. I've looked over the papers you were served, and I cannot find any grounds for a successful lawsuit. You didn't have a non-compete clause in your former employment contract, and even if you had, those are notoriously hard to enforce."

I let out a breath of relief. Isabelle stops pacing.

"That's good, right? It means we have nothing to worry about?" I ask.

"Natasha could try to prove you purposely undermined her company and turn this into suing for defamation—"

"Oh God!" I slump into one of the seats in front of his desk.

"I'm not done," Alan says, not unkindly. "When you asked if working with Julian Humphrey was fair game, you mentioned she still had your work in her portfolio. That is strong evidence in your favor."

"I still don't understand why she keeps those," I say honestly.

"Maybe because you and I did the best damn jobs in that company?" Isabelle suggests.

"Which brings me to the most probable reason for this bogus lawsuit. I've seen this before. It happens far too often, given how rarely it brings results. A company loses employees, those employees then open their own business in the same industry, and of course use the same ecosystem of suppliers, distributors, etcetera. Old clients prefer to switch over. Revenue goes down. In all likelihood, Natasha's lost considerable revenue since the two of you left, and she's hoping you'll be willing to settle so you don't go to court."

"Will we have to settle?" I ask, already panicking.

Alan smiles warmly. "Not if I have anything to say about it, and I happen to have a lot to say. I'll get on this right away, and everything should be closed by the end of the week."

"That's three days away," Isabelle remarks.

"I'm very good at my job," Alan replies simply.

"One more thing. Remember I told you about having to report to Family and Social Services regularly. The social worker in charge of our case overheard me talking to you—"

Alan holds up his hand. "Leave me his number and I'll keep him up to date."

"Can you emphasize that this won't affect our business?"

"Absolutely."

I breathe with relief. Isabelle finally sits down on the chair next to me.

"How much do we owe you, Alan?" she asks.

"Nothing. And before you both get up in arms, no, Christopher isn't paying. I owe him for a personal favor. He said this is personal when he told me about you, so it's quid pro quo."

Chapter Twenty-Eight

Christopher

As I walk inside Victoria's house on a Saturday morning two weeks later, everyone is in a frenzy. Victoria is running up and down the stairs for no apparent reason. Sienna is rearranging the plates in the dishwasher for the third time in the span of five minutes. Lucas and Chloe are huddled in a corner, whispering to each other. Judging by the way they jump whenever their older sister passes by them, my guess is they're trying to keep their conversation from her. Since it's Victoria's birthday today, I suspect the little punks are up to something.

"Did you all accidentally drink coffee or something?" I ask a flustered Victoria as she slips into her boots, ready to leave the house. She's been on edge for the last two weeks, since the e-mail from her former employer. When she told me about it, I wanted to eviscerate Natasha Jenkins and her company. No one messes with Victoria and gets away with it. Alan talked me out of it, assuring me he would handle it, and he did. Within days, the issue was completely off the table, and Alan assured Victoria that her former employer wouldn't bother her anymore. But she's still on edge, and I don't like it.

It's just the two of us in the foyer, the kids having slipped into the living room.

"No, just don't want to be late," she offers with a weak smile. "You're really great for coming by today."

"No problem. I like hanging around with the kids." She's meeting a new client today, and I offered to keep the kids company. Usually Sienna can hold her own watching the kids for a few hours at a time, but it's easier if she's not alone. That's where I'm stepping in. "By the way, I have a surprise for you tonight."

"What do you mean?"

"I mean, it's your birthday. I have a surprise for you."

"Okay."

"So you'll allow it?"

"Do I have a choice?"

"Not really."

"Thought as much."

"Can you stand still for more than one second at a time so I can give you a proper happy birthday kiss?"

At once Victoria stills, watching me expectantly. Her hair sticks in a million directions, giving her a wild appearance. I know what goes with that look. I kiss her thoroughly, cupping her at the back of her neck, tunneling my hands in her hair.

"Wow," she whispers when we pull apart. "I'll pretend it's my birthday every day if it earns me a kiss like that one." Checking her phone, she curses. "Shoot, I'm going to be late. Let me give you a rundown of—"

"Victoria, relax. I'm going to watch the kids, and I promise we won't burn the house down. I've been in charge of my younger siblings often as a kid."

"How did that go?" she asks.

"I don't recall the details, but I think a fair summary would be that no one went to the hospital with a life-threatening injury, just a couple of broken arms and legs, and we accidentally set a doghouse on fire. The dog wasn't in there, obviously."

"Very reassuring." Shaking her head, she laughs, some of the tension bleeding from her shoulders. I walk with her outside, but we linger on the porch.

"Why are you so nervous?"

"This is a new client, and he seems fussy. He said he wants to work with me, but he didn't like any of my proposals. I've been brainstorming like crazy for new ideas, hoping something will impress him."

"So it's a man."

Victoria glances up at me with incredulity. "The male brain will never cease to amaze me. I just told you I'm worried about not signing him as a client, and all you worry about is that he's a man?"

She clenches her hands into fists, tapping her foot against the floor. My woman woke up with an extra dose of fierce today, which I love, except when said fierceness is directed at me.

Right, time to lay on the charm.

"That's because I know you'll impress him. You're very good at your job."

"You're not fooling me with compliments," she replies, completely unimpressed. "Yeah, he's a man. Proud owner of the Y chromosome, and a penis."

"Does he know you have a boyfriend?"

"Caveman much?"

"Very much." I advance to her, and she backs against the wall of the house. "The thought of other men hitting on you, wanting you, drives me crazy."

"He's a client."

"So was I."

"And I'm yours now. I can't decide if this alpha behavior is sexy or annoying."

"If I give you another birthday kiss, will I tip the scale in favor of sexy?"

"You can try."

I lean into her, covering her mouth with mine.

As if through a dense fog, I hear Chloe's voice. "I knew they were doing the kissing."

"Of course, silly. That's what happens when people are boyfriend and girlfriend," Sienna enlightens her. "And it's called kissing, not doing the kissing."

Sienna's voice snaps me back to reality, and I instantly step away from Victoria, who stares at her hands, red in the face. She's never looked more adorable.

"How did you two get here?" I ask the girls.

"Through the back door. And you two don't need to sneak around. We all know that couples *do the kissing*," Sienna says, barely withholding laughter as she glances downward at Chloe.

"I really have to go," Victoria says. If possible, her cheeks are even more flushed. "I should be back in about four hours. Call me if anything is urgent."

***

After Victoria leaves, the kids announce that they're going to spend some time in Lucas's room, helping him on a science project. Call it a sixth sense, but I immediately become suspicious. Possibly because Sienna and Lucas are exchanging guilty glances, and Chloe says science project with a self-confidence that tells me they rehearsed this, again.

"What kind of science project?" I inquire.

"You know, science stuff," Lucas says. Clearly, they weren't expecting me to question them.

"Buddy, my siblings and I invented the art of sneaking around. I know something's fishy here. Why don't you all fess up?"

"What's fess?" Chloe asks.

"Confess," Sienna and I say at the same time.

Lucas rubs the side of his neck, glancing at his older sister.

"Let's tell him," Sienna says. "Maybe he can help."

"What's going on?" I ask, already imagining worst-case scenarios. They're kids, goddamn it. How much trouble can they be? Well, if I look back at my own childhood, the answer is a lot.

"But it's our present," Chloe says.

Some of my paranoia vanishes at the word 'present.'

Taking a deep breath, Sienna says, "We want to build a vanity table for Victoria."

"A what?" I ask blankly. "I didn't know she wanted one."

"A makeup table. We found some pictures of one in her office, and also some instructions on how to build one," Sienna explains.

"She didn't mention anything to me," I reply.

"To us either," Sienna says. "But ever since Mom and Dad passed away, she hasn't bought fancy stuff for herself. She buys us everything we need, but…."

I'm about to tell them that I'll gladly pay for a vanity table before building one when

Sienna continues. "I bought all the parts, and we have the instructions, but neither of us knows how to build stuff. Victoria told us you built the gazebo for your parents, so—"

"Let's get started."

***

An hour later, we're knee-deep in glue, nails, and

wood bits. We moved to the living room because Lucas's bedroom is too small for this 'science project'. Sienna and I do most of the work, and I'd be twice as fast if I weren't looking at Lucas every few minutes, making sure he's not gluing together his own fingers or something. It was easy to find Chloe a job. I told her no gift is complete without a handmade card, and now she's furiously drawing one. But Lucas insisted he wanted to help, and gluing was the safest task I could find for him.

"How are we doing with the time?" I ask.

"Two hours to go until Victoria said she'll be back," Sienna replies, frowning in concentration.

"Okay. Plenty of time to finish this."

We focus on the vanity table for the next hour, exchanging instructions and trying not to mess anything up.

"Just so I'm prepared, do you guys want to build Victoria something for Christmas too?" I ask.

"We haven't thought about that yet," Sienna replies. "We still have two weeks." Chloe finishes her card, which she insists features a phoenix bird. All I see is a red mess. If I squint, it *almost* looks like a butterfly. But I smile and nod because I'm not a heartless bastard. Chloe proceeds to draw a second card—this one with unicorns—so Victoria can choose her favorite. Lucas has finished gluing everything there was to glue, so now he just hovers around, eyeing the hammer hopefully.

Nope. Not gonna happen. Not on my watch.

"Buddy, why don't you go outside and practice until Victoria comes back? Sienna and I have this covered."

Ah, I can practically see the two thoughts warring in his mind. On the one hand, he wants to be part of this; on the other, the soccer call is strong.

"You have to practice if you want to be the star of the team," I insist, and his resolve breaks. With one nod, he's out the door.

Great. Potential disaster handled.

For the next hour, I'm doing most of the work because Sienna stops often, typing furiously on her phone.

"Is that Victoria?" I ask.

"Nah, it's Ben."

I turn in her direction so fast I swear my head snaps. *Who the fuck is Ben?* I take a few seconds to calm down, trying to remember how it was to be that age. I remember two things. One, I hated adults meddling in my business. Two, groping girls was high on my priority list.

I already hate Ben.

"Who is Ben?" I ask her in as calm as a tone as I can muster.

"A guy from school. We're working on a biology project together."

Over my dead fucking body.

"And Victoria is okay with this?" I ask, even more calmly. Predictably, she shoots daggers with her eyes at me.

"Yes, yes she is."

Well, Victoria has never been a seventeen-year-old boy. I'll have a word with her when she returns. Why can't girls start dating only after they graduate college? That's about the time men start thinking with their brain, not their cock. I don't insist on the topic, instead focusing on my work.

"You're cool for hanging out with us today, by the way. And thank you for helping us build this."

We finish a while later, but instead of sitting back and enjoying the result, we realize the living room looks like it's been a war zone, with bits and pieces scattered everywhere.

"Sienna, can you bring a trash bag? Chloe and I will start cleaning up."

"Sure."

Chloe shoves the new card under my nose just as Sienna leaves the room.

"Do you like the unicorn?" she asks. I'm on my knees next to her, inspecting the card.

"Yeah. It looks…." *Not* like a unicorn is what I want to say, but hey, at least it has four legs. "Well done."

Unexpectedly, she throws her little arms around my neck in a hug. "You're the *bestest*, Christopher. Thank you for helping us build the vanity table."

"No slacking allowed," Sienna says, having returned with a trash bag. "Come on."

We barely start cleaning up when Lucas bursts through the front door.

"Victoria's car is pulling in," he announces.

***

Victoria

When I return home, I'm bone-tired, but at least the day was a success, and I signed a new client. Now I have my birthday and the entire weekend stretching out, which I get to spend with my family and a wonderful man. What more could I ask for?

When I enter the house, the sound of hushed voices coming from the living room alerts me to some possible wrongdoings. Standing in the foyer, I strain my ears trying to make out individual words, but fail.

"I'm here," I say unnecessarily; if they haven't seen my car, they heard me open the front door. The whispering doesn't stop, nor do they greet me back. *Oh boy.* That's never a good omen. Gathering my courage, I head for the living room and do a double take.

What on earth?

There are bits of wood and colorful paper scattered around the living room. By the bulging trash bag, I assume there was even more lying around before. Sienna and Lucas freeze when they see me. Chloe smiles brightly, and Christopher has the distinct look of someone being caught during mischief. The three of them are standing in a straight line, so close you'd think they're glued to each other, or trying to hide something.

"I made you two cards," Chloe says, running toward me. "One is with a unicorn, one with a phoenix. Which one do you want?"

Stunned, I take both cards from Chloe—neither even remotely resembles a phoenix or a unicorn—and lower myself to her level, then kiss her forehead. "Thank you, pumpkin, I'll take both."

"We saw all your pictures of the vanity table in your office and wanted to surprise you," Sienna says. In unison, she and the boys step to the side, revealing a vanity table, which looks suspiciously like the one I have been desperately searching for... for a client.

"Do you like it?" Christopher asks, and I swear the four of them are holding their breath. And you're not telling the four people you love more than anything on this earth, who've spent hours working on this, that you were looking at it for a client. Nope, I'll take the secret to my grave.

"I love it." It's not even a lie; the only problem is that I have no need for one. I'll remedy that as soon as possible. "Thank you."

"We were going to clean up before you arrived,"

Sienna explains, "but we got carried away."

"We'll do it together," I say, hugging each of them. When Christopher's arm hooks around my waist, I can't help but melt into him, wishing we could stay like this for hours.

***

Rain starts pouring shortly after lunch, confining us to the house. Lucas and Chloe are taking a nap, the excitement of the morning clearly having worn them out, while Sienna's on the porch, talking to Ben on the phone. I have to start working on the festive dinner I have in mind for tonight soon, but there's still time.

Christopher and I are alone, and as he shuts the door to the living room, I'm convinced he's preparing for an hour-long cuddling session. But then he says, with no traces of his usual good humor, "We need to talk."

I sit up straighter on the ottoman, my stomach coiling instantly. "What's going on?"

"What do you know about Ben?"

I squint, sure I must have misheard him. "How do you know about Ben?"

Christopher paces around the room, jamming his hands inside his pocket. "Sienna was texting him constantly while we were building your vanity table."

"So?"

"She said you allowed them to do work on a project together."

"I did."

He opens his jaw, stopping midstride. Then he throws his hands up in the air like I just announced I'm planning to run the marathon naked or something. "Are you insane?"

"Huh?"

"Do you know what all seventeen-year-old boys have on their mind?"

"I've dated seventeen-year-old boys. I know very well. I know Ben. He's nice, and he's one of her closest friends and her lab partner. They often work together."

"You might not know this, but working on a project together is usually code for making out at their age."

I can barely keep back my laughter as I watch him. He's all but breathing fire out of his nostrils.

"I know for a fact it's not the case. I'm very close to Sienna, and she tells me everything."

"When can I meet him?" Christopher barks, resuming his pacing. His features have softened a little—but *very* little.

"Judging by your lunatic reaction, never." I try to work severity into my voice, but utterly fail because all this shows me is how much he *cares*. Decisively, his caveman tendencies are hot, not annoying. And in this moment, I know I've fallen in love with this man. The realization is humbling and exhilarating at the same time.

"I don't get it," Christopher says, snapping me back to our conversation.

"As a general rule, if you tell a teenager not to do something too often, they'll rebel against you. I'm saving my nos for situations that will truly require it. As I said before, know Ben, and he's trustworthy. They only meet here anyway, and usually sit in the kitchen or the living room. If they're in her bedroom, she knows she must leave the door open all the time."

"And she's okay with that?"

"Yeah."

He huffs something along the lines of "I'll believe

it when I see it" and "I still don't trust a seventeen-year-old boy."

I can't hold back any longer. With a grin, I cross the room and lace my arms around his neck. "You losing your shit about Sienna and Ben is the most adorable thing you've done so far, Bennett." Including building me a beautiful vanity table I don't need. Leaning in, I inhale his delicious scent. I will forever associate pine and mint with him.

"I was a seventeen-year-old, and I know what's on their mind," he repeats.

"Ben's trustworthy. You don't have to judge anyone by your appalling standards, you know."

"What's that supposed to mean?"

"That you use every opportunity to feel me up."

"I was under the impression that you were enjoying it."

"Never said I didn't, but that doesn't make you less of an opportunist."

"I see. So when you ask me to kiss you, I should just be a gentleman and keep my distance."

"Now you're twisting my words. That's not what I meant. Can I tell you a secret?"

"Do tell." He feathers his lips at the nape of my neck, turning my skin to gooseflesh.

"Sometimes when you're asleep in the morning, I kiss all around your chest and shoulders."

"Confession time? I know."

"What?" I jerk my head back, heat rising up my cheeks. "How?"

"Because I'm a light sleeper, so I wake up as soon as your precious mouth touches me."

"Why didn't you tell me?"

"And deprive myself of the constant proof of

how much you worship my body? No way."

In response, I simply pinch his arm. This does not deter him from teasing me in the slightest.

"So, since we established you kiss me when you think I'm asleep, who's the opportunist now?"

Looping an arm around my waist, he flattens me to him, sliding his hand further down.

"Since you're currently groping my ass, I think that means it's still you."

"You're too sassy for your own good. So, since I fessed up about knowing about your morning shenanigans, can I give you some tips? There are some parts of me you have thoroughly neglected."

"Really," I challenge, resting my hands on his shoulder. "And what would those be?"

He wiggles his eyebrows. "You have three guesses."

"You're impossible."

"Wrong choice of words. If you want to receive your present tonight, I suggest you play along."

This gives me pause. "You just gave me my present."

"No, that was all the kids. I just helped them build it." Something on my expression gives me away, because the next thing I know, Christopher lets go of me, stepping back. "Did you really want a vanity table?"

Oh hell, I don't want to lie to him, but I also don't want to come across as ungrateful. I weigh the pros and cons of each course of action in my mind and ultimately go for honesty.

"No, all those pictures were for research. For a client."

"Damn it, I had a feeling."

"I shouldn't have told you." Biting my lip, I add,

"But it was really nice of you to build it."

"Telling me is a good idea. I'm a big proponent of honesty. Pain now saves pain later. Otherwise, you could set yourself up for a lifetime of bad presents."

I try very hard not to swoon at the word "lifetime," but I swoon anyway. I chastise myself, because he could have been referring to a lifetime of bad presents from the kids.

He hauls me up against him, kissing the tip of my nose, making me swoon again. Pinching my lips together, I hold back the love declaration threatening to spill out of me. Despite everything, I don't know if he's there yet, and I don't want to scare him off, or for him to feel pressured.

I really hope he's there too, because the feeling of having his arms wrapped around me, and his warm breath on my neck? I don't want to be without it ever again.

Chapter Twenty-Nine

Christopher

Preparing the birthday dinner is a wild affair. The arguments start the second Victoria announces she'll start cooking—alone. Sienna makes the case that the birthday girl must be spoiled. Victoria stubbornly holds her ground, refusing to let Sienna and me cook or order food. That's when I step in and save the day, if I do say so myself. I pull her into an empty room, kiss her thoroughly, and let her know she won't receive my present unless she relents. No one said saving the day couldn't involve playing dirty.

Victoria agrees, with the caveat that she help too. I give in. I think it's called a compromise. Of course, once we start working, Lucas and Chloe poke their heads in the kitchen, insisting they want to help too, eyeing the set of knives on the counter while practically salivating at the idea of chopping vegetables… or fingers. I toy with the idea of giving them something benign to do, like I did when we were building the vanity table, but the damn kitchen is a death trap.

In the end, Victoria offers to watch a movie with Lucas and Chloe, effectively leaving the kitchen to Sienna and me. You'd think we planned this. Judging by the smug look on Sienna's face, she might have.

"Did you put Chloe and Lucas up to this?" I ask.

She shrugs, retrieving the ingredients out of the fridge. "It was their idea to help. I just told them to focus on the knives excessively."

"When did you talk to them?"

"When you pulled Victoria away to talk to her alone, I'm pretty sure that talking included 'doing the kissing.'" She imitates Chloe to perfection.

"I'm impressed."

Two hours later, the guests arrive: their Aunt Christina, her husband Bill, and their kids. Christina sizes me up, and I can tell dinner will be a test, but I'm confident I'll pass. We first enjoy the roast beef with herb crust, alongside caramelized shallots and mushrooms that Sienna and I cooked, then the cake that was delivered from Alice's restaurant. By the time the guests leave, it's almost midnight.

"Where's my present?" Victoria asks afterward, once Sienna has taken Chloe upstairs to prepare her for bed and Lucas is in his room. "And I swear if you just made it up to convince me earlier, you'd better improvise fast."

"I didn't make it up," I assure her.

"What did you get me?"

"You'll see."

Just as Victoria opens her mouth, Chloe steps inside, clutching her old fairytale book to her chest. Ah, so tonight will be a reading night. A few times a week, she asks Victoria to read to her until she falls asleep.

"I'll be right up to read, sweetheart," Victoria says.

"Can Christopher read my story tonight?" Chloe asks, bouncing back and forth on her toes. This is the first time she's asked this. Victoria lets out a loud breath, and it takes me a second to realize she's interpreting my silence as hesitation.

"Sure, I'll do it," I say. "It would be an honor, Chloe."

Chloe takes my hand, leading me out of the living room and up the staircase, then down a narrow hallway. Her room is all the way to the back.

"Do you like my room?" she asks shyly as we walk in, pink assaulting my eyes from every direction.

"It suits you," I reply.

She points toward the big beanbag opposite her bed, saying, "Victoria usually is there when she reads to me."

"Beanbag's mine, then." Grabbing the book from Chloe's hand, I plop myself on the surprisingly comfortable seat. "What do you want me to read to you?"

Climbing in her bed, Chloe pulls her brows together. "Cinderella. It's my favorite one."

The book cracks open at the page where Cinderella starts, which means it's been opened at this exact place numerous times before. In fact, this book is coming apart at the seams.

"Why don't you buy another book?" I ask. "This one's going to fall apart soon."

"It was Mom's," Chloe says in a small voice, hugging her pillow. "She had it from her Mom."

"Ah, a family heirloom." I rack my brain to come up with something funny to say to cheer her up, but I draw blank.

"When Victoria reads to me, I sometimes imagine Mom's reading," Chloe continues. "Now I can imagine Dad's doing it."

Her voice is hopeful, almost cheerful, but I feel like someone just stabbed me. This little girl is climbing in my heart, taking permanent residence there. *Jesus.* No one should lose their parents, much less at her age.

Chloe falls asleep midway through the story. I place the book on her nightstand, then leave the room carefully without making noise.

***

Victoria

Pacing my room/office, I'm on pins and needles as I wait for Christopher to join me. I all but melted when Chloe asked him to read her bedtime story. My little girl has completely let him in her heart, as have I.

When I hear the floor in front of the door creak, I swirl around, zeroing in on his imposing frame. I'll never tire of drinking him in: the beautifully groomed three-day beard, the broad shoulders and the expanse of his chest, those strong arms capable of making me feel cherished, protected, and wanted when they close around me.

"You didn't say you had a surprise for me." His rough bedroom voice jolts me from my thoughts, and I cross my hands behind my back as Christopher undresses me with his eyes. Not that I'm wearing much… just a black lace, strapless camisole with matching lace panties, which I bought especially for this occasion. He seems to greatly appreciate them.

Stepping closer to me, his gaze becomes more predatory by the second. Making a man like him lose control sends delicious tingles down my spine. Tipping my head back, he gives me a kiss as rough as it is breathtaking.

"You're gorgeous." He whispers the words against my skin as his lips trail down my neck, resting at the base, where my sweet spot is. "But before you unleash your seduction plan on me, don't you want your present?"

Ah, decisions, decisions. On the one hand, the man is coaxing my sweet spot. On the other hand, I'm a present junkie. My dark side wins, and I step back, holding up my hand expectantly. The corners of his mouth twitch.

"Turn around." His voice is low, commanding, and oh-so-alluring.

"Are you trying to trick me into having office sex with you?" I tease but turn around, wiggling my butt against his crotch for good measure.

"I don't need any tricks for that, Victoria." Sweeping my hair to one side, he kisses the side of my neck, while I feel him rummage in his pocket. Seconds later, he holds a necklace in front of me. The pendant hanging on the thin white gold thread is a beautiful diamond, and I'm stunned.

"Christopher!" I whisper.

"Do you like it?"

"Of course, it's beautiful. Thank you, but I…." My words trail as he clasps the necklace around my neck, the diamond resting on my skin. There is a mirror on the wall behind my desk, and we have a direct view.

"It looks perfect on you." Wrapping his arms around my waist, he pulls me flat against him.

Feeling the need to look straight at him, and not just merely through a mirror, I turn around.

"You didn't have to buy me this. I would've been happy with anything."

"You deserve something special."

I touch the stone with one hand, his chest with the other, my love declaration on the tip of my tongue. I'm being silly. There's no reason to be nervous. This is Christopher—*my* Christopher.

"I love you." With those three words, I feel as if I've put my heart in his hands. Loving someone means giving them a part of you. When they walk out of your life, they take that part with them. Love is scary, but tonight I'm brave.

Christopher exhales sharply, feathering his thumb over my bare shoulder. "I love you too, Victoria."

"Yeah?"

"I thought the diamond might have tipped you off."

"Words are better." I mold my body against him, needing the connection.

"It's funny, you know. I wasn't looking for anything when you came in my life. Crashed into my life, actually."

I pinch his chest playfully, but what can I say, the man is one hundred percent right.

"You fit in so perfectly, I have no idea how I lived without you in it before," he continues.

Oh, heavens. I melt on the spot.

"You're quite the romantic," I whisper.

"I warned you. It's a trait I rarely unleash, but—"

"Don't worry, I'm a sponge. I can soak it all up."

His hands glide down my back, resting on my ass for a brief second before he hoists me up in his arms. My legs hitch around his waist, already knowing where to settle for maximum stability. Christopher carries me to my bed, placing me on it swiftly.

He removes my camisole and panties with lightning speed, but I'm right there with him in my race to get him naked. Finally, I move to the center of the bed, beckoning him by opening my legs. Christopher smiles ruefully, cuffing my ankles with his hands, kissing along my legs up to my knees. When his mouth ascends to my inner thighs, all hot and sinful, I almost break out of my skin. I need to touch him too, and just when I think I'm about to, Christopher props himself up on his knees.

"Turn around."

Anticipation and regret war inside me. Anticipation because I know he'll do wicked hot things to me, regret because I won't be able to touch him. But I'm putty in his hands, driven by the promise of pleasure. So I turn around, flattening my belly against the bed, holding a pillow nearby in case I have to muffle moans or cries. All my senses are on high alert. Biting my lip, I try to anticipate where Christopher will start with the delicious torture. He chooses the back of my neck, trailing his mouth down, sending tendrils of anticipation straight to my center.

He drags his thumbs across my ass cheeks, down in a straight line, then back up in tiny circles that have me convulsing. When he traces the same pattern with his tongue, first one cheek and then the other, then swiping his tongue once along the crack between, I nearly black out. My entire body has transformed into a sweet spot under his expert hands and mouth.

Fisting the sheets, I seek to regain my composure, but what little I manage melts right away when he nudges my legs open with his knee. One rumbling sound later, a condom package is being ripped open. The next seconds seem excruciatingly long… until Christopher pushes inside me, stretching me. I bite into the pillow to muffle a moan. His thrusts are measured and deep, filling me completely.

"So good," I murmur, almost out of breath.

"Perfect." His hot mouth feathers over my shoulders, and I lose myself in the pleasure. Making love to him has always been beautiful, but tonight it's surreal. I feel closer to him than ever. When I'm so near the edge that my entire body quivers, one of Christopher's hands feathers up to the side of my breast and then back down. Slipping between my body and the bed, he presses on the tight bundle of nerves. His hot breath on the back of my neck is a sinful whisper. His thrusts grow more passionate with a desperation that mirrors my own. He loves me with unrestrained passion until we both find relief in a shattering wave of pleasure.

Chapter Thirty

Victoria

Chloe asking Christopher to read to her was apparently just the beginning. On Monday afternoon, they go on their first shopping trip to a nearby toy store, just the two of them. I warned him that Chloe could be a little extortionist when it comes to toys, but he insisted he'd manage.

I'm helping Sienna with a science project when my phone rings, Christopher's name appearing on the screen. The corners of my mouth lift in a smile as I put the phone to my ear, imagining he needs my expertise in negotiating with Chloe.

"Victoria!" Urgency drips from Christopher's voice. My stomach coils at the sound.

"What happened?"

"A car crashed into us on the way to the store."

"Oh my God."

"We only have a few scratches, but Chloe and I are in the ambulance right now, and the ER insists we go to the hospital to check for any internal damage from the impact. We need you there because you're Chloe's guardian."

Every wisp of air leaves my lungs at the words "internal damage." "Of course. I'm on my way."

"What's wrong?" Sienna asks after I click off,

panic flaring in her eyes.

Biting the inside of my cheek, I force myself to sound calm. "Christopher and Chloe were in an accident. Nothing major, don't worry. I'm going to them."

"I'm coming too."

"You and Lucas stay home. It's nothing," I promise.

I fight the cloud of panic threatening to swallow me up all the way to the hospital. My hands shake on the wheel, and my mind races with made-up images of blood splattered on the asphalt and cries of agony. I listened intently when I was talking to Christopher, and I didn't hear Chloe cry in the background. Christopher's voice didn't seem to hide pain.

Calm down, Victoria. Calm down.

Repeating that mantra is futile. I know I won't relax until the doctor clears Chloe and Christopher. They'll be all right. They have to be. Still, as I speed in the direction of the highway, I can't help remembering another phone call urging me to head to a hospital nearly a year ago. Aunt Christina called me close to midnight on a Friday, telling me to head to the hospital, that something had happened during my parents' boating trip and they were taken to the hospital.

At that time, I was in town enjoying a girls' night out. Reluctantly I got into a cab, and all the way to the hospital, I worked on a joke. I'd walk in and tell them it was time they left romantic dates to the young ones if they couldn't even make it through a boat trip. I imagined something like them falling over in the water and getting a scare. It was ridiculous, but at that time, I couldn't imagine anything serious happening to them. In my mind, my parents would live forever. When I arrived at the hospital, Christina was sobbing. I had never seen her sob before, and the joke froze on my tongue. When she calmed down enough to talk, she told me my parents' boat had collided with a poorly lit buoy, and they were both dead.

The entire world imploded.

Maybe I've become paranoid, but as I step inside the hospital, I have the sinking feeling that everything is about to implode again.

I find Christopher and Chloe in the crowded emergency waiting room, both sitting on chairs. *This is good. Sitting is good. If they have any real damage, they wouldn't be sitting, would they?* If they were hurt, they wouldn't be in the waiting room. I know jack shit about internal damage, but I keep telling myself that sitting is a good sign.

"Victoria," Chloe squeals when she sees me, jumping in my arms when I step in front of her. I hug her closely, breathing her in. She smells like candy and my perfume, which she sprayed on herself this morning when she thought I wasn't looking. There are no traces of blood anywhere that I can see.

Christopher pulls both of us between his arms, and he too seems unharmed. His grip is as strong and reassuring as ever, and my knees nearly buckle with relief.

"We're waiting for a doc to see us, but based on the preliminary checkups in the ambulance, we don't have anything more than a few scratches," Christopher explains after we pull apart and I place Chloe on the chair again.

His voice sounds strong and reassuring too. He couldn't sound like this if he were hurt, could he? And Chloe couldn't muster up this smile that lights up her entire face if she had internal bleeding, could she?

"What happened?" I ask. The seats next to Chloe and Christopher are occupied so I just stand before them.

"Some schmuck ran the red light. Slammed into the passenger seat from the side. Thank God Chloe was sitting in the back."

"And then Christopher's airbag went boom," Chloe exclaims, extending her arms up in the air.

"You weren't scared at all?" I ask her gently.

"Yes, I was, but Christopher said...." She frowns, resting her chin dramatically on her palm. "I don't remember, but now I'm not scared anymore."

I throw my arms around Christopher's neck, practically choking him. Chuckling, he loops his arms around my waist.

"We're fine, Victoria," he whispers. "We're absolutely fine."

"Sorry to interrupt," a low, brisk voice says from behind me. As I step to the side, the nurse surveys me. "Are you the little one's guardian?"

"Yes. I'm her sister."

"Okay. I need you to fill out some forms for me."

Afterward, the nurse suggests I remain in the waiting room while she takes Christopher and Chloe for a checkup. Usually the parent or guardian goes in with a child, unless the child has serious injuries. In our case though, Christopher needs to be checked out himself. I only agree because I think it's best for Chloe. I am beyond nervous, and I think my presence in the ER room would distress her.

Once they're gone, there's nothing for me to do except wait as two of the most important people in my life are being checked for potentially life-threatening injuries. I briefly consider calling Sienna, but there's no point right now. I'll call once I know that they're all right.

They *will be* all right.

I don't know how much time passes before I hear my name.

"Ms. Hensley, where is the minor?"

My spine stiffens as Hervis Jackson steps into my field of vision. At the back of my mind, I remember him saying in one of our earliest meetings that in case any of the kids were brought to the hospital, he'd know. That didn't even seem like a possibility back then. One of the reasons I hate interacting with him, besides his permanent air of superiority, is that he always throws around words like "guardian," "minor," and "case" instead of "sister" and "family." It's all so cold.

"Where is the minor?" he repeats slowly, as if convinced my IQ level can't comprehend his words.

"They've taken her back for a checkup."

"What happened?"

"Car accident, but Chloe wasn't injured."

"Then why was she brought to the hospital?"

I flex my hands, trying not to ball them into fists. Hervis has the unique ability to make me see red less than five minutes into a conversation.

"It's just a precaution—"

"We're back. The doc cleared both of us. No damage, so we're free to leave," Christopher announces, having just arrived with Chloe. He cocks a brow in Hervis's direction.

Hervis spares Chloe a fleeting glance before focusing on Christopher. "Who are you?" Hervis asks.

"Christopher Bennett," he replies, helping Chloe sit on a chair. "Who are you?"

"Hervis Jackson. I'm the social worker assigned to the Hensley case."

Hearing those damn words again is like a physical punch to my gut.

"And your relationship to the family is?" he continues.

"He's my boyfriend," I reply.

"Were you with the minor and Ms. Hensley when the accident happened?" Hervis asks Christopher.

"Yes, I was the one driving. Victoria wasn't with us."

A heavy silence follows, and I can practically feel the weight of Hervis's disapproval smack me in the face. I feel the need to explain more, though I don't know what to say. It's my right to leave the kids with whomever I see fit. Panic slicks through my veins, clouding my judgment.

"I've been around the kids for months. It's not like I'm a stranger," Christopher says, his voice strained. Obviously he feels the same compulsive need to overexplain as I do.

"Were you inebriated?" Hervis inquires.

Christopher, who is standing next to Chloe's seat, goes rigid.

"No."

"Were you under the influence of drugs?"

"No." He squares his shoulders. My gaze automatically lowers to his hands, which he balls into fists. Hervis notices too. I swallow bile, opening my mouth. No words come out, so I merely move over to Chloe's other side, placing an arm around her shoulders.

"Were you past the speed limit?"

"No," Christopher answers through gritted teeth.

"Would your answers remain the same if you were under oath?"

My throat constricts, air escaping me. Chloe tenses under my arm, glancing up at me with confusion, not fear. But I have enough fear for both of us.

"Yes. You can take a look at the police report. The accident was not my fault."

"Look—" I begin, having found my voice again, desperately needing to stop this, to protect the kids, Christopher, and me. Hervis holds up his hand, stopping the words in my throat.

"I'm talking to Mr. Bennett now. I would appreciate no interruptions. I certainly will check the police report. Do you have any felony convictions?"

"Fuck no," Christopher all but yells, making both Chloe and me flinch.

"That's a bad word," Chloe whispers to Christopher.

Hervis's gaze slides to my sister. I want to tell Christopher to calm down because this is what Hervis does. He pushes buttons until you snap, then holds said snapping against you like a damn gun. But there's no way I can pull him away and talk some sense into him with Hervis here.

"Are you employed, Mr. Bennett, or do you rely on Ms. Hensley for financial support?"

"Who do you think you are? Coming here, insulting my girlfriend, insulting me? Do you live under a rock? I'm a fucking shareholder in Bennett Enterprises. In case you don't know what I'm talking about, here's the cliff notes version. The company is worth billions. I suggest you spend more time brushing up on your obviously nonexistent knowledge on current affairs rather than harassing us."

I breathe in deeply, hoping that will calm my racing pulse. I want to defend Christopher and smack him in the head at the same time. He's making this worse.

Hervis blinks, scrutinizing Christopher.

"Have you ever taken anger management courses, Mr. Bennett?"

My body goes rigid with shock, as I realize what he's doing: searching for any angle to paint Christopher in a negative light. And Christopher is about to serve it to him on a silver platter. Raising one hand, he points at Hervis with his forefinger. His face is red, a vein pulsing at his temple.

"I have enough money and power to make sure you never work again in this country. Scratch that—on three continents, if I put in the effort. And believe me, I'm willing to put in the effort. Take your attitude and get out of here."

Now I'm downright angry at him. This is not a pissing contest, or him flexing his muscles. He can't threaten the social worker, or anyone for that matter.

"Christopher—" I start, but Hervis holds up a hand to silence me. Again. Sometime in the past few minutes, Chloe has shifted closer to me.

When Hervis looks straight at me, I can see on his face that the implosion is about to start.

"Ms. Hensley, I'm afraid the situation is much worse than I imagined. You have exposed the minors in your care for months to a man with clear anger issues. One of them has been put in a potentially life-threatening situation because of him. As such, I deem that you are not capable of being the guardian of the minors."

Wham! My eyes burn with unshed tears, even as the rest of my body feels as if I'm in an iceberg.

"Hervis," I say as calmly as possible. "This is all a big misunderstanding, and I—"

"That will be for a judge to decide. I will petition for an emergency trial as soon as possible, the end of this week at the latest."

"No!" I bellow. "Can't you at least wait until after Christmas?"

"These kids are her family. Heck, they're my family too," Christopher says angrily. "You can't do this."

"As a matter of fact, I can, Mr. Bennett. I have been assigned to this case to keep a close eye and determine if the minors are not cared for properly, or if they are in danger. You are obviously a danger, and Ms. Hensley is incompetent. I knew this from the first time I visited their home, but I gave her the benefit of the doubt. I shouldn't have. Ms. Hensley, you will be informed of the trial date as soon as possible, but it will be no later than Friday. Until then, Mr. Bennett, I suggest you stay away from Ms. Hensley and her siblings."

Somewhere at the back of my mind, I register that Hervis's voice is softer, and he used the word "siblings" for the first time. Too little, too late. I'm holding even tighter to Chloe, who is now sobbing. She might not understand everything, but she understands enough.

With a curt nod, Hervis turns around and leaves. I become aware that everyone in the emergency waiting room has been watching us.

I lift Chloe in my arms and, almost robotically, place one foot in front of the other, reassuring her softly. She's streaked my sweater with tears, and I'm afraid I'll break down in front of her any minute now.

Christopher walks silently behind us until we reach my car, which I parked a block away from the hospital. Without even looking at him, I place Chloe in her car seat.

"That idiot won't get away with this," Christopher says the second I shut the door. "He's just some over-eager social worker. He—"

"This is not a pissing contest between you and

Hervis, Christopher." Instantly, my blood begins to boil. Squaring my shoulders, I make myself taller, facing him.

"I know, but the stuff he was saying was unbelievable." He runs his hand through his hair, shifting his weight from one foot to the other.

"This was not about winning a popularity contest. It was not about winning at all. It was about the kids."

"Victoria, I can help."

"Really? Because all you did back there was nix my chances of keeping custody of the kids. You going on and on about your money and power didn't help jack shit. On the contrary, you just gave Hervis reasons to paint you as a raging lunatic and me as an idiot for allowing you anywhere near the kids." I want to cry out in rage, to drill in to his skull just how much harm he's done, but I keep my voice as low as possible for Chloe's sake, hoping she can't hear us from inside the car.

"I know it wasn't my finest moment, but I can help."

"You heard Hervis. It's best if you stay away."

"But—"

"You plan to threaten the judge and who knows who else just like you did with Hervis?" Christopher's expression is stricken. "You've done enough. This… mess? That was your *help*."

Chapter Thirty-One

Victoria

When I finally climb into the car, Chloe is asleep, probably exhausted from all the crying and sobbing. I swallow a sob of my own, not wanting to wake her up. I barely keep it together on the way home. She jolts out of her sleep as I park the car in front of our house.

"Victoria!" That's all she manages to utter before sobbing again. In less than a minute, I climb out of the car and join her in the backseat.

"Are you giving us away?" she whispers, breaking my heart into a million pieces.

"No, sweetheart. Of course not. There's been a misunderstanding, that's all." My voice falters, unsure how to put what's happening into words—words that won't scare the living daylights out of her.

"Chloe, I am not giving you away. I love you."

Her sobs subside a little, but she still doesn't look convinced.

"But what if they take us away?" Chloe presses. "Will you still want us back?"

"Of course, sweetheart, but no one will take you away." Freeing her from the car seat, I pull her into a hug. "I love you to the moon and back."

"To the sun," Chloe corrects. "The sun is farther away."

"I love you all to the sun and back," I say, my

voice uneven again. "Everything will be all right. Let's go to Lucas and Sienna."

I briefly considered not telling Lucas and Sienna about the possibility that they'll be taken away from me by the end of the week, but that wouldn't do anyone any good. They need to be prepared, and Chloe already knows and she could never keep the secret.

Breaking the news to my other two siblings almost undoes me. Lucas goes into shock, asking if they could move in with Aunt Christina. My heart breaks as I deliver my answer: a firm no.

Right after our parents died, when my abilities as a guardian were being questioned, I naively thought Aunt Christina could just sign up to be their guardian if the kids were taken away. The problem is that once the kids are in the state's custody, a potential guardian must be deemed fit by the authorities. Because Aunt Christina is a homemaker and her husband is the only breadwinner in the family, it was determined that their household income could not sustain three additional children.

Sienna keeps remarkably calm, given that she knows the ramifications of all of this.

"I know a great lawyer," I tell her, thinking about Alan. "He'll help us. I have to call him."

With a nod, she directs her attention to the little ones, who are sitting on the couch, hugging each other.

"Chloe, Lucas, you both have to go to bed," she says. "It's late. Come on, let's get both of you upstairs."

As soon as they're out of earshot, I call Aunt Christina. I know she can't help, but I just need to talk to someone who isn't the kids about this. Christopher… I can't talk to him just yet.

I relay to Aunt Christina what happened beat by beat, barely holding it together.

"I'm really sorry about this. I'll fix it," I say.

"I know it's not your fault, Victoria. State agencies are very rigid. But a great lawyer will get you out of this mess."

"I'm letting Mom and Dad down," I whisper into the phone.

"No, you're not. You've put a solid roof over the kids' head and given them all they need. Heck, you've given them more than they need. Your parents would be proud of you. Tell me if there is anything I can do."

"Thank you."

After hanging up, I barely wipe away my tears when my phone rings again. Jackson Hervis. That bastard.

"Ms. Hensley, we have a date for the hearing," he says the second I answer. "It's this Thursday at two o'clock. You will be served papers tomorrow morning. I know this is hard," he continues in a tone that conveys how clueless he is, "but it's for the best for you and the minors. They deserve a proper home, and you're obviously in over your head."

Even while grief looms over me, his words stab me, and I bleed anger.

"Hervis, with all due respect, you have no idea what you are talking about. From the moment you were assigned to us, you put a label on me. Then you started looking for anything that you could use against me. You are misjudging me, and Christopher. You look at us through checklist-framed glasses and miss the most important part: we are a family."

"Family is not always a safe haven, Ms. Hensley."

"I'll see you in court." I hang up before he has a chance to answer. Panic flares through me, but I can't break down just yet.

I need a plan first, so I call Alan Smith. He informs me that Christopher has already called him and relayed all the information. As usual, he remains calm and warm, assuring me we can build a rock-solid case even in the short time span. It takes all I have to listen intently and absorb the information about the next steps, tucking it at the back of my mind, from where I can pull it out tomorrow morning and act on it.

After the call is over, I hurry upstairs, checking on the kids, fully expecting them to still be awake. Instead, I find them asleep in Sienna's bed, all three huddled together. The thought that they might have cried themselves to sleep has me sobbing. I want to hug them, but that would certainly wake them up.

I run downstairs, locking myself in my room, needing to let the anger out. Because I am *so* damn angry. At Hervis, the system, myself… and Christopher. Oh, I am so angry with him. The worst part is that I know he meant well, and when he said the kids are his family too, I nearly melted. Hervis was pushing his buttons, but the result is all the same. I have to go to court to fight for the kids, and I might lose them. It takes mere seconds for me to break down. Opening the door to crying is a dangerous endeavor because it might end up consuming me, but I have to let the tears out of my system.

Tomorrow I will be strong again.

Chapter Thirty-Two

Christopher

"There are bad Mondays, and then there's this." Blake places a glass of scotch in front of me, and I take a large gulp with no hesitation. I stepped into his bar a few minutes ago, heading directly to the counter. He started pouring me scotch before my ass was on the barstool. "What happened?" he inquires.

"Long day" is all I say for now. My brothers will arrive shortly for our Monday gathering, and I'm not up to repeating the story more than once. We originally chose Mondays to meet here because they were slow nights for Blake, but that's no longer the case. The place is full almost to the brim, to my annoyance. Too many voices to drown out.

Logan joins us by the time my glass is dry, sitting on the barstool next to me.

"Sebastian is still at the office," Logan says. "He won't make it today."

"That means it'll just be the three of us," Blake replies. "Daniel's busy, and the girls are a no-show, again."

"Don't take it so personally. They just all have busy schedules," Logan says.

"They never miss any gatherings at our parents' house," Blake points out.

"Yeah, but Mom always has chocolate cake for dessert. That's much more of a draw for the girls than alcohol. But not for me. I'm thirsty. Give me a scotch." Turning to me, Logan cocks an eyebrow. "Where did you disappear to this afternoon? You've been ignoring everyone's calls."

"Interesting," Blake remarks. "So this Monday is even worse than I predicted."

I quickly tell them what happened this afternoon, trying—and failing—to ignore their expressions, which change from grim to dismayed to pissed. In that order.

"Let me get this straight," Logan says after I'm done. "The social worker was riding your ass and instead of playing the part of the Dalai Lama, you somehow managed to convince him you're a raging, dangerous lunatic?"

"Yeah."

He groans. "You're lucky Victoria didn't strangle you."

All I can do is nod because I want to strangle myself. I've replayed that scene in my head over and over again, trying to make sense of it. I'm usually a calm guy. The people I work with can attest to that, as can my family. But I'm man enough to admit I was scared out of my wits the moment I realized that Hervis was grasping at straws so he could make a case against Victoria. Apparently fear turns me into a moron.

Drumming my fingers on my glass, I become aware that Blake isn't saying anything, which is unlike him.

"What?" I bark.

"Tell me you're not here sitting on your ass and drinking instead of fixing things, or I'll put chili peppers in your next drink."

"Why do you think I ignored everyone's calls the entire afternoon? I was fixing things." Gripping my empty glass tightly, I shove it in Blake's face. "Another scotch. No chili peppers. I'm working with Alan—he's Victoria's lawyer—putting all my resources at his disposal so he can build a bulletproof case."

"Alan is a great lawyer. Can we help in any way?" my older brother asks. "You might have sounded like a pompous pig to that social worker, but we actually do have enough influence to turn all of this in Victoria's favor."

"I know. I'm pulling all the strings. I'm handling this, but I appreciate the offer. I'm making one thousand percent sure she's going to win."

"Have you talked to Victoria?" Logan continues.

"Alan said it's best if I keep my distance from her and the kids until the trial. I'm not sure she wants to hear from me right now, anyway."

Blake is handing out drinks to a group that's lingering in front of the counter, but I can tell he's still listening to our conversation.

"Look at the bright side," he says once the group leaves, retreating to a table at the back.

"Oddly enough, I don't see any."

"You have time to come up with a grovel plan," he informs me.

"Don't start with your crap." I down the whiskey in two gulps.

Blake smirks. "Free drinks come with my crap."

"I'll pay for my drinks, then."

"I know Blake can be obnoxious," Logan interferes, "but he makes a good point."

"You've now managed to offend and praise me in one sentence. Congratulations." Blake raises my empty glass, tipping it in Logan's direction. Logan clinks his scotch against Blake's glass. I can't believe I'm witnessing the least probable alliance in the Bennett family. Once upon a time, when Blake's full-time job was partying, Logan was riding Blake's ass continuously. It came from the brotherly concern that Blake was wasting his life, but it was fun to watch. At any rate, much more fun than seeing these two team up against me.

"Just because you're ensuring the result of the trial will be in Victoria's favor, it doesn't mean she'll take your sorry ass back," Blake clarifies. "It'll require some serious groveling. Now, my usual weapons of choice are flowers or presents. They've rarely failed me. Then again, my antics were of a different kind. More of the 'I forgot your birthday' variety." After a brief pause, he adds, "Or the 'I slept with your best friend' variety."

Logan and I snort at the same time.

"How did groveling go after you pulled that stunt?" I ask.

Blake shrugs. "It was the first time I legitimately feared a woman might cut my balls off."

"I would've paid good money to see that," Logan remarks with a shit-eating grin.

"I want to hear the whole story."

"It wasn't precisely a groveling case. I broke it off with that chick, Monica, and she and I agreed to stay friends. You know, in that way where neither of you actually want that, but it's the least awkward thing to say. About a year later, I met her best friend at a party. She was complaining how she'd had a dry spell for months."

"The horror," I mutter sarcastically.

"Exactly. I thought I'd help her out." Blake clearly hasn't picked up the sarcasm. "I'm always happy to take one for the team."

"Except you weren't on her team," I point out.

"I change teams according to my interests," Blake says seriously. "She confessed everything to Monica afterward. I never understood why."

Logan leans over the counter, stealing a jar of peanuts. "Might I suggest remorse?"

"That makes no sense. Monica and I had broken up an entire year before the event, and we'd been together for a week."

Shaking my head, I shove some peanuts in my mouth. "And you say you know women."

"How did you end up groveling?" Logan asks, mystified in honest.

"Showed up at Monica's door with flowers. I honestly don't know what got into me."

"Some of that Bennett honor reared its head, and you wanted to come clean," Logan suggests.

"Its ugly head," Blake corrects. "Anyway, enough about me and one of my less-than-stellar moments. Our boy Christopher is the one in need of counsel."

Damn, I don't want this conversation to circle back to me. I know what's at stake.

I make a grab for my glass but narrowly miss it. I miscalculated the distance and my vision's blurry; no more scotch for me. Pressing my palms against my eyes, I attempt to do away with the fog. An image pops at the back of my mind: Chloe shoving the two cards with the phoenix and the unicorn under Victoria's nose, and Lucas and Sienna proudly showing her the vanity table we built. The thought of losing Victoria and the kids is excruciating. Ever since I left them this afternoon, there is a physical pain in my body. They all mean the world to me, and I will get them back.

"I will pretend I didn't hear that." Blake's voice

snaps me out of my pity party for one.

"What?" Looking from Blake to Logan, it's hard to tell which one's grinning wider. I have the sinking suspicion I might have voiced some of those thoughts.

"You said something about a unicorn, a phoenix, and how Victoria and the kids mean the world to you and some more mushy stuff," Blake informs me. "Too much cutesy there. My masculinity is being threatened."

Logan clasps my shoulder. "Christopher doesn't need our advice. He'll do well on his own."

"Suit yourself, but no more scotch for you, Christopher, or you'll add a dragon to the mix so the unicorn and phoenix don't get lonely."

"Blake!" I warn.

"You know what the best part is about all of you getting hitched?" Blake continues undeterred.

"No, but I suppose you'll enlighten us," Logan deadpans.

"The best part is that I can watch you mess up and avoid the same mistakes when my time comes."

I snort. "You take the cake, anyway."

"When your time comes?" Logan asks our younger brother skeptically.

"Five Bennetts down in four years." Blake shudders, grimacing. "There's definitely something in the air. Before I know it, that damn virus will get me too."

"It definitely will if Pippa and Alice have anything to say about it." Logan downs his scotch, handing Blake the empty glass, then turns to me. "Go get those kids back."

Blake points his finger in my direction. "And the girl."

I nod. There is one thing I've learned since I met Victoria. You have no say when the people who will become your whole world walk into your life. But it sure as hell is up to me not to let them walk back out.

Chapter Thirty-Three

Victoria

I arrive at the courthouse fifteen minutes before the scheduled start of the trial. I ditched my usual multicolored outfits, opting for the dark blue suit I wear during bank visits, hoping this will contribute to establishing my image of a responsible adult.

The doors to the courtroom are open so I peek inside, not feeling brave enough to walk in by myself. I wish Alan were here already. The courtroom resembles what I've seen on TV, albeit smaller. Hervis and his lawyer are already inside, sitting at one table. An empty table is on the other side of the room where I assume Alan and I will sit. The judge's table is in the center at the far end, and the witness box next to it. Right now, it looks like a stake to me, one where I'm about to be burned. There is no jury in custody litigation cases, Alan told me.

Eventually, I walk inside and take the seat at the empty table, because I look ridiculous pacing around outside. My palms become sweaty with each passing moment, and I try to wipe them discreetly on my skirt. My pulse races and my mouth is as dry as cotton. *Everything will be all right!*

I repeat this to myself a few times, to no avail. Breathing in and out of my nose, I remind myself that Alan has built a rock-solid case. I've been running around like mad the past two days, asking everyone from the kids' teachers to former clients of mine for references. The aim is to build my credibility. Christopher has been doing the same, and Alan has been updating me on his involvement this entire week. I haven't spoken to Christopher directly, and Alan strongly advised that he should not come by our house, since Hervis will use the outburst at the hospital against him.

I was not in the right state of mind to call Christopher. When I wasn't running around asking for references, I was around corners crying out of fear of losing the kids, or pouring all my energy in holding back the tears when I was around them. Alan arrives five minutes before the trial is set to begin, sitting next to me.

"We'll do great," he says in a confident voice, offering me a reassuring smile. I cannot muster the energy to return it.

I glance up at Hervis, who is whispering something to his lawyer. Alan and Christopher did some background research on Hervis. Turns out he grew up in a children's home for the first years of his life, then went from foster family to foster family, suffering abuse in many households.

I have found some sympathy for him, imagining he chose this job so other children don't have to endure what he did. It's commendable, really, but since he's fighting against me today, an almost maniacal wish to throttle him drowns that sympathy.

Once the judge, Carina Williams is here and everything begins, my mind all but shuts off, experiencing everything as if in a dream, only hearing snippets. When Hervis is asked why he's adamant that I shouldn't be in charge of the children, I wish I could shut off my ears altogether. Unfortunately, I can't, so I hear him talk for what seems like an eternity, bringing up every item on his blacklist: losing my job shortly after my parents passed away, using the life insurance to purchase a house, refusing to find another job but instead working on my own and subjecting the children to the risks of an uncertain income.

"And then there was the matter of her previous employer's lawsuit against her," Hervis continues.

Alan springs to his feet. "Your Honor, I have represented Ms. Hensley in that matter. The previous employer dropped the lawsuit. I have personally explained to Mr. Jackson all the details, and why Ms. Hensley was absolutely not at fault. I can reiterate all the facts right now if necessary."

"That won't be necessary," the judge says.

Hervis's lawyer speaks up. "Even so, it's proof Ms. Hensley is prone to run-ins with the law."

Alan's nostrils flare. "So are speeding tickets. Would you hold those against her too?"

Hervis's lawyer shakes his head, but not in defeat. Instead, he's confident. Next, Hervis brings up Christopher, insisting that the mere fact I've allowed him in our life proves I can't decide what's best for the *minors*, and that the car accident is irrefutable proof. By the time he's done, he almost convinces *me* that I'm not good enough for the kids.

I look at the judge most of the time, trying to gauge the impact Hervis's words have on her, but Ms. Williams has the best poker face I have ever encountered. Her expression remains stoic. Under the table, I clench and unclench my hands so often that my nails have carved dents into my palms.

When I'm asked to speak, my spine stiffens, but I clear my throat and square my shoulders, gathering my wits. "When my parents passed away, everything changed. I admit I was not prepared for all the responsibility, and the start was rocky. I had no experience raising kids, but I'm a quick learner. I'm not afraid of hard work or ashamed to ask anyone for advice—teachers, therapists, or anyone who has more experience than I do. They are my family, and I'm willing to do anything to make sure they will grow up to be responsible, well-adjusted adults. Don't take them away from me, please."

The judge nods, clasping her hands together on the table. Afterward, it's Alan's show.

"Your Honor," Alan says, exuding confidence and competence, "I would like to shed some light on Ms. Hensley's financial situation. While it is true that she was fired from her previous job, her employer cited as reasons the fact that Ms. Hensley became less flexible and had to cut back on the hours she worked, frequently arriving late and leaving early. Of course, it's illegal to fire someone for suddenly having a family, so the employer's report leaves out that the reason for Ms. Hensley's apparently sudden disrespect for the company schedule was because she needed to drop off and pick up her younger siblings from school. I have two small kids myself. Frankly, they are the reason I started my own law firm because I could no longer abide by the draconian schedule of my employer."

"There is no need to bring in personal examples, Mr. Smith," the judge says firmly, but not unkindly. Still, my heart stutters. She did not interrupt Hervis once. This can't be a good sign.

"Of course. Back to Ms. Hensley. I would like to submit her financial records for your consideration, showing her income in the months since she was fired. It is stable and can provide a comfortable living for the children in her care. This was possible because Ms. Hensley acted quickly after her parents passed away, immediately assessing that she would not be able to afford the mortgage, thus selling that house and buying one that was affordable using the life insurance. I understand that cashing in the life insurance is sometimes done for the guardian's benefit—and I applaud social services for investigating the matter—but in this case, it was clearly for the welfare of the children."

The judge doesn't say anything, her face as blank as ever.

"On the subject of their welfare, we have obtained written statements from the children's teachers and educators. All of them praise the children's academic performance and involvement in extracurricular activities, insisting Ms. Hensley has always shown an active interest in her siblings' development. We also have a statement from the children's therapist. She affirms that the children coped with their grief in an age-appropriate way, and that Ms. Hensley's actions indicate she has the best interest of the children at heart, putting their needs above hers. As an example, Ms. Hensley called the therapist before engaging in a romantic relationship with Christopher Bennett, wanting to make sure it would not hurt the children emotionally. I would also like to emphasize that Ms. Hensley took the children to a therapist of her own initiative, hoping it would help them in dealing with their grief."

Alan pauses, taking a sip of water from the glass in front of him. I had no idea someone could speak so fast for so long. After placing his glass back on the table, he continues.

"On the subject of Christopher Bennett, I will first shed light on the subject of the car accident. As the police report states, the other driver was at fault, running a red light and slamming into Mr. Bennett's car. Furthermore, we obtained statements from the nurses and other personnel who were in the ER waiting room. They all attest that Mr. Bennett was very affectionate with Chloe when they arrived, constantly reassuring her and attempting to cheer her up."

My heart swells at this, as if I've just hugged a kitten to my chest. This is my Christopher. Oh, how I wish he could be here right now. Alan flat-out said no, for obvious reasons. But obtaining all these statements in two days would have been impossible without Christopher's help.

"He was in no way a danger to the girl, quite the contrary. He only became unnerved when Mr. Hervis Jackson began launching accusations at him without first listening to a full explanation from either Ms. Hensley, Mr. Bennett, or Chloe. The personnel have used words such as 'unfair' and 'aggressive in his questioning' to describe Mr. Jackson. You can read their complete declarations in the written statements. There is also a written statement from Mr. Bennett."

Afterward, the judge retires behind closed doors to assess our case, and Alan tries to encourage me, insisting the case is rock solid. Despite his assurances, I bite my nails like a madwoman. I don't know how much time passes before we're told the judge is ready for us.

"I have considered all that has been said in the courtroom and the written statements from the defending party. On that note, I'm surprised the accusing party did not present any such statements—interviews, reports or declarations from third parties who would support the claims."

Hervis's lawyer speaks up. "Your Honor, Mr. Hervis Jackson has extensive experience when it comes to such cases."

"Experience can lead to a subjective interpretation of observations, which is why third-party statements are welcome. Frankly, I'm dismayed you have not interviewed teachers or any of the personnel present at the hospital." Hervis flinches. The judge's tone is as neutral as ever, but hope blooms in my chest. She isn't done. "The concerns you mentioned could have been put to rest with thorough investigations." She directs her gaze to Alan and me next. "I commend the defending party for doing such extensive work to paint a full picture of the family situation, especially in such a short time. The written statement from Mr. Bennett was very heartfelt, and considering the third-party references and statements, truthful. As such, I am convinced that Victoria Hensley should retain full custody of her siblings."

It takes a few seconds for her words to sink in, and when they do, I barely restrain myself from leaping from my chair and hugging the judge and Alan. Euphoria flows through my veins, filling me with an infectious energy, and apparently turning me deaf. The judge is still talking, but I don't hear one word. All I can think about is leaving this room and sharing the news with my siblings, and with Christopher.

Chapter Thirty-Four

Victoria

I call Sienna the second I step out of the courtroom. At this time of day, the kids are all home. My words come out rushed and borderline unintelligible, but she understands, squealing at the top of her lungs. As she relays the information to Lucas and Chloe, they start squealing in the background. After clicking off, I hurry after Alan, who is exiting the building.

"Thank you so much for all you've done," I tell him once I catch up with him outside. "Can I ask you one thing? What did Christopher's statement say?"

"How did it go?"

I spin around so fast that I almost lose my balance. Christopher stands before me, tall and handsome, a hint of dark circles tinting the area under his eyes. His hair is disheveled, a sign he's run his hand through it repeatedly. His proximity sends my senses into a tailspin, and all my instincts crave to soothe him, to jump in his arms and kiss the living daylights out of him. With the trial no longer hanging over my head, I can focus on him. His brow is furrowed, and I do not like those lines on his forehead one bit.

"Christopher!" Alan exclaims. "You didn't say you'd be here."

"I was planning to wait at home for your call, but

I got anxious and drove here a few hours ago."

"Hours?" I ask, voice strangled with emotion. He was probably here outside while we were waiting for the judge to decide.

"Yeah. I have now skipped going into my office for three days straight. First time ever. There's a distinct possibility I'll never be allowed to step inside Bennett Enterprises again. I take it the judge ruled in your favor?"

"Yes," I reply. "Yes, she did."

Relief melts his frown, lighting up his expression.

"I'm sorry I can't stay and celebrate with the two of you, but I have to put fires out for another client," Alan says. Christopher and I bid him good-bye, and then Alan heads toward the nearest crossing.

Taking my hand, Christopher pulls me away from the entrance to the courthouse, turning into a narrow side street. We stop under the gold and copper streaked crown of a massive tree. A strong gust of wind blows, ruffling my hair.

"Thank you so much for everything you've done." I raise my hand to shove my hair out of my face. Christopher reaches for me too, and our hands collide briefly. With surprise, I realize we're both a little nervous.

"It was the least I could do," he says.

"You went above and beyond. Thank you. I'm sorry I didn't call, I was just so wrapped up in preparing for the trial."

"I was too. I'm sorry for the outburst at the hospital. You know that's not who I am."

"I know. I was just so scared."

"Me too. I haven't stopped being scared for three days straight. The thought of the kids being taken away from you, of losing all of you…."

His voice is pure silk, and I wish I could drape

myself in it. God, I missed his voice and his laughter. I just missed *him* terribly.

"I missed you."

"How much?" The corners of his mouth lift in a smile. "I'm warning you. I won't accept anything less than 'a lot.' Just to tip the scale in favor of 'a lot,' do you want to hear my statement? I heard you ask Alan about it."

"You have the statement with you?"

He tips one forefinger against his temple. "It's all here. Prepare to be blown away."

"Let's hear it." I fight to keep a straight expression, but utterly fail. My face cracks into a smile before Christopher opens his mouth.

"To whom it may concern, I met Victoria Hensley when looking for a decorator. From the first moment, she made an impression on me as a consummate professional. As I began to know her on a personal level, I discovered she was a sweet and nurturing person, determined to do right by Lucas, Chloe, and Sienna. I have fallen in love with Victoria and come to care very much for her siblings. When Chloe and I were in the car accident, my first instinct was to make sure she was unharmed. The outburst at the hospital in front of Hervis Jackson was unusual for me. Anyone who knows me can attest that I am a calm person. In that moment, I was overcome by fear that Victoria might end up losing custody of the little ones. I cannot imagine my life without all of them. I want to be there to mark every inch Chloe grows on a wall, to train Lucas for soccer, and fend off any subpar suitors asking Sienna out—"

"Oh stop, you'll make me cry." My eyes sting, emotion clogging my throat. Sometime during his speech, he curled his arms around my waist. I don't want him to take them away, not ever.

"I didn't even get to the good part." Leaning in, he kisses my forehead, and I feel his lips stretch into a smile against my skin. My man is about to get romantic again. "I love you, Victoria, and I want to spend my life with you. I want to be your partner in crime for everything, from making sure no one chops off their fingers to wrestling you to bed."

"You didn't include that last part in your deposition, did you?" I ask suspiciously, resting my palms on his shoulders.

"Thought about it, then decided it could come off as inappropriate. So, let's recap. How much did you miss me?"

"I love you, and I want to grow old next to you."

He offers me the first truly Christopher-sized grin for the day. "That will do."

I make a silent promise to myself to give him a reason to grin like that every single day. This wonderful man deserves this and so much more. I shift closer to him until our chests touch, soaking in his warmth. The weather today is on the chilly side, but I don't mind as long as I have him to warm me up.

"Are you about to climb me again?" he asks longingly.

"I think I'll wait until we're in a more private space."

"You know, I thought about including your climbing activities and how much they mean to me in the statement."

"What made you decide against it?"

"Instinct."

Another gust of wind blows, about a thousand degrees colder than the last. I swear it turns me into an icicle. Christopher isn't faring much better.

"How about going to your house and celebrating with the kids that this awful week is almost over?" he asks. His teeth are chattering.

"You've read my mind. One thing though. Never mention your intentions to 'fend off any sub-par suitors asking Sienna out.' It's for your own good."

"I love it when you're looking out for me." Kissing my forehead, he places an arm around my shoulders, leading us back into the main street.

***

I barely push open the door to the house when Chloe and Lucas sprint toward us. Lucas wraps his arms around my waist, squeezing me in a tight hug.

"Sienna said the judge allowed us to stay with you," he whispers, as if afraid to say it out loud.

"She did. We're all staying together."

Lucas is so happy I think he might even let me smother his cheeks with kisses in public today. Chloe jumps straight into Christopher's arms.

"I grew a full inch since Monday," she tells him with conviction. "But Lucas says it's not true. He says I'll always be a midget."

Christopher touches the tip of her nose with his finger. "We'll measure you today."

Sienna descends the stairs, her hands on her hips, a wide smile on her face. "Let Victoria breathe, Lucas."

Lucas merely hugs me tighter. Damn, my boy is stronger than I gave him credit for.

"We're going to celebrate," I announce.

"Where?" Lucas and Chloe ask in unison.

"I'm craving cheesecake," Sienna says, and there's a general murmur of agreement. "Oh, and we really should go buy a Christmas tree, or all the good ones will be gone."

"We'll go after the cheesecake," Christopher says.

Sienna glances from Chloe to Lucas. "Okay, let's get you two dressed up."

Lucas disentangles himself from me while Chloe asks Christopher to put her down. They have a pep in their step as they follow Sienna up the staircase.

"They're going to do the kissing, aren't they?" Chloe asks just before they disappear from view.

Both Christopher and I laugh heartily.

"I'll change quickly too." I'm about to go as well, wanting to rid myself of the blue suit and dress in something that looks more like me, when Christopher clasps my wrist. Turning to him, I cock an eyebrow. In response, he hauls me against the nearest wall.

"First, let's do some kissing."

Chapter Thirty-Five

Christopher

"This is wicked," Lucas exclaims a week later, inspecting the Disneyland tickets for the hundredth time—my Christmas gift to them. The kids and I are at a coffee shop near my office, enjoying some hot chocolate. Victoria is with a client, and I've offered to watch the kids for the afternoon. I've been waiting for a chance to be alone with them the entire week.

"Kids, I need to talk to you." Three pairs of eyes focus on me with curiosity. "As you know, I love Victoria very much, and we're happy together."

Sienna sips from her cup of hot chocolate. I suspect she might be trying to hide a smile.

"I want to ask you for her hand." My words are met with complete silence, which I won't lie, freaks the hell out of me.

"He means he wants to marry Victoria," Sienna tells her siblings, not bothering to hide her smile anymore. Lucas and Chloe erupt in cheers, and I breathe in relief when I hear distinct yeses among those cheers. I thought long and hard if asking them before talking to Victoria was the best idea, but it felt like the right thing to do. She might not have parents I can ask, but these little punks are her family. Soon, they'll be mine too.

"Does this mean there will be another baby?"

Chloe asks, now positively glowing.

"I don't know when, but there definitely will be more than one baby," I say.

She pumps her small fist in the air, giggling.

"Did you already get her a ring?" Sienna asks eagerly.

"No, I haven't. But my office happens to be in walking distance, and the new collection of engagement rings is ready."

The kids finish their hot chocolate in one minute flat.

***

As we walk into the creative department of Bennett Enterprises a short while later, Sienna elbows me. "Were those tickets to Disneyland a bribe so we'd say yes?"

"You're insulting me. Those were just my Christmas gift." Sure, I strategically gave them the tickets first, knowing it would put them in a good mood, but bribing? That's not my style.

Pippa smiles when she sees our little group heading toward her desk. The creative department is the only one in the company organized in an open office. There are a dozen people milling around the space. Personally, I detest open offices because I can't concentrate with constant chatter around me, but to each his own.

"Hello, lovelies," Pippa greets us. "Yes, everything you see around here are gemstones and diamonds."

I am so used to seeing jewelry or stones about to be made into jewelry around the office, I forget people find it surprising. The kids are looking around with gaping mouths. Sienna is practically salivating over a pendant with an outlandish design. When Pippa first showed us the sketch, my brothers and I weren't sure, but Pippa insisted that young, sophisticated women would find it appealing. As usual, it turns out she's right. My sister has a talent for predicting these things that cannot be taught or learned.

"Pippa, we're here to see the engagement rings for the new collection," I inform her as the four of us come to a halt. Her desk is far enough from the other ones that it offers *some* privacy.

"I know."

"How?"

Her response is prompt. "Intuition and some sniffing around. When you asked on Monday if the rings would be here this week, you were drumming your fingers on the table. You only do that when you're nervous. I put two and two together."

My sister is a little too perceptive for her own good, or anyone else's. Without another word, she rises to her feet, heading to the wooden storage closet behind her desk. She returns with a large rectangular box, which she places on her desk. Opening the lid, she reveals twelve engagement rings.

"They're all so pretty," Sienna exclaims. I lift Chloe in my arms because she can't see anything from her level.

"Wow," she exclaims.

"Not to be rude," Lucas says, "but they all look kind of the same to me."

Sienna gives him the stink eye, but Pippa chuckles. For the next half hour, my sister patiently explains the difference between each cut, each stone, and why she chose certain combinations. I already know most of that stuff because it's in the marketing copy we included in the catalog, but watching Pippa explain is a different experience. She lights up, exuberance dotting every word. An hour later, we have our ring and are on our way out of the building, the kids walking a short distance in front of me.

"What happens after he gives her the ring?" Chloe asks Sienna.

"They get married."

"And after they get married?" Her words are a whisper.

"They make babies."

Chapter Thirty-Six

Victoria

"I can't believe they're open," I exclaim as Christopher, the kids, and I walk up to the front door to our favorite coffee shop. Sienna mentioned that she was in the mood for cheesecake, and I backed her up because I never say no to cheesecake. Since she had the brilliant idea at nine o'clock in the evening though, I was certain we'd have to go someplace else, because Ms. Winters usually closes the coffee shop at eight. Sienna insisted she checked online, and it would be open until ten o'clock.

"Told you," Sienna says smugly.

As we step inside, Ms. Winters greets us with an excited wave, telling us to sit wherever we like. The place is empty, which makes me wonder why she's closing later.

As soon as we sit in the booth, she takes our order, winking at Christopher as she leaves. That's my first indication that something's up. My parents first brought me here when I was twelve, so I've known Ms. Winters for more than seventeen years. She's not a winker. My second indication is that Lucas and Chloe haven't been bickering since we arrived. Sienna and Christopher are exchanging accomplice glances every few seconds, further adding to my suspicions.

"Okay, what's going on?" I ask no one in particular, scanning everyone.

"Nothing," Chloe quips.

"Wrong answer. Now I know for sure that something's up."

Lucas plunks his elbows on the table, resting his head in his hands. "Told you we shouldn't have said anything to Chloe. The midget can't keep secrets."

"Lucas!" I admonish.

"I'm not a midget," Chloe volleys back, frowning at Lucas.

I zero in on Sienna and Christopher, expecting an explanation, but both remain tight-lipped. Opening my mouth, I intend to use some old-fashioned emotional blackmail to get them to spill everything but Ms. Winters arrives, placing the cakes in front of us.

"Wow, you've outdone yourself with the cake decorations, Ms. Winters," Sienna comments. As the woman in question thanks my sister and saunters away, I inspect the cakes. Truly, Ms. Winters has perfected her winter decorations. Lucas's and Chloe's cakes have a snowman on top, Sienna's a snowflake. Christopher's has a green fir tree.

Mine has a white fir tree… and a ring.

"Oh my God." My pulse ratchets up instantly and furiously as I blink, and blink again. The ring is not part of the frosting. It has a white gold band, and in the center is the most beautiful diamond I've seen. "Is that…?"

My voice fades as emotion takes over, clogging my throat and warming my chest. Out of the corner of my eye, I peek at Christopher. Sitting right next to me, he beams. The kids are on the opposite side of the table, watching intently. Wordlessly, Christopher takes the ring between his fingers and holds it out to me.

"Victoria Hensley, will you be my wife?"

Drawing in a lungful of air, I glance at this

wonderful man in front of me, wanting to memorize every single detail about this moment. The way Christopher's chest rises and falls in rapid succession, showing that he's as consumed by this as I am. The way the kids lean over the table, as if afraid they'll miss the word when it finally tumbles out of my lips, showing they want this as much as I do.

"Yes," I answer, my voice rich with emotion but strong at the same time. "I do. I want to be your wife."

Christopher slides the ring on my finger, and I have no time to admire the way it looks on my finger before his mouth comes down to mine in a sweet kiss. After pulling back, he draws tiny circles with his thumb on my wrist, a soft move that awakens all my senses. His eyes hold a mischievous glint full of promises. This man is as hungry for me as I am for him.

The kids choose this moment to erupt in cheers, hopping over to hug and us. Ms. Winters also congratulates us, revealing that Christopher called ahead of time, asking her to stay open longer today so we could come in and have the place to ourselves.

I'm still too overrun with emotions to make any long speeches, but under the table, I squeeze Christopher's hand, letting him know how much this means to me. There will be plenty of time for words later.

"We have to start searching for your dress," Sienna says, once everyone is back in their seats and focusing on their cheesecake. "And a location. And—"

"Breathe, Sienna." Chuckling, I add, "We should set a date first."

"As soon as possible," Christopher declares, curling an arm around my waist and pulling me close to him until our hips collide. The touch electrifies me from my center to the tip of my fingers.

Sienna grins. "In other words, as soon as we find a dress and location."

Chloe and Lucas start talking at the same time, their questions directed to Sienna.

"I can't wait to get home," Christopher whispers to me.

"And why is that, Mr. Romantic?" I ask in an equally low tone, even though the kids are talking so loudly there's no chance they'd hear us.

Christopher trails his fingers up and down my exposed forearm, igniting my skin. Anticipation courses through my veins. As he brings his lips to my ear in a seemingly innocent gesture, I know I'll see more of his Mr. Sexy side later.

"Because I have *plans*."

Epilogue: Four Months Later

Victoria

"This was a bad idea." I survey the chaos in front of me, crossing my fingers that by the end of the day, all the kids in the backyard will still have their fingers intact. It's Lucas's tenth birthday, and we're celebrating in style with fifteen of his school friends, plus Aunt Christina and her family. The Bennett clan is here too, of course, and that brings the total number of guests up considerably. Our yard is filled with people of all ages and heights; conversation, laughter, and the occasional cry fill the air. We'll move out of this house by the end of the month, and we wanted to host one huge party here before leaving. When Christopher and I decided it was time to move in together, it was clear my house was too small. We chose to restore his apartment to the original five bedrooms it had.

"Successful party," Christopher comments, watching the chaos as well. "Everyone's having a blast."

It's true. Even Pippa's daughters, Elena and Mia, are laughing their asses off, even though all they do is sit in their infant seats and wave at everyone. They're adorable. Chloe is once again shadowing Mrs. Bennett, who doesn't seem to mind in the slightest.

I lean against Christopher, almost purring with joy when his strong arms enclose me, protective and loving.

If someone would have told me eight months ago that on Lucas's birthday I'd be head over heels in love with a gorgeous man and be surrounded by his family, I would've dismissed it as a crazy idea. I was the girl with the plan to put my personal life on standstill until the kids were older, but there you go. Sometimes letting go of the plan and taking a chance leads to wonderful things.

"Do you think they'll miss the yard?" he asks.

"Nah, they love your roof." *Love* is an understatement. Lucas and Chloe have declared they never want to leave the indoor pool. Sienna proclaimed that the rooftop is the best reading spot in San Francisco. "You're so good to us, Christopher."

"You deserve it."

"Don't you two make a lovely picture?" Pippa says as she walks up to us. Sebastian's wife, Ava, joins us too.

"I swear if I get any larger," Ava says, "I won't fit in my car anymore."

"You look great," Pippa assures her. Ava huffs, patting her round belly. She still has a few months to go until she gives birth.

"Christopher, you've got to see this," Lucas calls from the other end of the yard. My fiancé lets go of me, heading to my brother without another word.

"You know," Ava says to Pippa, "I remember Christopher proclaiming loud and clear that he wouldn't fall for your matchmaking games."

Pippa shrugs, pushing her beautiful blonde hair back. "So did Max. My brothers were under the impression I'd given up my ways after getting married, but that just made them easy prey."

"Isn't it too much on top of work and your daughters?" I ask, handing her a second serving of pie from the nearby table. Ava hesitates for a split second when I hand her a plate, but then she digs in, eating with gusto.

"Oh no," Pippa says solemnly. "It relaxes me, almost like a hobby."

"What will you do when you run out of siblings?" Ava asks with fake horror.

Pippa holds her finger up as if saying, 'I have the solution for this scenario of doom.' "We have an alarmingly high number of single cousins. That won't do."

I burst out laughing without the slightest remorse. I would put more effort into hiding my amusement if Pippa wouldn't have so much fun at her own expense.

"But Alice is next in line now," Ava says with a knowing smile, pointing at the sister in question, who is deep in conversation with Sienna.

"Oh?" I ask through a mouthful of pie.

Pippa and Ava exchange a sheepish look before the former points her fork at me. "Before we give you any details, we have to know if you're with us or the boys."

"I'm not following," I say honestly.

"The guy we have in mind for Alice… let's just say my brothers will flex their alpha muscles when they find out," Pippa explains.

Ohhhh, they don't approve. This is exciting.

"So you have to choose a side," Ava repeats.

It takes me a split second to decide. "I'm on your side."

"That's my girl." Pippa nods, launching into a detailed explanation.

A few minutes later, Christopher emerges from the house, carrying Lucas's cake and placing it on the table outside. Damn, I hadn't realized it was time already.

"All right, everyone," I say loudly. "Time for

Lucas to blow out the candles."

The crowd parts for my little brother to walk through, and he smiles mischievously when he sees the candles on the cake. He insisted he wanted one candle for each year as opposed to two candles indicating the number ten.

From behind me, I hear Blake whisper to Christopher, "I bet he won't blow out all ten on the first try."

"I bet against you," Christopher hisses from the corner of his mouth, and I can't help chuckling.

"What?" he inquires.

"Sienna and I made the exact same bet when we bought the candles."

Alice appears on my other side, clearly having listened to the conversation. As we all turn to watch Lucas, she whispers conspiratorially, "You lot fit right in with us."

THE END

Other Books by Layla Hagen

The Bennett Family Series

Book 1: Your Irresistible Love

Sebastian Bennett is a determined man. It's the secret behind the business empire he built from scratch. Under his rule, Bennett Enterprises dominates the jewelry industry. Despite being ruthless in his work, family comes first for him, and he'd do anything for his parents and eight siblings—even if they drive him crazy sometimes. . . like when they keep nagging him to get married already.

Sebastian doesn't believe in love, until he brings in external marketing consultant Ava to oversee the next collection launch. She's beautiful, funny, and just as stubborn as he is. Not only is he obsessed with her delicious curves, but he also finds himself willing to do anything to make her smile.
He's determined to have Ava, even if she's completely off limits.

Ava Lindt has one job to do at Bennett Enterprises: make the next collection launch unforgettable. Daydreaming about the hot CEO is definitely not on her to-do list. Neither is doing said CEO. The consultancy she works for has a strict policy—no fraternizing with clients. She won't risk her job.

Besides, Ava knows better than to trust men with her heart.

But their sizzling chemistry spirals into a deep connection that takes both of them by surprise. Sebastian blows through her defenses one sweet kiss and sinful touch at a time. When Ava's time as a consultant in his company comes to an end, will Sebastian fight for the woman he loves or will he end up losing her?

AVAILABLE ON ALL RETAILERS.

Book 2: Your Captivating Love

Logan Bennett knows his priorities. He is loyal to his family and his company. He has no time for love, and no desire for it. Not after a disastrous engagement left him brokenhearted. When Nadine enters his life, she turns everything upside down.

She's sexy, funny, and utterly captivating. She's also more stubborn than anyone he's met…including himself.

Nadine Hawthorne is finally pursuing her dream: opening her own clothing shop. After working so hard to get here, she needs to concentrate on her new business, and can't afford distractions. Not even if they come in the form of Logan Bennett.

He's handsome, charming, and doesn't take no for an answer. After bitter disappointments, Nadine doesn't believe in love. But being around Logan is addicting. It doesn't help that Logan's family is scheming to bring them together at every turn.

Their attraction is sizzling, their connection undeniable. Slowly, Logan wins her over. What starts out as a fling, soon spirals into much more than they are prepared for.

When a mistake threatens to tear them apart, will they have the strength to hold on to each other?

AVAILABLE ON ALL RETAILERS.

Book 3: Your Forever Love

Eric Callahan is a powerful man, and his sharp business sense has earned him the nickname 'the shark.' Yet under the strict façade is a man who loves his daughter and would do anything for her. When he and his daughter move to San Francisco for three months, he has one thing in mind: expanding his business on the West Coast. As a widower, Eric is not looking for love. He focuses on his company, and his daughter.

Until he meets Pippa Bennett. She captivates him from the moment he sets eyes on her, and what starts as unintentional flirting soon spirals into something neither of them can control.

Pippa Bennett knows she should stay away from Eric Callahan. After going through a rough divorce, she doesn't trust men anymore. But something about Eric just draws her in. He has a body made for sin and a sense of humor that matches hers. Not to mention that seeing how adorable he is with his daughter melts Pippa's walls one by one.

The chemistry between them is undeniable, but the connection that grows deeper every day that has both of them wondering if love might be within their reach.

When it's time for Eric and his daughter to head back home, will he give up on the woman who has captured his heart, or will he do everything in his power to remain by her side?

AVAILABLE ON ALL RETAILERS.

The Lost Series

***

Lost in Us: The story of James and Serena

There are three reasons tequila is my new favorite drink.

• One: my ex-boyfriend hates it.
• Two: downing a shot looks way sexier than sipping my usual Sprite.
• Three: it might give me the courage to do something my ex-boyfriend would hate even more than tequila—getting myself a rebound

The night I swap my usual Sprite with tequila, I meet James Cohen. The encounter is breathtaking. Electrifying. And best not repeated.

James is a rich entrepreneur. He likes risks and adrenaline and is used to living the high life. He's everything I'm not.

But opposites attract. Some say opposites destroy each other. Some say opposites are perfect for each other. I don't know what will James and I do to each other, but I can't stay away from him. Even though I should.

AVAILABLE ON ALL RETAILERS.

***

Found in Us: The story of Jessica and Parker

Jessica Haydn wants to leave her past behind. Hurt by one too many heartbreaks, she vows not to fall in love again. Especially not with a man like Parker, whose electrifying pull and smile bruised her ego once before. But his sexy British accent makes her crave his touch, and his blue eyes strip Jessica of all her defenses.

Parker Blakesley has no place for love in his life. He learned the hard way not to trust. He built his business empire by avoiding distractions, and using sheer determination and control. But something about Jessica makes him question everything. Not only has she a body made for sin, but her laughter fills a void inside of him.

The desire igniting between them spirals into an unstoppable passion, and so much more. Soon, neither can fight their growing emotional connection. But can two scarred souls learn to trust again? And when a mistake threatens to tear them apart, will their love be strong enough?

AVAILABLE ON ALL RETAILERS.

***

Caught in Us: The story of Dani and Damon

Damon Cooper has all the markings of a bad boy:

- A tattoo
- A bike
- An attitude to go with point one and two

In the beginning I hated him, but now I'm falling in love

with him. My parents forbid us to be together, but Damon's not one to obey rules. And since I met him, neither am I.

AVAILABLE ON ALL RETAILERS.

***

Standalone USA TODAY BESTSELLER
Withering Hope

Aimee's wedding is supposed to turn out perfect. Her dress, her fiancé and the location—the idyllic holiday ranch in Brazil—are perfect.

But all Aimee's plans come crashing down when the private jet that's taking her from the U.S. to the ranch—where her fiancé awaits her—defects mid-flight and the pilot is forced to perform an emergency landing in the heart of the Amazon rainforest.

With no way to reach civilization, being rescued is Aimee and Tristan's—the pilot—only hope. A slim one that slowly withers away, desperation taking its place. Because death wanders in the jungle under many forms: starvation, diseases. Beasts.

As Aimee and Tristan fight to find ways to survive, they grow closer. Together they discover that facing old, inner agonies carved by painful pasts takes just as much courage, if not even more, than facing the rainforest.

Despite her devotion to her fiancé, Aimee can't hide her feelings for Tristan—the man for whom she's slowly becoming everything. You can hide many things in the rainforest. But not lies. Or love.

Withering Hope is the story of a man who desperately needs forgiveness and the woman who brings him hope. It is a story in which hope births wings and blooms into a love that is as beautiful and intense as it is forbidden.

AVAILABLE ON ALL RETAILERS.

***

Your Inescapable Love

Published by Layla Hagen

Published: Layla Hagen 2016

Cover: http://designs.romanticbookaffairs.com/

***

Acknowledgements

There are so many people who helped me fulfil the dream of publishing, that I am utterly terrified I will forget to thank someone. If I do, please forgive me. Here it goes.

First, I'd like to thank my beta readers, Jessica, Dee, Andrea, Carrie, Jill, Kolleen and Rebecca. You made this story so much better!!

I want to thank every blogger and reader who took a chance with me as a new author and helped me spread the word. You have my most heartfelt gratitude. To my street team. . .you rock !!!

Last but not least, I would like to thank my family. I would never be here if not for their love and support. Mom, you taught me that books are important, and for that I will always be grateful. Dad, thank you for always being convinced that I should reach for the stars.

To my sister, whose numerous ahem. . .legendary replies will serve as an inspiration for many books to come, I say thank you for your support and I love you, kid.

To my husband, who always, no matter what, believed in me and supported me through all this whether by happily taking on every chore I overlooked or accepting being ignored for hours at a time, and most importantly encouraged me whenever I needed it: I love you and I could not have done this without you.

<<<<>>>>

60748352R00200

Made in the USA
Lexington, KY
16 February 2017